I0533748

THE LIBRARY OF
PANOPTICON

Alexandria Nolan

The Library of Panopticon

Alexandria Nolan

Copyright © 2015 Alexandria Nolan

All rights reserved.

ISBN-10: 069240564X
ISBN-13: 978-0692405642

Cover Art : *Ecritoire et livres* , 17th century.
Attributed to Jacques Bizet
All other images within book culled from *Girl's Own Advice*, @girlsown
on Twitter

Also By Alexandria Nolan:

Shears Of Fate:
A Novella Of Memory & Madness

Wide, Wild, Everywhere:
Short Stories For Wanderers

Starlight Symphonies Of Oak & Glass

DEDICATION

To my mother and father, who read me as many stories as I demanded, and never thought any of my own stories were too silly or fantastic. Allowing my mind to romp fearlessly through the ordinary and dip into the extraordinary.

For Detroit + all of Michigan, who will, I am sure, rise again like the Phoenix. A place that was the home of so much fantastical hope and invention cannot be held down for long.

And for Terrence, who continually opens the world of adventure to me, fueling my imagination with stories waiting to be told.

CONTENTS

FOREWORD

Imaginations, fantasies, illusions,
in which the things that cannot be take shape,
And seem to be, and for the moment, are.

—Henry Wadsworth Longfellow
Michael Angelo: A Fragment
Part First, I. Monologue: The Last Judgement

I am part of everything that I have read.

—Theodore Roosevelt, 1906

expected more, perhaps an explosion or the sound of g… breaking. But instead, it was only the sound of a book, used roughly, and then its collapse to the floor, pages askew.

Julian looked at the book, and then at her, and then began to wail pitifully. He loved to read, or to pretend as he looked at the pictures, and did it more often than he spoke. This was a child that treasured books, and she did not want him to feel otherwise. But, as much as it broke her heart to cast away *these* books, she knew this time had been very close. Too close. She reminded herself that these were not ordinary books, after all, and she could not think of them the same way as those tomes she wished to share with her child, her heart.

Mia set him in front of the television, something she never did normally. She kissed him, cuddled him, and wiped his falling tears on the hem of her oversized sweatshirt. He had just calmed down and had begun to tell her the story he had read from his little red book, and to describe in his childish babble what it was like to fly through the air with the birds. She listened carefully, nodding, and smiled at him until his attention was captured completely by the TV. Leaving him sitting on the edge of the sofa, his little legs swinging to and fro, to the rhythm of the cartoon music, Mia then stepped quickly into the kitchen to call Finn at work. Out of the corner of her eye, she noticed that the orange cat was back again too, as obnoxious as the books if not as dangerous. She shooed off the windowsill and onto the balcony. How was it continuing to get in?

Julian's laughter in the living room and the steady hum the refrigerator calmed her nerves. She breathed out vly and grabbed the handset off the wall, checking the iber to his office, so recently inked into the little ess book.

was time to move again.

PROLOGUE

If only mother were here. It was a thought that Mia had almost daily now. And not in the way one does when almost anything is going wrong and one wants comfort. No, Mia longed for her mother because she was probably the only person who would know what to do with Julian.

They kept finding him, no matter what. Or, perhaps he was calling to them. No matter how the discovery was achieved, it spelled trouble. From Madrid to Helsinki, Tokyo to Connecticut, their little family was never truly free. Her husband, Finn, pretended that it wasn't a bother, their constant gypsy roving around the world, but she knew it was. It always was. How long could he go on pretending? At least they were safe for now, here in this little house on the outskirts of Rotterdam.

She peered into the nursery door, though it was almost time that he was too old to have his bedroom called such. His little head bobbed in tune to music only he could hear, and his little voice whispered secrets into the air and to his toys, secrets that she would never know. Childhood already held so many mysteries, he didn't need to have any more circling about him menacingly.

Julian's hair was still downy fine, black duck fluff that called to be stroked and caressed by her hands. She stepped closer so that she might do so, and maybe steal a kiss on his chubby cheeks, too soon losing their roundness to age. As she stooped down she noticed his skin looked lighter, not the dark olive tone they normally shared. As he turned to look at her, his eyes too were light...and growing lighter.

She looked at his hands and saw a small red leather book, just the size for a child, clutched lovingly within his fingers. He grew paler before her eyes, and his own attention was drawn back toward the book.

In one movement, she snatched the book from hi small hands and threw it hard against the wall. She'

The whole secret of a successful life is to find out what it is one's destiny to do, and then do it.—Henry Ford

CHAPTER THE FIRST
A Disappearing Act

The first time Julian had seen the small leather-bound book, he thought it unusual. It had been stubbornly sitting on his desk as if it had always belonged there. He even had the eerie feeling that he had at some point placed it there himself. But, a second glance and a thumb through had given him the impression that it was both utterly foreign to him, and somehow familiar. For a moment he was reminded of other books, other moments such as these from when he was a boy. But he had shaken the memories or fantasies, whichever they were, off and turned his attention elsewhere. And so he soon forgot the little tome though, and shut it into his desk drawer, his mind playing back the more pressing moments of his day.

But, the book kept returning, seemingly seeking him out intentionally. He would find it in his leather satchel, or in his backpack on the university bus. It would be lying on his bed when he tried to retire for the night. It would appear on his desk at lectures, as he rapidly scribbled notes, in a place where he knew it had not been a moment before. Then a second glance, and it was there no longer.

Strange too was the writing itself. A swooping, flourished script written by a lively hand in an old style. People simply didn't write quite that way anymore. It reminded him of the writing in an ancestral recipe book, or the signatures on old documents from his research. Handwriting like art, each letter more beautiful than the last, practiced often—so very different than the scribbled chicken scratch people made now in letters. A lost art, handwriting, something that used to be an identifiable part of a person, as welcome to the eyes as their very face.

With the new semester came the descent of summer into fall. He loved the crispness of autumn, the last bright flare of life before the cold death of winter. The crunch of the leaves beneath his soft Italian leather soles, measuring every step he took to class. It was football season at University, but he'd never understood American Football. It was…artless. He much preferred the international concept of football for its elegance and skill, probably a hold-out from his years growing up abroad. He liked the school and the atmosphere of this midwestern college town in a way that he never would have expected. The climate was so much like Munich, Arles or Lugano. A certain bite in the air, touched with the sweetness of sunshine. "All the best things grow in this climate" his father had often said. But this, his last fall as an undergraduate, felt different. A shift in his soul, and the damn book that kept coming back.

He had glanced through the pages once or twice, thumbing them warily this way and that. But, he was afraid to read it. Julian did not know why or what mysterious force blocked him from doing so, but he felt an outrageous trepidation to let the words string together in meaning within his mind. And so, for as many times as the strange book appeared, Julian would always find it had just as elusively disappeared, only to stumble upon its musty pages unexpectedly another time.

The past few years had been difficult ones for him. Perhaps, difficult was an understatement. The past few years had been a maddening maze of depression and confusion. He had spent the entirety of his life roaming the world with his parents. A traveling gypsy life, never residing anywhere long enough to put down roots—six months here, two years there and a lazy year somewhere else in between. His mother, in his memory, was adorned continually with ink-stained hands and her travel notebook open as she feverishly jotted down thoughts and typed up memories reconfigured as articles for demanding editors. Whimsical descriptions of places they'd been that he remembered much differently than she wrote them. In her writing, rainy days transformed into sunshine and dreadful seasickness became a blissful, blue sea cruise on the Mediterranean. It was from her that he learned the love of books and the power that words had to paint and reimagine reality—even as it was happening. If his mother was words and poetry, his father was logic and order. His position as a contracting specialist in petroleum engineering allowed them to pack up and go wherever he could find work, which seemed to be anywhere his mother could think up. His father worked long hours, but had a way of listening to you that made you feel as if his whole life's aim was to give you his full attention. He was quick to forgive and collected idioms, doling them out incorrectly in every situation. He was a lean and muscular man, exuding a silent, misunderstood strength many never looked close enough to see—or mistook for weakness. His parents were opposite magnets, that couldn't help but cling together.

They had teased him a few years back about these upcoming college years. Poked and prodded at him about having to stay put for four years at one time when he started his university classes. He had cringed at the thought, and replied back that he had plans to crash their retirement. He'd had grand aspirations of study abroad programs and his studies being a whirlwind of exotic locales and online coursework. They had laughed at him, telling him he would think differently when he got to college.

He was thinking of their laughter now, and could almost feel his mother smooth the back of his espresso brown hair, her hazel eyes flashing merrily into his own. He was sitting at his desk in his apartment, a picture of the three of them on the steps of the Sacre Cœur in Montmartre when he was younger, his parent's faces smiling benignly back at him from the photograph. He remembered everything about their flat in Paris and his mother's swishy black dresses and heels clicking on the steps of the church. He could almost taste that specific day in his mind, early spring and the sidewalk crepe vendors that were a favorite with tourists. He'd had no idea how sweet the memory would be until there was no hope of repeating it. He'd had no idea how trapped his four years of school would be.

All hopes of spring breaks in Vienna or Christmases in Lapland had been dashed that day in his senior year of high school. The seemingly harmless note to report to the counselor's office, passed to him by a bored student assistant during his calculus class. The greatest shifts in life always occur in the most mundane of circumstances, the blandest of details.

They had retired young from their respective work, although they both continued to dabble in their interests. His mother still wrote an occasional freelance article, his father composed and played music for hours on end. Their travels had only increased with retirement, and so they were now only home sporadically. They'd left the week previously and he hadn't even asked their destination. It hadn't occurred to him to do so. Many of their neighbors and his classmates parents' thought it was irresponsible to leave him alone for such long stretches, but Julian never had. He wasn't a possession of his parents, and they had their own lives. Though he was always welcome and loved when he was with them, the relationship between the three of them was built on respect, love and genuine friendship. They would no more tell him what to do with his life than he would tell them how to live theirs.

And so, the glum look on the principal's face and the words that came from his tight-lipped mouth were like another language. One that he had heard before, but couldn't translate. They were dead. Traveling in Russia, his father had crashed a helicopter and that was it. Their lives were over, their flames extinguished. He had stood, stoic, as the principal and the police officer explained it to him, as much as death can ever be explained.

They had never been like other parents, never scolding or chiding. Never punishing or establishing rules. But in many ways they were closer as a result, as if the three of them had raised each other. And for a moment, Julian almost laughed at the principal's description of the events. He could picture his father piloting the helicopter, mentally checking it off his "bucket list", he could see his mother rolling her eyes. But the laughter died in his throat.

He had continued to stand silently, waiting for the adults to stop talking. When they finally came to an end of the explanations and sympathies, they looked to him, preparing themselves to comfort whatever reaction he would give.

But Julian had no reaction. Instead, he had asked to return to class. He had gone through the rest of the day, the week, the month and the school year without a reaction.

He could not grieve them, because he couldn't accept that they were dead.

They were more than father and mother. They were his heroes, his greatest friends. From the beginning they had been three sides of a triangle or the holy trinity. Each their own face of the shape, but supported and somehow greater when combined together. They encouraged him, taught him and listened to his ideas. Every move, every relocation, each hop on the globe, his constants had been his parents and his books. If he could continue to retreat into Dickens, Tolkien and Vonnegut, he couldn't help but believe that his mother and father weren't going to come and knock on his apartment door. A lost book was always able to be rediscovered, wasn't it? Simply stashed in a place that one had forgotten. So, he believed that they would come, jet-lagged but bubbling with news of their travels, all the while scolding him for believing them gone.

But no matter how many times he looked into his mother's hazel eyes in the photo, or admired her honey hair. Nor how often he noticed his father's broad shoulders and faint sun-freckles reflecting back at him in the mirror—he never did hear that tap on the door.

Somehow he was finishing his fourth year of university with a degree in History and a minor in Art, and he hadn't left Michigan once. They'd been living in Detroit when it happened, and he had enrolled at the University of Michigan-Ann Arbor, hoping that if they came back, they'd find him more easily there. That's the first rule of being lost, isn't it? Stay where you are until you're found. And Julian was most desperately lost.

He had their urn, their ashes combined, sitting on the coffee table in the living room. He hadn't scattered them, because he couldn't reconcile his unflappable, lively parents with the cold dust of death that resided in the stark, small living room he shared with his roommate. For him, the once illuminated world had grown dark and small. The splendor of his past had dimmed and sometimes seemed a fantasy. Shades of dullness and ordinariness covered him head to toe, as he struggled to recall a time of vibrance.

Julian's head hit his palm and he yawned, blinking the tired from his eyes. He was supposed to be studying and researching the fascinating geo-political ramifications of the Boer-War on Afro-European relationships, when he'd been drawn into the photograph.

He noticed with surprise that the little black book had returned. It had settled itself on the desk near his forearm, opened up to the first page. The ink was a hand beckoning to him, pleading with Julian to give the pages a read.

Sighing, he ran his hands over his trouser legs, and gingerly reached for the little leather tome. Taking it in both hands, he brought it to his nose and inhaled. Julian loved the smell of an old book. He usually used his Kindle for reading, the family's constant jaunts around the globe made toting books too difficult. Still, he had a few of his favorites in hardcover and paperback, and he had always felt a magic in being amongst old, well-loved books in the libraries all over the world. The memory of those book treasuries recalled countless days among leather and paper, sitting near his mother in the library, both of them pretending to be as serious as possible, whilst trying to make the other laugh.

The scent of this book was familiar, musty paper and fingerprints. But it also had an unmistakable hint of cardamom and clove. The specific spicy perfume of this book evoked an image of a woman about Julian's age, dressed like a Gibson girl, long cinnamon curls hanging to her waist. She was crying softly and writing furiously into the book. The fountain pen bit so mercilessly into the paper that Julian was surprised it didn't bleed. Suddenly, the girl in his vision looked up, and her cool grey eyes stared at him, bewildered. Her mouth opened as if she would speak...

Julian dropped the book abruptly. It flapped harmlessly to his lap. He'd had a powerful imagination since those first stories his mother had read to him as a child, able to create whole worlds within his mind. He was an architect of his own museums, the protagonist in all of his novels. They were an escape whenever he needed one, and a home whenever he was lonely. Private galleries of his favorite artwork all hung together in his mind, alongside of an avenue containing every cottage, townhouse and flat his family had ever lived in. All these alternate realities and fantasies locked within him.

But this, this was…different. Julian's eyes bored into the black leather book and its brittle pages, half expecting it to fly into his face or suck him inside. Instead, it lay harmlessly in his lap. It had been so real.

He could hear her breath and see the bob and shake of her red-brown waves. He could feel the tension and confusion in her eyes when her gaze met his, felt the sorrow that lived inside of her, a harmony of sadness shared between them. That clove and cinnamon scent that had come from the book was fresher in her presence, new.

He covered his face with his hands and closed his eyes hard, shaking his head quickly side to side, clearing it. His eyes sought the comfort of his parent's photograph, and when he looked back down, the book had vanished.

CHAPTER THE SECOND
In Which The Unseeable Is Seen

It had been weeks since he had last seen the book, but now all he wished was to lay a hand on it again, a shooting star that passed before his wish had been spoken. He yearned to read the pages that before he had avoided.

Julian had begun re-reading Edith Wharton, E.M. Forster, Dreiser and Conrad, melting into the world of the turn of the century. He was looking for her. Trying to find her in this faraway, once-upon-a-time, and not knowing why. Who was she? Had she even been real? And if not, why could his mind no longer conjure her anew as he could with any other fantasy person? Why could he not invent the stories of her life? Perhaps because her life was not invention...perhaps because it was unfolding in her time at the same time his was unwrapping around him even now.

The thought made him shudder, the whole idea of parallel times and seeing ladies from books made flesh before his eyes gave him pause. But, as much as it scared him, he still set his mind to picturing her, with her wild long hair, the murky grey-violet of her eyes with tears that fell on her skirt as she leaned forward over the table to write. As if the tears from her eyes provided the ink to her pen, writing with her own heart's sorrow. Just that single memory, and nothing more. And that was the rub, it felt like a memory, not a dream, or a figment of his imagination.

He saw her in his mind with such clarity that it frightened him. She felt familiar and safe, as no other person had been for him in years. Growing up, he had been strange with girls, never understanding what it was they wanted from him. Not awkward, that was the wrong word. He didn't act uncomfortable or foolish, he simply did not spark when his life was struck with theirs. His novels had failed him, his favorite authors had lied—at least until now.

Julian's relationships in high school and college had lacked the easy companionship his parents had thrived on. They had always been connected somehow. His father's hand resting on his mother's knee or their thighs touching innocently at the dinner table. They held hands in the car and on the plane, and each of them was a shade paler when the other wasn't around. It wasn't a corny, romance movie marriage where they completed the other, it was just that they were both somehow *more* when they were together. Julian never felt that kind of comfort with anyone, except perhaps as a child, but never again.

His last girlfriend, Catherine, he had initially liked because of her name. Catherine Earnshaw, the same as the heroine of *Wuthering Heights*. But the name was where the similarities ended. They had met in his second year of college in the university library. She was from a suburb of Detroit—Rochester Hills, Bloomfield Hills, Hillsdale—something like that. She'd been pretty in a bland, predictable kind of way. Highlighted blonde hair, big eyes lined heavily in black and edged with metallic mauves and greys. She'd been bursting with borrowed opinions on politics, religion and family, plagiarized egregiously from her parents. She spouted these ideas in such a way that Julian could actually hear her father's voice when she spoke.

Her idea of travel was South Padre or Cabo San Lucas for Spring Break, and her idea of "wanderlust" was links that she pinned to her social media online. Cathy was a glorious lipsticked automaton without a soul. Eventually the very things that had attracted her to him, his skills with languages, his well-travelled globe-hopping past, his old fashioned, polished way of dressing—these things became the poisoned tipped barbs in her arsenal. He was old-fashioned, liberal, snobby, stuck up, and not "macho enough" for her. She was looking for marriage and babies, and from a man that loved her like her daddy did.

Julian wasn't these things, and even though now he couldn't believe he had endured Cathy as long as he had, it had broken him at the time. He'd hated so much of the relationship—hunting with her father, the way she tried to dress him, the golf outings and country club dinners. The very things that his mother said "suffocated a person's soul". Cathy's was the kind of life that many people would be glad to slip into, the Cinderella slipper of their destiny that fit *just so*. But, for Julian, that slipper was too tight. He had bigger dreams than these.

It had also served as a reminder for all that he had lost when his parents died. They had offered the world to Julian, no part of it off limits, and when they died it was like the world closed up around him. And so, he and Cathy had ended badly, with overly dramatic chest beating and exaggerated ugly cries of "I've wasted my best years on you!" and "It was all for nothing then!", which Julian could hardly understand.

She was engaged now, he'd heard from his roommate, Patrick, who seemed to know plenty about everyone else's life, even if he rarely shared the details of his own. Julian was happy for her, and a lot of his bitterness had found its way out of the place in his heart where he had locked it. And instead of jealousy he found that he was now able to reflect on some of her critiques of his character without anger—and found that many of them were spot on.

Late fall and its bright leaves and cinnamon spice, a daily tease of the girl in the book, had frozen into a blustery, sugar-coated Michigan winter. This was the first time in the last few years he wasn't spending the holiday with Catherine's family, which was a relief. In old holiday movies the characters are always begging someone to join them for Christmas or imploring them not to spend the holiday alone. But, Julian thought this was nonsense. Every

Christmas without his mother and father, without their annual Christmas trip to Edinburgh, London or Oslo, without their harp music CDs and traditions, it wasn't Christmas. There was no better way to be depressed for the holiday than to spend it with people who celebrated it the wrong way. Christmas was carols and stockings filled to bursting and a new city to explore.

And so it was that the fall term was ending and Patrick had packed up for home, asking Julian one last time if he was sure he wouldn't like to come? Holidays are too hard on your own, he was always welcome, etc. The sound of his truck starting up and pulling away from their apartment was the happiest Julian had felt since the semester started.

His carefully chosen books were stacked higgledy-piggledy next to his bed, easily reachable by an eager outstretched arm. The harp music played and with it, his mother's voice singing along in his memory. It hadn't been a beautiful voice, but she had sung with enthusiasm and confidence. It had seemed lovely to him, first sound he remembered hearing and all that. But, the music didn't make him sad, nor the season. Instead, he felt closer to that old version of himself than he had in years. He could picture his father on the couch flipping through travel magazines and dog-earing the pages he'd want to show everyone later. His mother, elbow deep in a book, stopping every few pages to read a sentence or two aloud, looking at Julian and saying "Hm? What do you think of that, Jules?" And then continuing on reading silently, not needing or expecting an answer.

He'd always been good at pretending, and this fantasy was easier than most, as he'd seen it in real time, so very often.

The whole city outside was a winter dream. The streets stood starkly silent, emptied of their usual bustling occupants. Most of the students had gone home, but all was white and green boughs with starburst lights winking in the trees. But, no matter how many hot toddies he made or how many old books he drank in over that holiday break, the little leather book never returned. He kept expecting to see it on his nightstand or find it in the cushions of the chair, but it was nowhere—as if in wanting it he had banished it back to wherever magical treasures dwell.

With January came the worst season in Michigan: slush. It was these days most—covered in dirty water, trousers rolled up and peacoat snugly buttoned—that Julian's gypsy soul began to tremble and whimper at his self imposed captivity. The soles of his feet would itch, and his mind could never stick to the present moment, drifting along like a tendril of smoke in the wind, blown every which way but the place he was standing. Instead he was in Southern Italy or Mykonos or South Africa. He was peering over cliffs and drinking wine on the beaches. The temperature didn't have to be different. Just the location. Memories were calling to him from the past, yearning to be relived, and memories not yet made called even louder, begging to be experienced.

But he had one semester left, and if he was being honest, he was still afraid to leave. He was worried that his parents would somehow show up, it was all a mistake, what a great lark they'd had all these years.

Most unsettling though, was that he didn't have anywhere particular to go. Not really. Or rather, he *could* go almost anywhere he chose, but Julian couldn't make his mind up. Just when he settled on the destination that would shake him from these four long years of inactivity, he would find some reason that it wasn't quite right. He'd been there too many times, or he hadn't been there enough, or he hadn't yet been there at all. He had too many friends in this city, or he'd remember a close friend had recently moved from that city to a different one. He'd dismiss a place because it reminded him too much of his parents, or maybe because his father had said in passing he wasn't interested in ever going suchandsuch a place. He never got any closer to deciding, and so he never made plans for anything. He was stuck treading water, moving neither forward or back, just perpetual tiring motion. Enough to keep him busy, but not enough to move on.

As graduation grew ever closer, the dirty grey snow of late winter melted gleefully into the first green shoots and pansies in a window box, he was no closer to an answer. Julian hadn't a clue what his next step was. Should he be writing something? Applying for grad school? Law school? A position in a gallery or museum? His friends and classmates looked expectantly to *next* and he could only shake his head in bewilderment. When had life grown so tedious? When had these opportunities become difficult conundrums?

The next opportunity he had to come up for air was in late March. He had been drowning for so long in research papers and trying to come up with a thesis that differed from all the other barely employable prospective historians in his classes. The one ray of hope was his final art projects that were fairly producing themselves. The only problem? They were all the same. Her. She, the girl in the vision reproduced in pencil, in charcoal, in oil and watercolor. Any medium he could get his hands on, and as soon as the brush or the pencil was in his hand, her face would appear, fresh as life. Not the stale, dead-eyed expression of old photographs, but real as life. He painted to remove her from his mind, he painted her to clarify what he had seen. But mostly he painted her to make the whole experience more real somehow, to bring her back. His art advisor had called it his "best work, his truest vision".

Julian's roommate, Patrick, was an art major, and for all of his pretended lack of focus, his disinterest in art elsewhere on campus, he knew his roommate was a talented sculptor. and gifted painter. Patrick took pains to hide it, drinking too much at parties and feigning disinterest in their classmates conversations over technique. But, Julian had lived with him for four years now and knew that there was nothing closer to his heart than his passion for creation. Julian had always been a great admirer of art, and had spent most of his childhood touring the museums of the world, feeding off of the masters. It was this that inspired his decision to make art his minor, a bit like taking classes with old friends, Titian, Monet, Cézanne, Rubens, Hals, Sargent...these were his comrades since he was a child, just as his favorite authors were. But for the first time, in painting *her*, Julian thought he felt the same passion for art that Patrick carried deep within him all the time. A force so powerful that he dared not let out that smoky mixture of creativity and darkness.

It was this element of mystery that swirled around Julian's brain as he and Patrick left the studio together after class and wandered over to the Brown Jug for a beer and something to eat. Sliding onto the familiar bar stools they both ordered whatever was seasonal from Bell's, a local brewery, and sat silently, companionably, for a few minutes as they sipped.

Julian had met Patrick freshman year. He had been confused at first, as to why this burly school spirit paragon was attaching himself to his side. It wasn't that Julian was unpopular with people, quite the reverse. His life abroad had taught him how to get along with virtually anyone. It was just that because he had moved around so much he hadn't much use for close friends or casual girlfriends. He had never been one for *needing* others. Julian had his thoughts and his books, and temporary acquaintances that served for a few months or a year before he moved on again. He stayed in touch with a few of these people, but only for a quick hello, or a text now and again.

But Patrick had been resolved on making friends, and

so they had now lived together all through college. They made an odd pair though, he and Patrick. His roommate was a giant of a man, six foot five, 250 pounds of muscle, dark ebony skin with a clear complexion, he was always getting them into places for free claiming he was on the football team. Between that and his uncanny ability to charm anyone, Patrick was intensely likable. Julian in comparison, was a very different physical specimen. Average height, with a kind of mediterranean handsomeness, lithe and lean-muscled with bright eyes and thick dark hair like brewed coffee. It was his clothing that really made him stand out; blazers, cardigans, and twill trousers. Pointy leather shoes and men's jeans in the Parisian style, cut tight with the appearance of tailoring. He wore pressed button-downs and in the correct shades for his olive coloring. The result was cosmopolitan and a little old fashioned. He was very definitely out of place in this Ann Arbor, Michigan college campus, but he liked it that way. Patrick beside him was wearing an oversized university sweatshirt and jeans that had collected some plaster and paint from his latest projects. They were an odd pair, indeed.

Julian had come to realize over the years that Patrick had pursued his friendship because of his differences from their peers. Because the self he was with Julian wore a very different face than the good-natured affable mask he wore for most of the day. They weren't close still, even after all this time, but they were content in one another's company, which is a horribly undervalued quality.

After drinking half of their beers, Patrick nudged him and spoke quietly, staring at the TV.

"Weather's supposed to bump up next week, just in time for spring break. You game for Cocoa Beach this year? Supposed to be crazy!"

Julian smiled and laughed, Patrick had invited him every year, and he'd never yet entertained the idea of actually going. But, it had become a kind of ritual to ask, and so every year he did, knowing the answer was no.

"No way, Pat. It sounds awful. Crazy is right, I'd have to be crazy to drive across the country with some of these people you hang with."

Julian chuckled at Patrick who was feigning offense.

"Besides, I have some work to do on my History thesis, and some tweaks on that oil painting."

"Well, I'm super jealous of you there. Though, I'm not sure how many more 'tweaks' you can make on that oil before it's just a big mess of paint." Patrick said with another big-toothed smile. They both sat comfortably, for a moment, the same thoughts on their minds, four years of being easy roommates would soon end. This was the last Spring Break of their college career.

"Well, what's next then, Pat?" Julian drained his golden brew and signaled to the bartender for a refill.

"Today? Or what's next in life?"

"In life, I suppose."

Patrick reddened a bit, but couldn't stop the smile from once again overtaking his face. His broad shoulders relaxed significantly, as if he had carried something burdensome on them all day and suddenly was offered the chance to put it down. He took a long pull on his beer before answering.

"Well, it had been a secret, but I guess there's no harm in telling you, Jules. I'm...I'm moving to New York. I've got a job at a gallery. It's not much but, well...I'll have enough time to keep making my own art, and hopefully rub a few elbows in the art scene there."

Patrick looked sheepish in sharing his news, his smile beginning to glide off his face, and instead the anxious need for approval took over as he bit his lip and offered Julian a look sidelong.

"Well done, you! When did you line all this up?"

"Oh, it's just recent. But you're the first I've told. You don't think it's...stupid?"

"I think it's absolutely brilliant, Pat!"

Patrick's smile finally reached his eyes.
"Thanks, Jules. Seriously. And, I mean, you'll have to visit..."

The words hung over them. Patrick knew that Julian had traveled and lived more places before college than he'd be likely to see in a lifetime, but he also knew that Julian hadn't been outside Michigan since they'd met. Changing the subject, Patrick cleared his throat and asked,

"What about you? What's next?"

His face was friendly and his inquiry kindly meant, but Julian was at a loss to answer. His eyes bored down into the effervescent gold of the beer and then flicked over the marred and well-used wooden surface of the bar.

"We'll see. I've got quite a few opportunities I'm looking into."

"That's great, Jules. I'm not surprised. Seriously, good for you, man."

Their glasses clinked and the conversation turned to art class and current events. But try as he might, Julian couldn't swallow Patrick's question alongside the beer. He ordered another to try and forget, but it stayed with him despite his efforts.

Later that next week on a damp evening, a volume of Sherlock Holmes lying forgotten on his knees, Julian was staring at an antique map of Italy he'd purchased in Naples years ago. The city names always sounded like music to him. Rhyming poetry names that seemed like fantasy lands instead of cities like any other. Venezia, Calabria, Positano, Torino, Firenze...beautiful. Patrick's question still ate away at his thoughts, demanding to be entertained. The truth was, he dreamed of leaving. He wanted desperately to go away. But, he'd lied to Patrick. He had no plans, no opportunities. He was too afraid to escape. How would his parents find him if they came back?

He was half a bottle deep in some California red blend he'd made an obsessive habit of buying. He was alone in the apartment, and practically alone on campus, owing to spring break. Julian was somewhere in the middle of reading for pleasure, researching through some articles for his history project and dozing. At the moment, dozing, distraction and the map were winning the day.

Setting the wine glass down and peeling his eyes from the map on the wall, its gilded frame needing a good dusting, he knew he really needed to make some headway on the research. His hands reached down for the heavy leather-bound *Sherlock Holmes* compendium to move it aside, when his eyes caught something strange on the table alongside the almost-empty wine bottle. He dragged a hand over his face, forehead to chin, and reached for it tentatively. His hands were trembling in anticipation, all thoughts of research banished. He brought it to his nose, and breathed in that same cinnamon, cardamom and clove scent. He gripped it firmly, afraid it would disappear again, and tenderly he opened it. The book was back, and this time he would read the pages. His eyes hungrily consumed the swooping elegant whorls, as the girl of his memories took shape, his own little apartment dissolving from sight.

CHAPTER THE THIRD
A New Voice Is Heard

From the Diary of Lively Lindenwood

Dear Diary,

No matter how many times I put pen to page, it is always with an odd feeling of trespass. Knowing that this was purchased to be filled with my dear papa's thoughts, ideas and confessions, creates in me a desire to write something worthy of him. It is a feeling that is immediately followed by intense dissatisfaction that I only did accomplish in scribbling dribbles.

But, for all of that, this little book has become over these months, as dear a companion to me as I could hope for. This little black and golden book, with an oddly smudged spine, as if papa had cut away the words that used to have been there, this tome is my constant. Even as the days and weeks slip me by, each moment I fill deeper with abhorrence of this place. Aunt Charlotte seems to always be about my ankles like a terrier, tripping me and hounding me through my days. Uncle is quite the opposite, as I've written before, but still it is no great virtue to have the intellect of a baked potato. As for the vapid cousins, I will try not to mention them for at least another paragraph as a kind of penance for my last entry on their shortcomings. Suffice it to say that it is a miracle they haven't violently murdered one another with boredom and ignorance.

Aunt Charlotte has persisted in calling me 'Olivia', though I have told her nigh on a thousand times that though my parents might have given me that name, to them I was naught but 'Lively'. Does the woman not understand that it would be comforting to be called by something familiar? That hearing "Lively" on someone's lips would give me welcome? How she can be so completely opposite to her brother, my papa, I can't imagine. Mama would of course urge me to try harder, and to love this family as I ought.

But…Papa was hardly ever cross. And if he was, he got it all out in one go so that sunshine could return to his features. Aunt Charlotte never smiles, nor Uncle George. I am inclined to think that Victoria and James are too stupid to know how to do so properly. Oh dear, I had meant not to mention them again.

I will repeat the same question that I ask in all of my entries. Why did they have to die? Why did they have to leave me alone in the world? My parents were peculiar, and our life together wasn't usual, but we needed one another. "The Three Musketeers" Papa always said. What is one Musketeer alone? Who am I without my other parts? Why am I left to fight my way through this life that feels foreign and strange?

Detroit is agony to someone who is used to the vibrance of the continent and the wonders of the east. I miss the sunshine, and the cities. I miss the twinkling lights of a million lamps, and the salt in the ocean air. Everything was more colorful with Papa, as if he painted it only for me. There is no mystery here in this blank place, and if there is, my aunt makes certain that I never see enough to encounter one. Never am I to speak of life abroad, probably aunt thinks it unfit conversation for her irritating children. So it is a kind of milk-toast life, desperately needing the seasoning of the spice of new experience.

I hear from my friend, my only friend besides you, little book, that Detroit could be a place of wonders. There is much happening here, as if it is the new epicenter of America. She hints at exciting happenings just beyond our doorstep, but I find myself held fast to the stoop. And so no matter the splendor of our former life, or the marvels that could be within reach, I am quite alone, except for this book and my memories within it.

Sometimes when I am writing I pretend that I am having a conversation with Mama and Papa. I write out all of the inane, ignorant things that someone in this house has said and I quite divert myself with the responses I imagine Papa would come up with. All the while, Mama chides me for my unkindness. But lately, I have seen <u>him</u> instead. I only saw him truly the once, unless it was a very vivid dream in a moment I did not know I was sleeping. But his face is burned into my eyes, searing them with his own. As if his eyes melted into mine and I can only see the world through the lens of our combined vision now.

And so I read over my words today, and I am ashamed of myself, as I think he would be. I do not know this young man, nor can I really believe he exists, but there is something different in me since the experience. A glowing hope that grows, and tells me I am capable of more and better things than these petty trifles I focus so closely on.

And so, I shall not denigrate the love my dear parents held for me with any more unkind words, if I can help it. Perhaps, too, this enigmatic man of my thoughts can lead me to behave better and to be grateful, as I ought.

She had been sitting on the settee in her bedroom, writing for some time. The room was friendly enough in hues of fresh lavender and a lazy French blue. But, to Lively, it was still a prison. She could hear Aunt Charlotte calling from the stair, but could not bring herself to answer. How many times had she asked to be called "Lively"? She knew it was childish, but to answer to the other name felt like abandoning her parents. It would be a kind of betrayal to her own heart, and a second death for them that had called her so lovingly by the name she preferred. When no one else called her by that name she had always known, she feared she would cease to hear it entirely, the memory of those that had spoken it so often, vanished into the dust.

Aunt Charlotte, she could tell by the heavy tread on the rug in the hall, rapped in tight succession on the door, and then stepped inside without permission.

"Olivia?"

The way she said it stretched out the word and gave the final syllable the most emphasis. From her mouth it sounded like "Oh-liv-ee-AHH", which made Lively cringe as much as the name itself.

"Yes, Aunt."

"We have been waiting in the parlor for you this past half hour."

"Oh?" Lively looked to her aunt with as much innocence as she could muster.

"Yes, Victoria and the Misses Fitzgerald are anxious to have your conversation and I am certain your tea has gone cold."

While Lively was certain the latter was true, the former claim she seriously doubted. She was sure that Victoria and both the Misses Fitzgeralds enjoyed her company every bit as much as she enjoyed theirs. That is, not at all. In all probability they thought her ill-mannered and boisterous, and she thought them as bland as twice-chewed saltines.

It was difficult for her to even look at her Aunt Charlotte. One always imagined one was speaking with a bulldog who has just sniffed something odious. Her mouth perpetually was drawn up in an expression of offended distaste, and sometimes Lively half expected her aunt to jump in her lap and force her niece to rub her stomach. Instead of bursting out in unrestrained hilarity, (as she had been known to do when she hadn't the time to prepare herself for the sight of her aunt) she swallowed and calmly acquiesced.

Lively's parents had disappeared a year ago this past March. She hadn't been with them at the time, which was unusual. Her father had left her behind at a convent in Southern France, the same that he told her that her mother had been educated in, though she'd never heard of her mother having lived in France as a girl. The École Primaire Sainte Odile in Montpellier was a charming place, and the nuns who were her teachers were kindness itself. But, even then she had felt bereft without her parents, and had not understood why they must do this new missionary work without her. Within a week of their arrival in Egypt, their letters stopped and within the month they were presumed dead. She hardly remembered the ship from Paris to Boston and then the journey here to Detroit. She had known that there were relatives here, but the knowledge was like a stocking in the drawer. She knew it was there, but it did not matter at all until she needed it. Their small life here and her ever having a part in it wasn't even a ghost of a thought in her mind.

And now it was October. She had lived here with a family she barely knew for nearly a year and had endured this weekly women's gathering for all of that time. Yet every time her slippered feet stepped into the parlor, it was a strange place, a scene from a hazy dream.

She had lingered too long on the stair. Aunt Charlotte had turned around offering her a strange look of such a mixture of confusion and idiocy that Lively snapped back to the moment immediately.

"Is it your pins, Olivia?"

"My pins, Aunt?"

"Hair pins. Giving you a headache."

She indicated Lively's hand still pressed tightly to her brow in thought that she had mistaken for pain. She took firm hold of the excuse and nodded. They continued down the staircase, all the while Aunt Charlotte muttered about Lively's needing company, less time in her room, and a plethora of other grumblings that she didn't approve of in her niece's habits.

Lively sailed into the parlor and sat demurely at the empty seat, trying to avoid the stale expressions on the faces of the assembled company. Her cousin Victoria seemed oblivious to her presence. She always had an air of confused vagueness, with blonde effortless curls and a small rosebud mouth beneath warm vacant brown eyes. As if reality didn't really exist and she was in a kind of humming daydream that made sense to herself alone. Plump, but shapely, obedient, sweet and charitable with her time, she was someone whom no one could find fault with. Yet, somehow Lively hated her. Perhaps because she was a reminder of what a proper young woman should be, and Lively's soul rebelled against all of the shoulds and supposed-tos that limited her gender. Victoria was... colorless. She was not greatly moved by music or art, and it was unclear if she had the wherewithal to read a novel. Not passionate about anything, just blandly bobbing on the current of her own life.

The Misses Fitzgerald though, were very passionate about a number of topics of which they understood very little but were enraptured to discourse upon anyway. They weren't twins, but they operated as one complete person. Lively often wondered what would happen if she locked one of them in the cellar for an hour. Would the other wander in circles silently until they were reunited? She very much thought so.

The conversation at the table had hardly varied for the past few months. The gala.

It had been the main point of discussion since word of it had trickled down the fashionable streets of Detroit. A brief rain shower of gossip had wetted wagging tongues for miles. In midsummer, Mr. LeBlanc, who was a partner at the bank with Uncle George, had let slip that his wife was making a big to-do over their son Anton's 20th birthday. Despite the obvious enthusiasm of the rest of the ladies in the city, every week Lively felt excluded from the conversation. Not because the others in the company did not seek her opinions and thoughts, but instead a personal detachment from it. As if distancing herself from events that were interesting to the créme of Detroit, she could pretend that she was not one of them. She had never had to *belong* anywhere, and the pressures of community and familiarity were a heavy burden on the silk shoulders of her grey dress. She also felt it very difficult to imagine what else there could possibly be left to discuss, as they had exhausted the subject every week.

"But ladies, what *are* you going to wear?"
Victoria gushed, pouring herself a cup of very cold tea. Lively began to take a sip herself, when the door opened abruptly and a welcome sight popped brusquely into the already cramped room.

"Bonjour mesdames! No one say another word until I'm seated and comfortable."

Madame Isadora sailed gracefully into the side chair before the maid could reach the doorway. Madame Isadora was a bit of a mystery, but she knew everyone and had presumably lived in France until her marriage thirty years ago. She lived just a few houses down on Woodward Ave, and was endlessly making the rounds visiting neighbors and friends, and then suddenly disappearing for weeks at a time. There was a rumor that she had a young beau in Chicago since the death of her husband some years past, which Lively could easily believe. Madame Isadora, or more properly Madame Isadora Bellevie, was tall and dark with hazel eyes that blazed gold when she was very interested in something. Her youthful prettiness had settled very elegantly into her advancing years. She wore her age as a new hat, jauntily and with confidence. Lively could believe there was a younger beau somewhere, but she didn't quite think it was true. Whatever Madame Isadora's secret was, Lively was glad she had one. It made life more exciting somehow.

Conversation had resumed and the Fitzgeralds were describing in their identical nasal voices the velvet monstrosities they were having made for the gala. Lively tilted her head from the gilded rim of the tea cup to see five sets of eyes looking at her expectantly.

"Yes?" she asked, unable to hide her confusion.

"Well, what are you wearing? What does the dress look like?"

Lively had gone to the dressmaker with her aunt and Victoria weeks before, but she had opted instead for a few every-day dresses suited for the upcoming cold weather. Of her dresses from Paris, she found they were too fine and designed a bit more avant-garde for the colder weather. The rest of her wardrobe had been pared down for the trip across the Atlantic, and she had grown out of many of her well-worn frocks.

"I hadn't thought of it" she replied, in a tone that dismissed further inquiry.

Lively dropped her eyes once again and stared deeply into her cup. The silence in the room grew awkward and expanded, suffocating further conversation. With a clatter, Madame Isadora dropped her tea cup back into the saucer and spoke in an oddly distracted manner.

"Oh, but Olivia, you'll look lovely in anything. All that heavy hair—and your figure! You resemble Evelyn Nesbit almost more than her reflection."

Lively reddened considerably, but Madame Isadora's eyes were far away, appearing to see through the walls of the room. The woman was there in the room with the rest of the party, but she was elsewhere too. Only vaguely making the correct comments in the right pauses of conversation, a recording on the gramophone.

Lively looked down, still blushing from the compliment and made to protest even if the compliment was well intended. Surely Gibson's girls were beautiful, but Lively felt uncomfortable with praise.

Aunt Charlotte had deftly reigned in the conversation though, and it had already sped past Madame's comment. The girls were now speaking enthusiastically, once again, about the upcoming gala, going over every detail of their dress and their hopes for their dance card. The room grew hazy, though it was only mid-afternoon, and as the darkness fell like a night sky with only pin-pricks of stars, Lively only had time to catch the table cloth.

When her eyes fluttered open, the sun had risen once again because all was light. Her eyes flicked over to the table where all had received a lap full of cold tea, and the colorful china had scattered on the carpet like wildflowers. Two of the maids had rushed in the room at the sound. One quickly began picking the little china buds on the floor and assisted the ladies at the table. The other pulled Lively to standing with the strength of a woman much larger than herself and dragged her to the stair, calling behind her,

"Nothing to worry about, Miss Olivia has just had a little attack of her nerves".

Her hand on Lively's wrist was a clamp of iron until they reached the safety of her bedchamber, wherein both maid and Miss threw themselves into the pillows, burying their faces to stifle their giggles.

Clara Howard was the upstairs maid in Mr. George and Mrs. Charlotte Maxon's house. More importantly,

Clara was Lively's dearest and only true friend besides her little black journal.

"God in Heaven, Lively! But one would almost think you'd planned it! Each of the ladies looked as though they'd pissed themselves!"

They pressed their faces harder into the pillows, stomachs convulsing in fits. When they had sufficiently calmed enough to speak, they turned toward one another and clasped hands, a devilish smile reflected from one face to the other.

"Oh, Miss Lindenwood, at least once a month you ruin your cousin's tea in some form or fashion. "

"I know, Clara. I can't seem to help it. Everything just goes black. As if my mind is so idle that it seeks to exit the confines of tea. And they're still discussing that damned ball."

"Oh, aye." Clara looked down at the floor, all traces of glee folded back into her features. She was not one given to moodiness, and so the change to her usual cheerfulness was marked.

"What is it, Clara?"
She looked up at Lively then, her neat maid's uniform clean and unwrinkled. She had perfect posture and no matter how hard she worked she was always fresh and sweet. Lively had taken ill on the voyage and had arrived thus in Detroit. It had been Clara and her stories of her family, her heartbreaks, and the fantastical ideas of horseless carriages taking over the streets of town that had healed her. It was painful then to see this vibrant creature grown so muted.

"What is it, Clara? What have I done?"

Lively pulled her closer and embraced her. Her aunt would have a conniption if she saw her niece so familiar with a servant, but it had always been this way for Lively's family. Anyone who was in her father's employ or helped her mother around their house was treated as an equal. She clasped the shivering little maid's hands tighter and waited for her to speak. Clara exhaled and pulled herself a few inches farther away, peering deeply into her mistress' eyes.

"Well, it's just that an invitation to Mr. LeBlanc's ball seems, well, it seems a rare treat to be sure. Many girls, including myself, would give their right arm to go. I...I know that you're not like other girls" she added hastily with a nod of her head toward the parlor. "But, it still is a shame to look at a grand night of dancing and amusement as a misfortune."

Lively had cast her eyes downward, wishing to sink though the floors and into the cool earth. Hot shame pounded at her temples. "Oh! Clara! I *am* sorry. You must think me a spoiled wretch. I wish...I wish it were you going in my stead."

Clara's mouth turned up wryly in one corner and she shook her head, her eyes turning skyward as if asking heaven if it was hearing this conversation.

"Aye, but it's not me. Now, I understand why you do not want to attend. We've both had enough sorrows to fill the River Rouge. You know my story...I've already had a chance with love, and I only escaped with a shattered heart and a hazy plan for revenge" She paused and breathed deeply summoning something within herself, her eyes never leaving Lively's. A flicker of resolution registered on her face, and she continued.

"But, Lively, would you go for me? And not just go like you go down to take tea with the young ladies—sort of a body without a soul. Only going because you must and it is expected. No, would you...for me, would you dance and smile and pretend you want to be there? That way, when you tell me of it later, 'twill be as if I went and had a lovely time too. And somehow, I think, my own sadness would seem less."

Her eyes, shining brighter and brighter as she spoke, finally flowed over with tears, as did Lively's. It was a silly thing, they both knew, but in the moment the gala wasn't just a silly party, it was a whole world. Clara would never go to a ball. She would never have a fine dress to wear or drink champagne surrounded by young men who flirted with her gallantly. The friends embraced, Lively pulling her friend to her breast.

"Yes, Clara, of course. And please accept my apology for all of my blubbering about it. How you've stood all my grumbling about it these past weeks, I have no idea..."

"Hush!" The mischief had come back into Clara's eyes. "That's enough of that. You're forgiven. Now, you must forgive me, I'm afraid."

"Forgive you for what?" Lively sat back against the headboard, catching her friend's mood like a fever. Clara walked across the room and pulled a dressmaker's box from the armoire.

"That moss colored satin your great uncle sent from London?"

"Yes...?"

"Well, I told Master George that you would be needing it for the ball. I took it down to the dressmaker's myself and had her use the measurements from your last fitting. The style, well, it's quite unusual. New and daring... and straight from Paris. It's worn only loosely corseted, but with a high waist of rose taffeta. Miss, the color will compliment the golden lights in your hair and the apples of your cheeks. You simply had to have it."

Lively embraced her again, not even attempting to brush away the falling mist of tears. Hearing her name on the stair, Clara's head turned, and her girlish smile vanished. She was once again the upstairs maid, no longer a bosom companion to one of her betters. She stepped to the door, but before leaving turned and spoke in an excited whisper.

"Now you must pretend to be excited, Lively Lindenwood, or you'll break my heart!"

She smiled like a cat with feathers sticking from it's mouth and was out the door.

Lively sat on the edge of her bed, still holding the heavy dress box on her lap. She knew she had made a mess of things downstairs, yet again. Her aunt and cousins thought her bohemian and rather uncouth. A sentiment that Lively was certain was shared by the Fitzgeralds and the other young ladies in their acquaintance. Her cousin James, Victoria's brother, was intolerably stupid in the way that spoiled boys are when nothing much is expected of them. But, he had the virtue of being genuinely kind and found her years abroad interesting rather than scandalous. She made her mind up to find him before supper and ask him about the dancing and so forth. He'd be better for asking, less likely to tease. She wondered at the reaction of her relatives at her sudden change of heart relating to the ball. Likely, they wouldn't notice. Yes, she really must go, and she really must force herself to enjoy it, if only for Clara's sake.

Lively carefully opened the box and ran a hand over the fabric of the dress, the intricate golden threads woven into the silk. It *was* beautiful, the way it flashed flaxen and seafoam in the changing light. Clara had been right, as always, the color was the perfect accompaniment to her hazelnut waves. How clever of her to have used the fabric

—it was much too fine for any other purpose.

The gala was ten weeks away. She had no particular beau to hope of dancing with or any particular friends with which to look forward passing the evening. Anton LeBlanc was handsome enough, and charming, and the rest of the young men would be different shades of the same. Not one man existed that sent shivers down her body or beat a familiar tattoo in her heart. Except, well, except the boy from the dream. He'd seemed so real though, his woodland eyes boring deeply into her own, dark unkempt hair and an olive face. She could have reached out and touched him, laid her hand on his own. He had been so close…but then not there at all.

CHAPTER THE FOURTH
A Fortune Is Revealed

Unexpectedly, the vision ended. His hands uselessly turned the pages, but they were empty. Surely...surely they had been full before? Covered in her swooping, sweeping hand, weren't they? Their blank whiteness stared back at Julian, settling as an opaque fog on the scenes that had been so vivid just a few moments before.

Everything in the room was as he'd left it. The wine glass, the bottle, the research notes, the hefty tome of *Sherlock Holmes*. Everything was unchanged, except for Julian.

What had begun as reading had become instead a completely immersive vision. He was reading her words, but he was also in the parlor with the ladies, drinking tea. He was in his chair at his apartment, but he was also sitting on the bed with her and Clara, giggling into their pillows.

Her. Lively. What a name for a woman. Appropriate for the quickness of her mind and animation of her features. The experience wasn't like that of other books, where one's imagination paints the story. No, this was... *real*. He could smell her sweet orange perfume and could feel the silk as she held it on her lap. And she had seen him too.

Julian loved the way she wrote. Her writing was like speaking, but in a cadence that was only familiar to him through novels. She was witty and clever, charming and blunt. If he were to meet her on the street, he should think they were already fast friends. The writing that at first glance he had thought old-fashioned now seemed fitting. It was bold and confident, blaring off the page, just like the woman herself.

He smiled and tilted his head back into the buttery softness of the old leather chair. It was an awful shade of mustard yellow, but it had been the first article of furniture his mother had purchased from an antique store in Ann Arbor when they moved to Detroit. "It has character, and it needs us" she'd said. The memory of the voice in his mind spoke crisply, was deceivingly sweet, but brooked no disagreement, much like his mother herself. His head fell deeper into the headrest and he absently chewed the pen he had been using for his research notes.

It was crazy, nonsensical…impossible, and yet, it *had* happened. He had read the words, but he had also seen her face. Heard her speak. Impossible it might be, but it seemed that this didn't prevent it from having occurred.

Julian settled more completely into the chair, still considering the startling events of what had previously been a tediously average night. The yellow chair gave off a faint scent of spicy pipe smoke and a kind of masculine musky smell mingled with a woodsy cologne the longer one sat in it. It was a scent that reminded him of his father, though his father was neither musky nor a pipe smoker. No, Finnegan Cole always smelled like fresh shower and the same cologne that Julian's mother bought his father for their anniversary every year. The chair reminded him of his father simply because that masculine tang would emanate from its yellow depths as his father typed away on his computer or pored over his work binders. Scent and music seemed to have the keenest link to his memories. Julian would catch part of a song playing in the bookstore and suddenly he was in Ireland, riding in the backseat of a rental car, while his parents disagreed on directions, the same tune playing softly on the little radio. Or a certain unknown perfume, usually worn by older ladies, would take him back to their Paris flat and the indomitable Mme. LaChance who favored the scent and small yapping dogs. Peppermint oil always brought visions of his mother, slathering her arms and shoulders in it after her bath. Links lying in wait in his mind, patiently biding their time until something would come along and connect them.

Memories had ceased to be painful for Julian, and instead they served as a bridge between now and then, and they were beginning to forge a path between now and what lay silently ahead. Julian could not be sure what shape that future would take, but he'd begun to feel 'normal' again.

When had it stopped hurting? He didn't know. The death of his parents, his fear of leaving, the purpose of his life had been carried painfully in his stomach like a gnawing tumor eating away at his insides. A dull, heavy reminder of his own limitations—and then like elastic on an old pair of socks, it had slackened. Bit by bit, it had hurt less, so minuscule a change that it was not noticed in the process, until one day he realized that the pain simply, no longer was. He was not burdened as he once had been, and was instead freer and lighter, though still conflicted.

But still, when these memories came, unsought, unbidden, the first feeling was of sucking sadness. A cold punch to his stomach, but then it would lessen and he was able to relive the moments with a light heart.

For the rest of spring break, the book was nowhere to be found. All the same, Julian thought about Lively daily. He saw her in his dreams and imagined her life as he slogged through merciless Michigan lake winds swirling around campus. He wondered about the gala and her life before Detroit. He wondered if she missed her parents like he missed his, and in what way they had perished. He mostly wondered *how*. How was this happening and what did it mean? How did the magic work? And was there such a thing as magic? And why were they both provided this window into one another across the decades?

The break from classes had succeeded not only in giving him the long awaited peep into his mystery woman's life, but it had also provided ample time for Julian to study, to complete a few canvases and to create and extrapolate on the graduation thesis for his history degree. He'd trashed an oil painting of her, begun carefully a month previously, when he had realized to his chagrin, that he hadn't captured the look of her at all. He had begun again, obsessed with the need to get the likeness correct. Julian was absorbed in the feeling of brushstrokes on canvas, Cole Porter blaring from his speakers, when Patrick came in the door.

It was some time before Julian even realized that his roommate was there, just behind his right shoulder, politely observing, not wishing to interrupt. A trait that he had always appreciated in this huge, gentle man. By the time Julian turned around, Patrick too was lost in the paint and the color. Julian saw his eyes flash back and forth, missing nothing. He almost could believe that Patrick could tell him the exact order he'd laid the strokes down.

"This is good, Jules."

"Thanks, Pat."

"No, I mean, this is really good. It's raw and human and yet...so animated and ethereal. It's almost like she's in this room, dude."

Putting the brush down and wiping his hands on a towel, Julian smiled. "Thanks, seriously. She's hard to capture. How was your trip?"

Patrick dragged his eyes from the wet paint before him, the girl on the canvas smiling mischievously at a joke he would never hear. His expression was glazed confusion.

"Trip?"

Julian laughed, "Now, that *is* a compliment. My humble painting is enough to make you momentarily forget the thrill of Florida and crazy half-naked girls in bikinis on the beach."

Realization bloomed, and his onyx cheeks blushed a shade of dusky scarlet.

"Oh, yeah. Man, it was nuts. Probably smart you stuck around here. Fights, hangovers, drama, drama, drama…let's just say I'm glad I went, but I won't miss it. You have an okay time here? Was it like this all week?"

Patrick gestured absently toward the window, spattered with cold spring rain relentlessly beating a tattoo on the panes.

Julian looked at the window, then back at Patrick, a bewildered look on his face. He opened his mouth to answer, but was immediately interrupted.

"Let me guess, you have no idea because your skinny ass hasn't left the apartment except to go to the gym in the dead of night?"

They both laughed and Julian tried not to look sheepish. The reason they'd picked this complex to live in three years ago had been the very gym that Patrick was referring to. It sat lonely and mostly unused in the basement, its only visitor being Julian as most of the students preferred the better facilities on campus. He went when he couldn't sleep, which was four or so nights out of the week. He always supposed it was because his body was still tuned to a different time zone and petulantly refused to adapt to America, much like Julian himself. Patrick, having enough eccentricities of his own, never asked questions and only teased him lightly.

"Anyway man, it's a good thing you've got that permanently tanned skin gene, or else you'd scare people with your Boo-Radley-Casper-the-ghost shit. This letter, along with about five pounds of mail was in the box, so I already knew you were either dead or a hermit this week. Here ya go, bro. I'm going to catch a nap, Chinese later?"

Patrick had handed him the letter and then had spoken the rest as he moved down the hallway toward his own bedroom door.

"Yeah, sure. Sounds good, thanks for grabbing this. Welcome back, Pat."

Julian heard Patrick's door close and the sound of his large frame hitting the bed. He wasn't kidding about sleep. Julian felt a momentary pause of guilt throb in his stomach. He'd kept the place clean, cut his own hair and had made a recipe or two in imitation of favorite dishes from local restaurants. But he had lived like a recluse this past week. Nose in a book, fingers stained with paint, phone off. He really needed to get out of there. Not just there the apartment, but *there*. This city. This country. This stage of his life.

Julian ran a hand through his dark hair and then pulled it out quickly, assessing it for any wet paint he may have inadvertently just combed through. He looked down at both hands and remembered the envelope, still held lazily in the fingers of his right hand, held so long it had been forgotten.

He almost never received personal mail. He had no family that he knew of, all of them dead, and neither of his parents had siblings that he'd met or heard mention of. The art of letter writing was just as dead as this unknown family, and if a friend had a message for him it was delivered via text or phone call. The only mail he received was bills or documents from the University, the bank, or his parent's solicitors in London.

This little letter didn't look like any of those. It was definitely from a solicitor, the outer envelope reading:

Daniele Anastasio & Associati
Studio di Consulenza Tributaria e Legale

with an address in the Naples business district that Julian
vaguely recognized. There was something about the letter
that quickened Julian's blood. The paper in his hands felt
cool, and he brushed his fingertips over the seal on the
back again and again, like a sorcerer searching for the
magic incantation necessary to reveal the message within.
He was stalling, and he knew it, but this strange letter
made him nervous. Pressing the paper to his nose, he took
in the well-remembered scents of espresso, grit, pizza and
death, a mix that was distinctly Neapolitan. Repulsive and
endearing all at once, all of Italy was a singing siren, but
Naples bubbled with the most vitality. Even with its total
obsession with the macabre, its heart beat, the pulse of the
joyful life of the city itself pounded throughout the streets.
Italy, the land of harmonizing opposites, deceit and death
and the sacred were charming bedfellows of beauty and
vivacity and frivolity.

A stirring in his chest brought the images back. The
summertime villa they had shared in Sorrento and his
father cruising a little white boat up and down the
Tyrrhenian. His mother had been ill, he remembered. She
loved the sea, but only when her whole body was covered
in the salty water, never from a boat.

All this while he held the little letter in his hands. It
was still warm, like a living thing, and he knew it contained
information that would change things. He was afraid.
Afraid of what it might contain, and what it might require
of him. For some reason, his first experience skydiving,
done on a whim with his father in Auckland, came to
mind. Knowing that a great leap lay before him and that
the next step was out into that unknown tumbling chaos.
Maybe because no one wrote him letters, or perhaps
because the letter seemed to contain a trace of that magic
from the black leather book. He knew that ever since he
had first spied that diary and read its pages, his life had

been whirring out of his control, and that was why he hesitated. Julian had been living in a kind of dreamy darkness since his parent's death and these beams of lights terrified him, lest they dim again and leave him concealed deeper in shadow.

He heard Patrick roll over heavily on his bed in the other room. For some reason, the reassurance of his being there gave Julian a kind of strange courage. Without another moment's thought, he ripped the envelope apart, as the first present of Christmas morning, and examined the note inside. It contained simple words, written in excellent English and although the verbiage was direct, the letters swam before his eyes, rearranging constantly into indecipherable patterns he could not understand. Taking a seat, Julian smoothed the thick paper out on the notched desk and read it slowly.

Signore Julian Cole,

I am writing to inform you that your grandmother, Sig.ra Argentina Di Leo has regrettably left this world. I offer you my utmost condolences.

With the death of your mother, Sig.ra Mia Di Leo Cole, you are left as the sole beneficiary of your grandmother's estate.

The Villa Azzurro has been left to the Provincia di Salerno as a historical landmark, but the bulk of the financial assets are now yours.

I invite you to telephone or visit the office of Daniele Anastasio & Associati in order to go through the necessary paperwork and documentation.

With condolences,
Daniele Anastasio

Julian read the letter twice, thrice, memorized the writing. The office phone number from the top and the fax number beneath that. He held the letter firmly, forcing the warmth and life of the message to seep in through his hands until the object itself was cold and lifeless again.

His grandmother? Julian had never known of any living relations. His father's parents had died within a year of each other soon after he was born. His mother had never spoken of her family at all. But he had always assumed that this side of his family was long dead also. Julian couldn't imagine why his mother would keep such a thing from him. He thought for a moment of tracking down the secret of whatever enmity that had existed between his grandmother and mother. But, catching his mother's eye in the photograph on the desk, he dismissed this idea from his mind. If she had wanted him to know, she would have told him. Even the dead should be allowed their secrets.

So then why did he want to possess Lively's mysteries? Why were those secrets not to be left in respectful silence?

Julian shook his head and crumpled the letter distractedly. Strange that Lively should pop into his mind at such a time. He remained sitting at his desk, considering what he should do. He would call Signore Anastasio in the morning. It was Sunday, the avvocato wouldn't be in his office now.

He wondered lazily what kind of fortune had been left him. What would he do with it? Travel again, finally? Graduate or Doctoral school? The possibilities gave him a headache. Thinking about money always did. Life was much easier with it, but worrying and thinking about money brought its own ugly terrors. There was freedom in money, but also servitude. It shackled one to growing it, maintaining it, ever increasing its amount—the fear it would run out. To be sure he was fortunate for his reserves left by his parents and now whatever treasure his unknown grandmother had left, but he would give it all back. Julian would trade it in a flash for the family that was now forever absent.

Morning came and with it the bouncing nervousness in his gut. He was nervous about this call, like the day of a class presentation or the first time he'd driven a car. The phone call had been on his mind all night, greedily cheating him of sleep. Julian had been tempted to get out of bed and call, as the time difference would have allowed it, but he stayed his hand. No need to rush headlong. It was not necessary to hurry destiny, it was already unfolding about him without any of his aid.

It was early still, and Patrick had only just left for an eight o'clock class. Julian hadn't discussed the letter with Patrick over their dinner, instead he was content to hear all about his roommate's spring break. The ridiculous stories helped cloud his troubled mind.

He rinsed his teacup in the sink and breathing out heavily, he reached into his pocket for his phone. He carefully pressed each number and held the phone to his ear. Julian walked over to the yellow monstrosity of a chair and sat lightly, too anxious to be comfortable. The phone buzzed once, twice, three times, four. A clear, formal Italian voice finally answered.

"Ciao, questo è l'ufficio di Daniele Anastasio."

Julian's eyes searched the table for a pen and paper to take notes as they spoke. He absently grabbed at the items he needed on the table and brought them to his lap.

"Ciao, si, questo è Julian Cole. Ho ricevuto la tua lettera…"

His voice trailed off into nothing. The solicitor was speaking now in English, offering condolences. But Julian wasn't listening. The notebook he had grabbed in his preoccupation with the phone call was the little black book, returned again. The ink glittered on the page and appeared as if it were still wet to touch. Reaching down hesitantly, Julian pressed his index finger down into the page and his mind filled with the turn of the century. Quickly, he tore his finger away, revealing a dark smear of ink on its tip. The book lay open on his lap, its warmth on his trouser legs making it feel like it had just come from the hands of another. A living, breathing magic spanning the years, and the proof of it was still inked onto his finger.

The solicitor's voice broke into his thoughts and Julian turned his attention to the conversation, now desiring nothing more than to end the call. He gave the man all the information he needed, the name of his bank, his lawyer in town, his personal fax number. Julian's eyes never left the book, throughout the exchange. He was terrified lest it disappear again without his chance to swim once again in the depths of its pages.

The conversation was ending, the phone call he'd been sure was the key to his future. Instead, the book had appeared like a tug on his sleeve, forcing him to consider its importance. The tale within its pages, the mysteries inside seemed so much more important to his future. But how could it, when it was lived so far in the past?

Just before they rang off, Julian asked,

"Oh, mi perdoni, but how much is this fortune my grandmother left?"

"Signore, unfortunately, the full estate is not coming to you. You are receiving a smaller portion."

"That's perfectly all right, I just was wondering so that I could think of my future plans."

In response, the solicitor named such a vast amount that Julian's mouth fell agape and his eyes mimicked the width of his jaw. It was an inconceivable amount of money. The man could just as well have said the number of stars in the sky or rocks at the bottom of the sea.

Signore Anastasio had said his ciaos and promised to send all the documents over as soon as possible, but Julian remained in the same attitude. Sitting in the chair, one hand holding the phone to his ear, the other clutching the little black book for dear life. His eyes stared into the photograph of his parents, wishing they could speak to him through the same enchantment the book did.

He looked down to the open pages in his lap and the words he saw there made his jaw drop anew.

Dear Diary,

Is he here? The young man with the forest eyes —the man who stirs my dreams—is he here? Or is he a phantasm of my tortured mind?

I cannot help but think he is real, and more than that…I think we are connected, he and I.

CHAPTER THE FIFTH
A Visitor To Woodward Ave.

Lively smoothed a hand over her hair, detecting some stray wayward strands that had fallen from her pompadour and low bun. Her hair was so thick and heavy that having it up higher gave her an aching head. She considered taking it down but the Misses Fitzgerald would be arriving for tea soon, and she would never be able to put it back up by herself before their prim knock sounded on the front door. She chewed on the end of her fountain pen and re-read the words she had just written. Yes, it was strange, but reading the entry in her diary, she almost felt him with her now, beside her. Perhaps she *was* going a bit mad, though it wouldn't be surprising with the company she was forced into.

The gala was still ages away, but with Clara's voice in her ear reporting what she'd heard had been ordered, the menu, the guest list, the rooms that had been redone at the LeBlanc household for the soirée...she would be barely human if she wasn't growing more excited. Even though she had thought the whole thing a tremendous waste before, now she saw it all in a much different, softer light. Clara had used her best skills in gossip trading to gather all she could from the LeBlanc servants, and hadn't kept any delicious detail from being whispered into Lively's waiting ears. She was still slightly surprised at Clara's insistence on her attending the gala, but if it would bring her friend happiness, she supposed she saw how it made the girl excited. And the feeling was utterly contagious.

The result had been that she had given herself over to the idea of a sumptuous evening. She was enraptured with stories of satin tablecloths and pristine snow white bowties and pressed black tailcoats. The whole scene sounded so... European, a blazing flame of the old world on the banks of the Detroit River. She pictured the tumbling curls of the ladies, just kissing the tops of a white décolletage and tight fitting bodices, each lady a delicate frosted tea cake, sugar and sweetness swirling about her. She could hear the strings of the orchestra and wondered what kind of music would be played. Surely Anton LeBlanc would insist on some new melodies, it *was* 1900, after all.

She could hear the maids scurrying downstairs and her aunt trudging about, giving the orders for tea, as if the maids didn't know what they were about. The American way of treating servants was very different than what she had observed in London and around Paris. But then, Detroit was a newer place where people were still seemingly uncomfortable with their wealth. It was said that Detroit had a varied and diverse population, with a large portion of those living in the city not speaking English. Lively supposed it could be understood that Aunt Charlotte might explain things again and again, and demonstrate the way of doing something to a newer member of the help a few times, before trusting it was understood. The world was changing, and somehow it gave Lively an odd kind of happiness that those changes were coming out of the city she now called home, even if it was done grudgingly.

Lively took the pen from her mouth and looked back to the page opened before her. She laughed under her breath, wondering what someone else would think if they were to peek at her scribbles. No doubt they would think her foolish or very wicked, or perhaps both.

She pressed the nib to the paper and then heard a scratch at the door. She made to get up when she heard a soft voice through the keyhole, Clara's voice.

"Lively dear, you've about a quarter of an hour 'til the Mrs. will expect you down."

Lively heard a rustle of skirts in the hallway and then silence. Enough time for perhaps a little more writing, then.

Conjuring her mystery man in her mind, she pressed the pen again to paper, and let her thoughts take her out of the room, out of the chair, and into the part of her world where she was truly free.

Any moment now the company will arrive and I will be forced to sit through the tedium of tea with the fish-mouthed Fitzgeralds and the empty glass doll's eyes of my cousin Victoria. Except this week, I must admit their mindless prattle will be much more welcome than it formerly has been.

I have never understood gossip, really. Well, until recently at least, and even now I do not profess expertise in the moving cogs and levers of it. Spreading secrets and off-hand comments, details of another's life being poured drip by precious drip from the mouths of those "in the know" into the ears of those who would like to be considered so. In all of our travels, Mama, Papa and I had no such pastime.

My father always said we were exploring the world in the vein of missionary work, though I cannot help but laugh when thinking of Mama and Papa as devout to anything but their library. My parents were the kindest, but least religious people I'd ever encountered. If they weren't conspiratorially whispering together, their noses were in a book or they were off at tea or parties with Lord So-and-So and Lady Whomever. As a child I was not invited, but instead sat with my Nanny, listening carefully to her tales. Stories of Persia, India and the exotic east, none were foreign to her. So entrancing was she that father and mother would stand spellbound at the door as she spoke, making them late to dinners or to bed. There was no room in this life we had for gossip or cattiness, there was too much treasure in her words, actual mysteries of the universe to entertain us.

Perhaps this is why the dark-haired youth doesn't seem so impossible to me. Like Ivan and the Princess in the Russian fairytales, or the story of La Belle et La Bête.

It is strange, it is madness...but that doesn't preclude it from being reality. I will wait, I know I will see him again, in my dreams or in the flesh.

She heard the tell-tale sound of skirts sashaying up the stair and the quiet soft-soles of Clara's shoes. Lively popped up quickly from her desk, shutting the diary, re-pinned a stubborn chestnut tendril, and gave her cheeks a good pinch. She opened the door just as Clara's fist had come to tap upon it, and the girl's smile shone sweetly in the shadowy hallway.

There was something about Clara Howard that always caught Lively a bit off guard. She had an angelic wickedness, a dulcet willfulness that attracted Lively to the upstairs maid. She was a few years older than Lively herself, and had a kind of tragic wounded quality that made her all the more interesting. Some might look right past Clara, but Lively couldn't understand how.

"They've only just arrived. Miss Victoria is showing off her new Zonophone Gramophone, and so won't they be shocked to see you waiting in the parlor for them for a change! And to hear you excitedly discuss the gala during tea—they'll probably choke on their spoons!"

"Hush, Clara! Aunt Charlotte might hear you."

Clara widened her eyes dramatically and feigned terror. They both giggled and Lively breezed through the hallway and down the stair.

She was looking forward to it, and not only for the pleasure of imagining the ball, but because any time she left her room she fancied *he* had been inside. How perfectly shameless! To imagine with titillation that a strange man was pawing through her room!

She sat down in the carved wooden chair and pressed her fingers to the smart little tie on her shirt-front. For the first time ever, she was the only one in the room. As the minutes dragged on, she stared at the teapot under its cozy, the small needle pricks of guilt in her stomach made themselves felt. So this is what it was like to wait for tea. It wasn't at all pleasant and her cheeks pinked a little with shame. How many times had she been less than punctual for this weekly ritual? Lively's eyes began to wander about her aunt's parlor, as if she were seeing it for the first time, and perhaps she was.

The parlor was handsome and colorful, although the style was a touch dated. It looked very much like the front rooms she had seen in London and in the fashionable homes of the British in India. Something of a William Morris and Walter Crane imitation—though quite a good one—donned the walls. Stiff, unmoving irises lined up in a neat row on the wallpaper, their blooms forever pointing toward the ceiling. The table was finely polished and laid with an intricate lace pattern that made her dizzy to imagine its creation. She turned in her chair and inspected the ornate carvings of a lion's head that sat regally on either side of the top of her chair. Its mouth was open in a perpetual roar, its carved wooden teeth sharp to her touch. It struck her that this room was frozen in time. The lilies on the walls stuck in continuous blossom and the lion in its everlasting snarl. The tea-parties and gossip trading persisted uninterrupted, so that even the current events were held in a kind of relentless perpetuity. She herself had been caught in this unmoving clock, unchanging except for growing more weary and disappearing deeper into its loop.

Until now.

Clara had changed all of that with the ball. Something to look forward to, something that breathed life and change under her unsteady wings. And he, the dark-haired stranger. He, too, had altered things irrevocably.

Lively had never seen hair so dark that wasn't black, and the way his body moved when he walked or bent over her writing, at least in her mind, was almost animal. Sinuous and confident, moving with an ease not seen in young people their age. His eyes weren't the cool blue pools of a romance novel, but instead a living, melting mixture of viridescence and earth.

And they were now staring into hers from the chair on her left.

Three quick inhalations and she clapped a hand over her mouth. Their eyes were locked and his mouth fell open a fraction. The room around her seemed to be coming to life after its unremitting stupor. In the corners of her vision the lilies in the wallpaper bobbed and undulated in an invisible wind, and she thought she could hear the lion lick his lips and sniff her ear.

"You can...can you see me?" His voice was soft, but deeper than she had imagined. Her lips moved for a moment or two, wordless, before she could get them to produce a sound.

"How did you...where did you?...Who are you?" She spluttered finally, her voice a trembling whisper.

"Your book, I have your book." He offered her a sheepish half smile, as if acknowledging to himself that this explanation was far from satisfactory.

Voices in the hallway, but she could only remain in place, dumbstruck, staring into his eyes. If they saw him, she would know he was real, but *if* they saw him, she wouldn't be able to explain him. Lively didn't know if she cared.

They were right outside the door now and he had begun to pale. She reached a hand out to reassure him, but

he wasn't paling, he was disappearing. By the time her hand alighted on the top of his, she felt only a whisper of warmth as his hand vanished. She heard his voice softly, perhaps the word "soon", and he was gone.

Aunt Charlotte and her cousin Victoria stepped into the room, smiling broadly at the sight of her. Victoria's face registered alarm at Lively's expression before she had time to readjust her features to greet the Misses Fitzgerald, coming in behind her aunt. One final figure entered the room, Madame Isadora Bellevie, whose eyes sought Lively's and locked into them before becoming languid again.

His brief presence, and now his absence, was palpable. Lively grinned idiotically at her cousin and guests as her eyes traveled from one corner of the room to the other. The irises in the wallpaper were once again standing vigilantly, blooms up, leaves outstretched toward its neighbor. The lion remained in its stalwart roar, jaws opened and teeth bared eternally.

All was exactly as it should be, all excepting Lively. The ladies had fussed and preened and finally settled down into their chairs. What had a few moments previously been an odd tête-a-tête, was now a chatty circle of ladies. And even though he was gone, and Lively was now sitting in a room that she'd always hated being in, with company that caused her discomfort, she couldn't stop smiling. Sometimes the world was filled with so much beauty and possibility and sweet mystery that one couldn't help but be filled with it.

And so they sipped and chewed and discussed. If Victoria or the Misses Fitzgerald were surprised in the change in her usual taciturn nature, they didn't let on. Instead, she was easily included. They offered her compliments and smiles in exchange for details of her dress, and descriptions of how she would pin her hair. In a word, it was lovely. Even if Aunt Charlotte mindlessly stuffed herself with biscuits and tea cake, which resulted in crumbs spraying from her fat lips, Lively was still in a cloud of comfort. She even noticed that Miss Ellen Fitzgerald's poorly pronounced French didn't grate her nerves quite like it normally did.

Until a few stray, chance comments burst into their conversation, leading to a revelation that sent her smiles scurrying from the oncoming storm.

It had begun innocently enough with Miss Lucy Fitzgerald asking Lively about her experiences with balls abroad.

"Oh, but I bet you've been to grand galas, Lively. After all the places you've lived."

"On the contrary, Lucy, missionaries are not often invited to balls. This will be my first."

The room grew quiet as her Aunt Charlotte turned her large bulldog face toward Lively and laughed.

"*Missionaries?* What a bunch of tosh! Is that *really* what Alistair was spinning? That's the strangest name for what he was that I ever heard. What a bushel of absolute nonsense!"

Madame Bellevie smoothed over her aunt's declaration, speaking of the eligible bachelors that would be at the party, adding that she hoped her own nephew might be present in time for the gala.

The girls either didn't notice Lively's altered mood, or pretended not to notice Aunt Charlotte's words when they had rung out, but the cruel syllables of them rang over and over in Lively's mind like the bells for church on Sunday. The sound of them resonating deep within her, only to clang again and again.

The rest of the visit passed uneventfully, and soon

Lively found herself back in the soothing lavender softness of her own bedchamber. Mechanically she sat down at her desk and looked into her only photograph of her parents. It didn't capture the life and brilliance of her father's features, or the mystery of her mother's eyes, but it was them. It was all that was left of them. This little black and white image that she'd taken with her little red leather Pocket Kodak a few years past. The rest of the film had been of this particular trip to Brussels and the International Exhibition. She hadn't thought to take more photographs of her parents. What child *would* when the Exhibition held so many delights?

But this solitary likeness of them and her memories were all that remained—and she had just been given reason to doubt those memories. She'd always known they weren't missionaries of course, but had never thought to ask what it was that they *did* do. She supposed it made a kind of sense, somehow she was ready to believe her ridiculous Aunt Charlotte, even if she didn't like her. When she was younger, she had thought a missionary was just another word for traveler, or a term for a man who is merry all the day long. To discover that it meant one who travels to a foreign place to aid those in need, and preach the word of God, she had been flummoxed. Her father and mother were kind and charitable and charming, but they were in no perceivable way spiritual.

What were they then? Why the mystery? Lively wondered as she drummed her slender fingers on the desk. She reached out and grasped the little leather book, its black cover gleaming with golden flecks like stars in an inky sky. How fitting that this was where all her dreams were sent, from the nib of her pen into the sky of pages. Every entry a kind of wish on one of those glittering stars.

She opened the book and flipped lazily to the next fresh page. Her mind burned with flickering tendrils of thought. The whiteness of the unmarred page called to be filled with the raging flames of her mind. But, before she brought her nib to the page, she had an inkling. A niggling in her mind that she had seen something on the last page, something unfamiliar.

Turning the page back, she realized she had been holding her breath. When she saw what was written on the page, she gasped and coughed at the sight.

Printed neatly in a strange hand was a message to her. He *had* been in this room, and not just her thoughts. His hand had touched this page, perhaps this very pen!

Dear Lively,

I apologize for trespassing in this, your personal book, and I am uncertain that you will ever see this note. But, all that was inconceivable now seems to have moved from the land of imagination to reality.

If you do read this, give me a sign. I am very far from you—what would seem an insurmountable distance—but I will find my way back to you. If only you will offer me a sign. You must think me terribly impertinent, but I mean no offense. I feel connected to you across this great distance, and would know you better.

Yours,
Julian Cole

She read and re-read the words until the letters swam before her eyes. What was this distance? Who was Julian Cole? How many secrets would she stumble into in the course of one afternoon?

A sign. She sighed and closed the little book. All of a sudden her mind was as blank as the pages she'd meant to scribble on. A sign he said.

What in the world was she to do?

CHAPTER THE SIXTH
A Reunion Of Sorts

Time had trudged on at an infuriatingly slow pace complete with a week full of sleepless nights. He *had* walked those rooms of the past; he *had* spoken to her! She'd reached out to touch him, he'd felt the heat of her skin, a spot of sunshine on his own.

And then he was back in his chair, staring at the black book, the page open but blank. A hand beckoning to him —mocking him, pulling him back into the past. He'd flipped through the pages only to find that again, what once had been filled with her familiar, recognizable hand was empty. As if it had never been there at all. As if those swooping letters hadn't pierced the soft paper as they too had been inked on his heart. Without taking his eyes from the book, his hand reached for the cup in which he kept his pens, and he'd written her. With no real hope that she, 100 some years earlier, could possibly read it. Impossible, fantastic, and yet...he could almost see those purple-grey eyes skimming the message now. A sign he had asked for, but closing the book, he wondered how it could be achieved.

After that delicious step into the past, the book had disappeared again. A dubious messenger between points in time. The gloomy Michigan spring undulated and swayed to the tune of the changing season. Soft premature summer sunshine held the college town in a cocoon of beauty to come. Julian had received the wire transfer of his grandmother's treasure, and for all intents and purposes he was set and contented. Except that he wasn't. Even with the money, his future was undecided. There was only one place that he yearned to travel—but it was much farther than he had ever dreamed before.

So it was that Julian was still lost in contemplation on his way home from history lecture. He crossed the street in front of the apartment complex, heavily burdened with books, his mind a hundred years away. Patrick was just closing the front door of their building. When he saw Julian, he greeted him with a puzzled expression and called out,

"I didn't know you had family!"

before replacing his headphones and running quickly toward the retreating university bus. He hadn't time to respond, nor time to consider his roommate's meaning. Julian wrinkled his forehead in confusion. Family? Had Patrick seen the wire transfer paperwork? But no, he'd returned it with the other documents in the safe, hadn't he?

His mind was whirring as he stepped into the tiny apartment. Shutting the door softly behind him, he felt that the air itself was different. That something in the attitude of the room had shifted. Stepping into the living room from the kitchen, he found an older woman, perhaps in her mid-50s, tall, with a shadow of something familiar to her features standing straight-backed on the oriental carpet. Yes, he had seen this woman before, but where? He could hear her animatedly speaking, but Julian could not see another person in the room with her. He realized that she was speaking to herself, or more correctly, she seemed to be speaking with his parent's urn. Alarm became panic as he bounded to the center of the room in an effort to somehow protect the little metal box.

"Erm, excuse me, but…who are you? What are you doing here?"

Her eyes slipped into his own. Eyes so familiar, and yet, he knew he hadn't seen them before. Julian saw that she was dressed with care. Not exactly stylishly, but in a way he would consider classic. Clean lines that spoke of high quality fabric and attention to detail. Her clothes were tailored perfectly, a silhouette that was different…but somehow something about her was so unabashedly recognizable to Julian. She was oddly beautiful, but not in a way that he was accustomed to. Her beauty was again, more of a classic beauty, an elegance that knew not time nor place. A woman in a painting, or a woman described in literature. Not a flesh and blood woman standing before him. What was this creature doing in his shabby living room? She parted her blood-red lips carefully, narrowed her eyes, and spoke.

"I've waited a long time, Julian. I think we both know why I am here."

He took a startled step backward and looked at her incredulously.

"I'm sorry, but I really haven't the faintest…"

"Pish-posh. I've been bobbing back and forth and in and out of the pages for nigh on 20 years, knowing that Mia's plan wouldn't pan out. Destiny in the end you know, pet."

She sat down primly, looking as though the living room were her private domain, any newcomer would have thought she'd sat there every afternoon of her life.

"I'm sorry, you said Mia? You…you, uh, knew my mother, then?"

Her hazel eyes flashed golden for a moment, and the resemblance was stronger now.

"Of course. As well as anyone can really know their younger sister, naturally."

Julian's mouth fell open, his jaw hanging idiotically, but he didn't notice. His mind opened instead to the particular movements he had seen but not understood until her startling revelation.

The slight tilt of her jaw and the familiar crinkle of annoyance in her forehead. The way her back rested ramrod straight, yet still appeared somehow relaxed. All of the subtle paint strokes came together on the canvas of his mind to evoke his mother. This woman was a few years older than she would have been, and perhaps taller, narrower. She was missing his mother's athletic curves and sunlight smiles—but yes. This woman could only be his aunt. But why? Another secret his mother had locked away from him.

"Why haven't we met before now? And what do you mean by 'bobbing back and forth'?"

Although the truth of her words was undeniable, Julian still couldn't make sense of them. A jigsaw puzzle for which he had all the pieces, but no larger picture from which to join them together. She was staring intently at the urn, his questions hovering above her head, like annoying flies buzzing about her that she was pointedly ignoring.

She let out a resigned sigh, and faced him.

"Well, I suppose you must know everything then. Or as much as I can tell you at any rate...Marcus will have to have his say of course, and then the others...but yes. No sense in engaging in any more of this cloak and dagger nonsense...though I suppose quite a bit of this *is* actually cloak and dagger, come to think of it. Certainly, I'll be glad to have this all out in the open, and so will Marcus, I'll warrant. No more of your interfering my dear, I told you again and again it would all be for naught in the end."

Somewhere in her response she had resumed talking to the urn, and to herself, Julian's presence either forgotten or unnecessary. She chuckled softly once more in the urn's direction before turning back toward Julian.

"Are you quite well, Aunt?"

"Aunt" felt odd vibrating through his vocal cords, like an unknown word in a foreign language testing its meaning on his tongue. Julian had begun to worry that perhaps he hadn't seen his aunt before because she was insane, a theory she seemed to be in a hurry to prove correct.

"Oh, don't you stare at me with that look in your eyes. You look just exactly like your mother. I'm quite well, thank you. Never better, in fact. How wonderfully pleasant it will be not to have to come back to this beastly 21st century. I declare for once and all that beauty is dead here. You may call me Aunt Isadora, by the by, but don't speak a syllable more, not just yet. I need a look at those eyes of yours once more."

With that, she resumed sitting, a slight smile tugging on the corners of her mouth. She pointed to the mustard colored chair, and her eyes directed him to sit. She brought her gaze to his and searched him for some time. His aunt seemingly memorized each of his features in turn. He could feel her eyes in his hair and on his jawline and along his shoulders. She was taking measure of him and somehow those same eyes held him silent the whole while. Finally, she blinked and the spell was broken.

"Yes, yes. Just as I thought. You've found your book then, and you've become a Lector. You're a reader."

Julian's face lit with anxiety at the mention of the book, and then confusion to be called the Latin and English word "reader". Hadn't he always been a reader?

"Oh do close your gob, Julian. I'm afraid your tongue will fall clean out."

His eyes bugged open again, wider, and he dutifully

pressed his lips together, staring at this strange woman who had appeared like a sudden storm and had now blown his ideas of his former life to wreckage. His aunt! His mother's sister! An idea occurred to him, suddenly, and he stood up excitedly, moving toward the safe underneath the desk.

"Then your mother, my grandmother...she's dead! I mean, she died. Recently. She's left me a fortune...and well, it's yours, then."

"Sit Julian. And do *try* not to interrupt. It will be difficult my pet, but make the attempt, won't you? There is much to tell. So much. Your mother should not have kept it from you, but...I suppose she had her reasons. And, please, don't speak of money, it's abominably vulgar."

With that statement, she leaned back into the sofa, tilted her head toward the ceiling, and let her words float and spin around the little room until Julian was so tightly bound to them he couldn't have broken free if he'd tried.

"We are a family of Lectors, or Readers, Julian. It is not impossible to trace of course, as you will come to understand, but I'm not familiar with the particulars of our line, myself. Suffice it to say that it is in our blood to walk through worlds by walking through words. I say Reader, but not in the way that you pore through volumes, consuming chapters by the dozen, smacking your lips on the poetry or prose of a well crafted chapter. No, to be a Reader is to...well, is to travel *through* the words on the page. To swim through a book as one does the waves. For some of us this means that we can become part of every story that we read, for others...it means that our place was always in another time, another place or another world altogether. The book becomes the door from which we pass through to our destiny."

She moved her eyes back from the ceiling to his face, and spread her hands apart, dropping them back onto the arm rests of the sofa. It was as if she was trying to grasp the words to explain, only for them to fly from her touch. Julian considered her words for a moment and then nodded, uncertainly. She continued.

"I do not know what it is like for the others, but for me, it began when I was young. The books would appear and I would read them. I could be in a fairytale forest, a diamond mine in Africa, and out at an Edwardian Ball, all before lunch."

Aunt Isadora smiled, her eyes far away in memory. Julian could just see the glimmer of a younger woman, stepping to the rhythm of music that was no longer played in the world around them. He hadn't really considered thus far if he believed her, he simply accepted it as truth. Just as a reader accepts the truth of the writer's words on the page. They appear in the mind and the reader strings them together in meaning, believing the words of the tale, no matter how fantastic or otherworldly.

"Your grandmother was a Reader. Might still be, I suppose, odd duck, my mother. Continually slipping between this time and the Italian Renaissance. She didn't discuss it often, but I knew that the older she grew, the more time she was spending in the past. Which definitely gave me and Mia some guesswork as to whom our unknown but obviously charming father might be. At any rate, I'm sure she was more than glad to have a grandson to pass her fortune off to, wherever it is she might have departed."

She chuckled again under her breath and cast a knowing glance toward the urn, sharing a belated confidence with her lost sister. Julian had been studying his aunt as she spoke, and watched as the years fell from her face as the words flowed. A dam breaking out with the story of her family. He tried to ignore the suggestion that his grandfather was some kind of Renaissance royalty, his mind burned with too much new information as it was.

"What about you and my mother? What time or place does your book take you to? What about her?"

Isadora didn't meet Julian's eyes, instead she stared at the urn and Julian thought her expression was angry. She smoothed her features, and spoke calmly, making Julian think perhaps he had been mistaken about her mood.

"Well, as for me, as a Reader grows older, it seems that they settle more. That there are fewer books that allow movement between worlds. It has to be a special book, a book that is linked to you somehow…"

Her words drifted off into a place that Julian would never see. He realized that this side of his mother, this secret would explain all the others. He didn't understand why she wouldn't have revealed it to him, but at least his aunt would surely have some of the answers.

"My mother…what was her time? Where? What were her books…"

A delicious thought occurred to him suddenly, and he fairly leapt to his feet with the realization.

"Is that where she and my father went? Are they… still alive?"
His voice croaked down to a shattered whisper on those last words, but a faint hope flamed dimly in his heart. Perhaps, perhaps…

His aunt's eyes opened widely and she looked from him to the urn and back again.

"Oh, dear. My sweet pet. She told you *nothing?* Not even a hint?"

Julian shook his head, black clouds of doubt rolling through him.

"Oh heavens. Your mother, Julian, she…she didn't have the gift. She loved reading of course, and encouraged the same love in you. Mia escaped into books as is customary for bibliophiles, but her destiny was always here, in her own time. With your father. He was quite an adventure himself, Julian. And they were very, very happy."

She looked at him sadly, her eyes crinkling in the corners and her age returning to her face.

"I'm sorry, pet. They are truly gone, no doubt about that. But, what about you? Living here in this coffin of a place? Shoveling the dirt of distraction and indecision upon yourself—burying your life here. You were destined for so much more."

It hurt more than he had anticipated, the bald truth, spoken so bluntly. A knife thrust into his gut, that he couldn't remove without all the little lies he was living spilling out.

"But why? Why all the secrecy? I don't understand. If she knew what was happening why didn't she tell me? Have books come to me before? Why can't I remember?"

"I'm afraid that it is my fault. You see, I was forever disappearing into one place or another, vanishing into times she only imagined. My world was so much more vast than hers. But also far more dangerous. Readers can die in other worlds, Julian. They can slip through the pages and never return. And so, when you were born and the books started to appear, un-bought, unbidden, searching for you… she wanted to protect you."

She said it so matter-of-factly that Julian could tell that she was angry with his mother about her decision, but was either too careful or too proud to say so. Realization swept over him, a raindrop that became a wave.

"Is that why we traveled so often, then? We were running away?"

"In a way, yes. Your parents did love to travel, but inevitably a book would creep in and your mother would find you with your little mitts on it. Next thing your father was applying for a transfer sooner than anyone had planned. Don't be hard on her, she couldn't lose you, you see."

Suddenly Julian had a glimmer of a memory, a sense of falling, the beginnings of being plunged into the pages of a long-ago book as a child. His mother's hands ripping the feeling away before it could take root. He thought then, that he understood her fear. Something in Isadora's voice had faded into sadness, a note in the melody of it shushing his other thoughts and questions. They sat for some long moments, each trapped in their own thoughts. Julian's whole universe had exploded before him, each piece of truth, each lie too small now to sort through or piece together properly. But somehow he felt that he had known all the while. Not the details certainly, but known that there were pages missing from his life story. He was excited more than afraid or doubtful. Their eyes met.

"Well then, without being able to satisfy all of your curiosity at present, do you feel that you are ready for your future?"

"Yes." Julian whispered, hesitation coating his throat like syrup.

"Even if it is in the past, even if it is in a different

world, in a reality that is utterly foreign to you?" The questions came out as a breathy whisper too, and her eyes twinkled.

Julian looked at her with consternation as she removed a brown leather-bound book from her handbag. She ran her hand over the cover and opened it. Her other hand shot out and grabbed his, lying forgotten on the arm rest of the mustard chair, and all was darkness.

He blinked his eyes uncertainly, and took in the strange glow of an unfamiliar lightbulb. The light it gave off was ghostly, almost the memory of light, an afterglow. It was attached to a series of wires, running parallel down the ceiling and walls. As his eyes adjusted to the supernatural light, he made out shapes of furniture and creamy walls adorned with gilded-framed maps of cities long renamed and countries that existed no longer.

Julian was on his feet, and sensed that all the while another person was near him in the strange room. A flower bloomed in his mind, the memory of all that had occurred blossoming into his consciousness. He turned toward his aunt's silent form, unsure what to say, or if there was something to say, and if there was, he wasn't certain how to verbalize it.

"Where...?" He began a bit awkwardly and turned wild eyes to her, asking the question with his movements that his mouth couldn't master.

"My apologies, pet. I'd forgotten that it was a different experience entirely if you weren't traveling through your own book. This is my residence in my book in 1900. One of the first houses in Detroit to be electrified, you know. I saw Mr. Edison about it directly after he moved his Menlo Park operations here. I have lived in this book for the past 30 years."

She sighed and met his gaze once again, a flushed confidence filling her features.

"It's a grand time to be in Detroit, you know."

Julian couldn't help but think how strange that sentence would be 100 years from now, and it made him sad. But still, he was back, returned to the past, which meant that Lively was near, perhaps even just a few streets away.

As if his thoughts had been written on his countenance, his aunt moved toward the shelves full of books against the wall and casually asked,

"What book is it then? Is it fiction or mystery? I do hope I have it in my collection. Or I suppose it would have to be the "The Paper Serenade" as well? Obviously, it could hardly be anything else. How silly of me. Too ironic."

His whole body recoiled backward with force and he settled himself into a stiff high-back chair that seemed to encourage standing. The question had pierced him, seeking to pluck out his great secret happiness.

She had the wrong of it though, and Julian wondered what it could signify.

"It is none of those, aunt. And I think it would be remarkable if you had a copy, because I believe the only copy that exists in this time belongs to another. It is, well, it's a young woman's private diary."

He flashed crimson, the heat of embarrassment starting in the pink of his cheeks and traveling to his toes, thankfully encased in his sturdy leather loafers.

Aunt Isadora was pacing in circles, faster and faster, following the ill-concealed whir of thoughts in her mind.

"Dear, dear. This will not do, pet. Not at all. It can be dangerous to use a book that truly *belongs* to someone else. Because they didn't simply buy it, but instead are inking their own life story on its pages. This is very sticky, indeed. I wonder what dear Marcus will think? Oh dear, dear. It must be impossible, I cannot think of how this would happen…"

She spun around and faced Julian, her eyes locked on his own.

"This *is* your story, though? And place? I could swear that I had felt you here, it was why I returned for you this time. You *have* been here though, correct? Vividly in your mind or perhaps, in the flesh?"

"Yes, aunt. I was here…in this time, well, a week ago yesterday."

She resumed pacing, but slower now, more controlled. "And do you happen to know whose book, whose life, you came through?"

She didn't look at him, but Julian felt uncomfortably studied all the same.

"Erm, yes. I believe, that is to say, she calls herself Lively Lindenwood."

"Olivia!" She stopped abruptly, her little black boots clicking together. "Oh, gracious. Good heavens, pet! But, it cannot be! But, I suppose it must be. Oh bother and biscuits. I suppose it does make a kind of sense… what *will* dear Marcus think?"

Her hand flew to her forehead, a movement that reminded Julian of his mother so much it hurt to look at. How many times had he seen his mother do the same? His aunt's drifting comments had begun to niggle at him. Who was this 'Dear Marcus' she kept referring to? And why was it so terrible to be linked to Lively, and what's more…why did it make sense? Nothing seemed to have made sense since they had arrived.

Aunt Isadora dropped her hand to her side, balled both fists, and walked in measured steps toward him. She grabbed his hands in her own, and rubbed her fingers over his palms. Scars and paper-cut marks from all the adventures he'd had with his mother and father and in his books. Every mark on his skin a memory of what had been.

"This version of Detroit is a grand place for a man like you, Julian. A man with dreams and creative visions. A man who has seen much of what the world is capable, and where it is lacking. A man not afraid to get the grime of industry on his hands, who is willing to bleed for his dreams. You will do well in this story, but it must be your choice. I can see already obstacles and hardships, mysteries and adventure awaiting you in this world. Though your mother would have wanted you to have the future to make your home in, and leave your mark on."

"I will have the future. I think…I believe that my future lies somewhere here, in this world" He didn't know what made him say it, but the truth of it covered him like an old sweater, forgotten in the wardrobe, but fitting him in all the right places.

"Well, then. I am glad of it—for the most part. I cannot tell you everything now, that is the job of another. For the moment you have enough to think on. The book that called you here, well, it is not usual, and perhaps it is best to let that all be explained later." She paused and her eyes turned soft.

"Come then, let me give you a tour before you return to your own time…"

Julian's head snapped around in confusion. "Return? But, I said I wanted…"

"Oh hush. You will be here, but an ounce of preparation is worth a pound of tears or something to that effect, eh? You have money to convert, clothing that will need to be ordered here, a degree to finish there. Leave me to preparing the house and your wardrobe here, and you tie up the fraying ends in your world."

"When will I be back?" Julian asked fearfully. She was walking up the narrow steps to the second floor, having pointed out the kitchen and parlor near the library they had begun in. The whole house was like a living museum, like the Ruben's house he had toured in Antwerp or George Washington's Mt. Vernon. The kind of place you could picture corseted ladies and men with periwigs slipping through the rooms, but here it was real. Wigs of course, were out of fashion by this time, and corsets suffering a languishing death too, but the effect was the same. But this wasn't any more a museum than his own apartment over a hundred years in the future, each equally fantastic and dull in the right light.

However, this was beginning to feel like home more than anything had since his parent's death. The dust of comfort and the scent of happiness wafted through every room in his peculiar aunt's presence and he found that he was in a rush to travel here for good and all. To leave the future that was his past behind him and to move forward, even if it was in a sense, backward.

"When…well, it will have to be by the LeBlanc gala, won't it? Especially since Miss Olivia has taken an interest in attending, what a delicious meeting that will be. Quite romantic, I should think if the pink in your cheeks is any indication of your feelings."

"You know her, then? I mean, you seem to know her

well, what can you tell me, aunt? Does she live close by?" A scene flashed in his mind, and he recalled why his aunt was familiar. He had seen her at tea in Lively's house. It wasn't just her similarities to his mother, he *had* seen her before!

Her eyes twinkled, glittering in the ghostly lighting as she wagged a finger at him. "I should think you know quite enough already, having read her private thoughts."

Blushing again, he closed his lips together, and found that she had led him into a seemingly unused bedroom. Aunt Isadora walked over to the desk, picked up an unusual book and held it lovingly. She passed it over to his hands, a look of genuine pride on her face. He opened the cover and stared at the title page.

The Library of Panopticon
A Novel
by Julian F. Cole
New York
Thomas Catwick, Publisher
2085

The moment the words entered his mind, the room dissolved into his own study, and instead of the book he had been holding, he was gripping the little black diary, the golden glints in the leather the mirror of his aunt's eyes.

CHAPTER THE SEVENTH
A Day Of Unexpected Pleasures

Diary of Lively Lindenwood
27th November, 1900

A sign he says. He writes in my private diary, appears like a phantom in the parlor, and then vanishes into the air—as invisible as the wind. His hand trespasses into my most secret thoughts, and he dares request a 'sign'?

"An insurmountable distance" he writes, though I cannot divine the meaning. Is this man then a spirit? A geist come from beyond the grave to haunt my thoughts and diary? It is as ridiculous as it is terrifying to contemplate.

To think that perhaps he—or it—is perusing my scribbles even now is almost too much to bear. One feels enough of a goose as it is when keeping a record of one's personal thoughts. How perfectly appalling to imagine they are being read for entertainment—and at my own expense!

But a sign he desires, and so a sign he shall get. So if my above rambling was not enough, to you Mr. Cole, if you are reading this, be you revenant or man, <u>Shame on you!</u> Shame for the insult of inspecting a lady's private thoughts. Any true gentleman comes through the front door and not into a lady's bedchamber when her back is turned!

But, stay. Please, do not leave me, no matter what you may be. I would know you better if I could as well.

Well that's a clear a sign as any if this isn't all just a stray figment of an overburdened mind. What if I am indeed going mad? Cousin James is hardly clever enough to imagine a trick like this, and very definitely lacks the brains to put such a scheme into action. Furthermore, his kindness in the past few weeks in teaching me the cakewalk and some new waltzes has been invaluable. I confess that I should have spent more time with my dancing master when we were in Paris, but, there was always something else to occupy my time. One never fully understands the skills one will need until the need is upon one. No, James is innocent, so there must be another explanation.

I shall wait and see, as that would be mother's advice. Always "wait and see", "patience" and "things reveal themselves in time". The patience, time and waiting are the very things that give me no end of trouble.

Besides the elusive Mr. Cole, my mind is full of mama and papa. Aunt Charlotte's strange proclamation the other day has given me no rest. It is true that the greatest mystery of one's life is one's true self—the puzzle of one's own existence, but I had not imagined it quite so literally. Who were these parents? What was this life that they lived that I imagined I shared so completely, but may not have ever really understood?

I cannot think on it anymore just now, I declare that every time I attempt it my head begins to pound and my eyes water fiercely.

A sound on the stair reached Lively's ear, and forced her pen to rest. It had to be Clara, though Lively was seeing her friend less and less. She would vanish after her duties, some of the other servants thought she had a sweetheart, others thought she was applying for other work. In either case, Lively thought that her closest friend had closed ranks against her, shutting off herself from confidences. The rift had been sudden, and though there hadn't been any specific row between them, there was certainly a coolness in their conversation, when they did speak, that had not been there before. Lively had felt very alone with her thoughts these past days, a feeling that she

had thought to have finally shed from the moment she'd met Clara. There was a feeling like her parents dying all over again, but not as sharp. To lose Clara would be an awful blow. But where was the girl going?

A few light taps on the door and in walked Clara, as if on cue. Humming happily a tune for which she alone knew the words and melody. She stoked up the dwindling fire in the grate and stepped behind Lively, as she hurriedly closed the diary she'd been confessing in.

Lively felt like she'd been overheard gossiping and turned scarlet. She became aware of her own simmering anger, which was tempered by her own hypocrisy in the situation. She was not divulging her secrets to Clara, why did she expect the same from her? Was she the only girl allowed to have private mysteries?

Clara's deft fingers combed through Lively's hair, tenderly ridding her cinnamon mane of snarls, smoothing it to a silky sheen. She was still humming, and though it was lilting and soft, it grated on Lively's ears.

"Enough of that cacophony, Clara! Won't you please leave me to myself? I'm a woman grown and completely capable of combing my own hair!"

She had cried the words in a bossy, shrewish tone that sounded unnatural to her own ears. Lively knew that she wouldn't have had the courage or rudeness to say those things had she been facing her friend. Her lip stuck out petulantly, and she longed for her mother. There was so much she wanted to ask her and confide in her, and only a mother's shoulder is the right balm for crying into when feeling lost.

Lively could sense rather than see Clara's tears. The humming had ceased and an icy air breathed through the room. Clara still had one hand on Lively's hair and the other was holding the little comb halfway through the long waving tresses. There was something in her manner that seemed off to Lively, but the sound of her friend's sniffling behind her made her push aside any of her doubts.

"Oh, do forgive me, Clara. I'm so very sorry. I don't know what came over me."

Lively spun around in her chair, but saw that Clara wasn't crying. Instead, she looked angry. But, in a moment the anger melted and her face turned sad. Clara was shaking her head, the comb dropped with a clatter to the floor, and her arms wrapped around herself. It struck Lively that it appeared that her emotions threatened to explode and her arms were all that was holding her together.

"Oh, Miss Lively… don't be cross with me. Please, please, forgive me, there are reasons…"

Not allowing another word, Lively wrapped her friend in an embrace and shushed her tears, begging her friend's forgiveness for her words. It was the first time they'd ever exchanged anything but friendship, and the moment was sobering. Though Lively *was* sorry for her behavior, there was something about Clara she couldn't pinpoint, something different. A different attitude, or a transparent veil that had fallen between them. It was one of those events that grows in intensity the more one ponders it. A touchstone for all of the events that would follow. Noticed but fleetingly at the time, but sticking out like a tree on the lonely, empty prairie ever afterward.

Another timid knock on the door, and before either of them could utter "come in", Victoria passed timidly into the room. Her voice was odd as she cleared her throat and her cheeks colored salmon. Her message came nervously from her tiny rosebud mouth, a muffled bell.

"Lively, mother has sent me to fetch you."

Lively's forehead wrinkled in confusion.
"Fetch me where, exactly?"

Victoria colored a little more deeply, seemingly studying the weave of the carpet.
"Madame Isadora Bellevie, and a Mr. Chasseur have invited us out for a day on Belle Isle."

Belle Isle was a public park that had been purchased, according to Lively's uncle George, for much too high a sum. It was a small pleasure island that many in Detroit had big plans for. There was talk of a greenhouse and trails, in addition to a conservatory and a lighthouse to be finished in the next couple of years. For now, it was mostly used as a leisure park. A place to admire nature and see clear across the water to Canada. Lively was pleased, the day was cold, and an abundance of snow had fallen in the past week. But on this fine November day, only a powdered sugar dusting remained on the ground.

"But who is Mr. Chasseur? I do not believe I've made his acquaintance."

Victoria raised her eyes to her cousin, and spoke softly, though her voice was clearer now, and her eyes had taken on a faraway look.
"Oh, but you have. He is an associate of Mr. Malcolmson."

"The coal merchant?"

"Yes, that's him. He came to supper a few weeks past, the one who has invested in the motor company."

"Oh, the younger man, then?"

Victoria smiled, "the very man. Mr. Chasseur is young... but oh, just think! Horseless carriages zipping up and down Woodward Avenue! Can you imagine?"

Her eyes bulged significantly and her face flushed with color. Lively had no idea her cousin could register so much excitement about anything.

"Yes, it is a rather invigorating thought. Wind in your hair, flying down the streets like magic..."
Lively left the sentence unfinished, and it floated through the air around her parted lips. "Like magic" there was a certain amount of that around already, fortunately no one else seemed to notice her unfinished comment, as Victoria fluttered out. Clara was hurriedly dressing Lively's hair whilst adding warmer layers over her heavy cotton blouse and cinched-waist wool skirt. She brought out the cold weather overcoat lined with satin and the mink stole, muttering under her breath how much better a matching fur coat would be than Lively's heavy wool one—satin or no.
Less than half an hour later and they were all bundled

up and buttoned, ready to be fetched by Mr. Chasseur and the indomitable Madame Bellevie. A strange noise could be heard coming down Woodward Ave. It wasn't loud or discordant, but instead, simply different. Lively couldn't help herself from opening the door to peek out and investigate. As the door opened, the sight of Mr. Chasseur and Madame Bellevie coming to a halt in an open black coach with what looked like four large bicycle wheels greeted her eyes. Their cheeks were bright and pink with cold, but both were glowing with happiness. They were laughing, and more than anything Lively wanted to be a part of that joke, whatever it was. A splash of color in the grey and white November day.

The two girls burst from the front door, Aunt Charlotte tottering behind them, her girth making quicker progress undignified and impossible. The younger women encircled the motor car with enraptured squeals. Lively noticed again, her cousin's changed demeanor. No longer far-away and simple, she was alive with exhilaration, though she could hardly credit the machine before them for the change.

"Oh please, Mr. Chasseur, how does it work? What is it called? Madame Bellevie, how daring of you! Was it glorious?"

Victoria's quiet stupidity all gone, as if this side of her had been hiding beneath a veil of propriety. A glance at Aunt Charlotte confirmed her own confusion at her daughter's behavior, and her disapproval.

Lively thought the little motor car charming, though it wasn't the first she'd laid eyes on. There were a few men in Detroit who had built or bought different designs. And she'd seen a couple of prototypes in Europe before she'd come across the pond. But never before had she seen one so close. She was near enough to sit in it, and she smiled to think of herself doing just that.

Aunt Charlotte had walked over to supervise their

own carriage being readied, and Lively frowned involuntarily. She would have loved a drive in the frigid air. The competing streetcar lines had merged in the beginning of the year, forming the Detroit United Railway. Climbing aboard the tram was quick, efficient and inexpensive, but such things didn't matter a whit to Aunt Charlotte. She wanted privacy, exclusivity and to feel her own superiority. Lively rolled her eyes pondering it.

Mr. Chasseur was in the process of answering all of Victoria's questions, and even James had sauntered out for a look. Lively turned her attention to Mr. Chasseur's discourse, and leaned in to better hear him.

"... This Olds runs on electricity, though this is only a few steps away from a prototype. We call it the Curved Dash Run About. 1 cylinder. She behaves better than a horse, and doesn't take fright like one either. Much safer..."

Though obviously Aunt Charlotte didn't think so. She had walked back over from the carriage to pluck Victoria and Lively away from the novelty. They arranged to meet just down the road, Belle Isle not being far, and the ladies had resigned themselves to watching the marvel motor past them in the carriage. Lively had taken a few steps toward the carriage when Madame Bellevie called her name. The older woman's eyes lit as she asked her if she would like to ride along with them instead. Something in her golden eyes glittered strangely and her smile was almost a challenge.

Without waiting for permission, Lively skipped over to the Curved Dash and settled herself in the back. Mr. Chasseur spread a fur blanket over her and started the motor, Madame Bellevie grinning like a cat. The last thing Lively saw was Victoria's pouting face staring after her in the coach window and Clara, looking out Lively's window, a cruel smile on her face.

The expression on Clara's face stayed with her, gnawing

at her, but she pushed it back to the recesses of her mind. So many things to ponder, traitor thoughts that sprang into her head, demanding to be entertained. But no, not now. Her companions in the front seat were speaking and she leaned forward to listen.

"Well done, Gabriel! It's so quiet." Madame Bellevie cast him an approving glance.

"Yes, and clean. Mind you, an electric car is no fun to tinker with, but it's quiet and doesn't make a mess. Mark you this, Madame, but I envision the streets of Detroit filled with electric motor cars in the future. It will be the ultimate symbol of status and style. As essential to man as his own two feet."

"Yes, but you forget the $600 price tag. No small sum for a working man."

Mr. Chasseur smiled and turned his head to include Lively in the expression. "I still keep to my prediction. Just you see."

He passed Lively a wink, and his eyes lingered a moment too long. Never much of one for propriety anyway, Lively didn't mind the more casual attitudes and behaviors between men and women in America. But, she'd be lying to herself if she didn't admit the frankness and openness in interest between the two sexes still caught her off guard. But, again this was a young nation still. With new ideas, in a new century.

Besides, Mr. Chasseur, Gabriel, as Madame called him familiarly, was a handsome man. Just a few years shy of 30 perhaps, with flaxen hair and a well groomed mustache. He was tall and fair and had something fine about his face, a solid warmth, a kind of confidence that was most attractive. Any number of women, including her cousin Victoria, would be ecstatic to receive his attentions.

But, thinking about Mr. Chasseur only made her mind conjure up the mysterious Mr. Cole and his clean-shaven boyish good looks. His dark, swarthy features and the ease of his movements. How she would love to be spending this motor car ride alongside of him. She wondered if he'd ever had the chance to ride in a machine such as this?

"You're very quiet my dear. Taking it all in are you? We're taking a scenic route, but if you're too cold, I'll tell Gabriel to turn straight toward Belle Isle."

"Oh no, really, I'm having a lovely time. It's so freeing, As if the wind is pulling me inside of it." Lively smiled at the older woman.

"Quite right, what a thought that is. I'll have to add that exact sentiment to my *diary* tonight"

She turned with bright eyes toward Lively, but something in her voice gave her pause. Why would she bring up her diary? Was Madame Bellevie teasing her? The older woman continued, not missing a beat.

"Gabriel's employer has just invested in a brand new motor company, right here in Detroit. He's helping to establish a Mr. Henry Ford. The man apparently has some novel ideas for the production of these marvelous machines. It is my hope that Mr. Ford will employ my nephew in some capacity."

Lively's memory searched and then latched onto that snippet from tea a few weeks past.

"Your nephew, oh yes. I did not imagine he was so old as to necessitate employment, I had thought him to be a boy still. When does he arrive?"

Lively was interested, but more for the desire for a fresh face in her acquaintance. She knew asking too many questions would be rude, but Madame Bellevie was not the type to be offended. Indeed, she offered her the same inexplicable look, her eyes flashing briefly, before answering.

"He will be out in society in time for M. LeBlanc's soirée. He is coming a great distance and will be weary from travel when he first arrives."

"I understand the weariness of travel all too well myself. I will look forward to meeting him at the gala."

Lively paused a brief moment and considered the conversation before adding,

"Can I infer then that if you would like him to work with Mr. Ford's company, that he is much interested in motoring?"

Though Lively had merely asked out of curiosity, she recoiled at Madame Bellevie's reaction. The older woman, handsome and refined, leaned forward and laughed into her hands. Lively's eyes widened and she met Gabriel's gaze, who shrugged and shook his head, as if accustomed to his friend's odd behavior.

In between giggles, Madame Bellevie managed,

"Yes, yes. I daresay Julian will have taken an interest in motoring at one point or another."

To which Lively sensibly replied that she was sure he would find the Curved Dash a fascinating leap forward, to which Madame, begging her pardon, said that she doubted it very much, before settling into another round of hysterical laughter. She was just wiping the tears of hilarity from her eyes as they approached the wooden Belle Isle bridge.

The bridge was nearly a half mile long, but rickety in places, and Mr. Chasseur did not want to chance the weight of the Curved Dash on it, even though others, including Aunt Charlotte were perfectly content to trust the wooden planks with their heavier horse-drawn carriages. The Dash came to a halt, and Mr. Chasseur helped the ladies out, Lively murmuring her gratitude and delight quietly. They all stepped into her aunt's carriage and Victoria's big brown eyes darted from Lively's to Mr. Chasseur's and back again, and something she saw removed the stricken attitude from her features.

But now it was Lively's turn to look stricken, as the carriage plodded along the bridge, the Detroit River waving hello and goodbye. Lively's face grew hot as her mind skimmed over the words she had heard in the carriage but hadn't processed.

Madame Bellevie had said her nephew was coming a great distance. Her nephew, Julian.

CHAPTER THE EIGHTH
A Spectacular Journey Is Undertaken

The past to him had always been like a burst firework, its ghostly smoke tendrils floating across the sky. The color that had filled the moment faded to gray. But he saw now that the past was a vibrant rainbow of lives, an exploding sequence of stories as bright as any bursting moment he'd lived.

Julian couldn't make sense of what he had seen with his aunt. She, like the experience, seemed beyond belief. But, if everything she said was true, a lot of the missing puzzle pieces of his life were coming together. He'd never had an ordinary life, but *this* was ridiculous. Wasn't it? This would propel his life into something more sensational than any fiction he'd lost himself in.

And he knew the life she was offering was something he'd be glad to throw himself into. But what about now? What about his life in Ann Arbor? And Patrick, the whole wide world of the future waiting for Julian Cole to make his mark…wouldn't retreating into the past be like losing his parents in a different way? Just another place to hide himself? His head hurt thinking about it, and so he'd had an aching brain for the past few weeks.

Julian had called the lawyers and liquidated some of his accounts, though he had left most of his money right where it was. No sense cutting ties completely with the outside world. He'd bought some 1900 currency from dealers and brushed up on his Michigan History. He had prepared himself the way his aunt had advised, but he still wasn't certain his whole heart was in the enterprise. Was he doing this for the right reasons? Was the past his destiny? Could he live within the pages of a book? Or was he simply mad as a hatter, completely off his block, and the whole thing merely a distressing illusion of a diseased imagination?

Part of his hesitation came from the elusive black and gold book. He had not seen a single page of it since he had written in it. It had been weeks now since he had glimpsed its pages, much too long since he had seen her face and read her thoughts.

Classes were winding down and the only thing on anyone's mind was graduation. Patrick had come home on a number of occasions with new clothes, new suitcases, and had developed a noticeable spring in his step. His upcoming move to New York was life-changing and not only because it was going to actually change the circumstances of his life. But also because the break with Ann Arbor, Michigan seemed to be a breaking of a chain he had forged around himself. A disconnect with the person he pretended to be to most of his friends on campus, a self-inflicted guise to be sure, but a facade all the same. Finally, he would escape to a place where he felt that he would be accepted for himself. Julian had never understood why Pat placed such restrictions on himself in the first place, but he supposed it really wasn't that strange. Don't we all concoct our own walls and obstacles?

Julian's steps were springier too, coming home from a final exam. Soon, he would walk the stage…and soon after that…move into a new life also. He'd gotten a weird tickling feeling in his stomach during the test, and after that he couldn't complete it quickly enough. Julian just knew that the book was waiting for him at home, and he was anxious to see if she had left him a sign. If the connection between them flowed both ways. There was so much he wanted to tell her, so much he wanted to explain. He imagined her face at the gala…how would they act? Would they run into one another's arms? No, he was sure that wasn't correct at a 1900 society function. In that time, the gala would fall on the 31st of December, perfect timing for his new beginning with the new century.

He tripped up the steps in his building two and three at a time, and his hand shook as he turned the key in the lock. Upon opening the door he could feel it already. A shift in the air, just as before. The room itself felt more vivid and alive, some kind of magic dust scattered over the blades of the ceiling fan and the books on the shelf. He bounded to his room and his eyes pierced his desk, hungrily. A little black leather book sat innocently on the top, right below his parent's photo, with a post-it note unceremoniously stuck to it.

As he stepped nearer to the desk, he realized that the book was new, and not Lively's little gold and black book at all. His stomach plunged in disappointment and his face fell. He grabbed the washed-out yellow note and brought it closer to read, his eyes slightly unfocused. It was probably just something of Pat's that he left on the desk without thinking. His roommate's things were kind of everywhere and nowhere as he was preparing to leave.

The writing was not Patrick's though, and the note was addressed to him. He brought it closer for inspection.

Julian,

Hot off the presses! Your very own reader's manual. Guard this with your life. Inside, please find all the answers. See you soon, pet.

Affectionately,
Isadora

He picked up the book, sniffed it, and the scent of new ink and new paper and the impersonal scent of new leather invaded his nostrils. It was utterly unremarkable. He turned the book to the side and read the spine,

*L*IBER *L*IBRI

was embossed in large gold letters. He snorted, and shook his head.

Turning it back around, he sat down in the desk chair, preparing to read it. "All the answers" she said. Well, knowledge was power, so he figured he'd read a few chapters and see what it was all about. Julian still had a sinking feeling in his gut after not finding the little diary, a feeling like the first time your mother drops you off at school and leaves you. Alone. That's how he felt.

The cover seemed heavier than it looked, and as he opened the first few empty leaves of the book, Julian scanned for an introduction or table of contents. But the book was empty. Blank pages stared back at him mockingly, and just when he began to think that it was all a bizarre joke from his aunt, he realized his error. The whiteness of the pages surrounded him on all sides and the ringing of bells, like on a shop door, enveloped him completely.

All at once, he was standing on a highly polished hardwood floor, in a brightly lit room with shelves of books on all sides. All of the books were the same width and height, but all were different colors. Khaki greens, and bright reds. Buttercup yellows and electric blue. He stepped close to the shelf nearest him and saw that they each were embossed with the same golden letters, "Liber Libri", but in a myriad of fonts.

Julian's hand reached toward a lime green guide at eye-level and a voice behind him scared his grasping fingers away.

"Wouldn't touch that if I were you. No telling where you'll end up. Not your book anyway, my boy. Yours is the new black leather, bound it myself yesterday."

Turning around to face the voice, Julian's eyes had to move startlingly high upward to find the face. The man was smiling at him now, but in a way that suggested he didn't see enough people to know the way of it. Besides being uncomfortably tall, his hair was long and greying, his skin pale. He had just enough of a gut on his otherwise gangling form to make him seem human. Altogether, this was an odd specimen of man, indeed. Julian decided that he immediately liked him, something in his face made it impossible not to.

"Begging your pardon, you'll be Julian, then?"

"Yes sir, Julian Cole."

"Quite right, Marcus Birdwhistle, at your service. Why don't you step into my office, better lighting, warm tea and better for awkward conversations."

Julian agreed, and followed the giant of a man through row upon row of shelves, each completely full of books. So *this* was the Marcus his aunt had been speaking of. Julian thought she could have done more to prepare him for this strange character, but perhaps to her, Mr. Birdwhistle wasn't odd at all.

The air was surprisingly light, not weighted with the heady scent of numerous tomes found in libraries or old bookstores. Instead it smelled like the sweetness of a spring afternoon in the sunshine.

"You're wondering about this place, I'll warrant"

Mr. Birdwhistle commented much more loudly than Julian felt comfortable within a room full of books. It felt sacrilegious somehow. There seemed to be no end in sight, row after row, stack after stack of the same rainbow books. Each unfailingly embossed "Liber Libri" on the spine, the gold letters glittering and winking at Julian as he passed.

"Yes, it feels like it's as big as a city. And Liber Libri... that just means 'book' in latin, right?"

"Yessir. You have the right of it on both counts, though I'd say this place feels the size of a small country on these old legs some days. Your nose was missing that old book smell, I'd reckon, but for myself, I like to set an enchantment for springtime. I so often miss the seasons with my work, you understand."

Julian most definitely did not understand, but nodded agreeably to the old man who'd turned around to speak these last words. They walked on and on, Mr. Birdwhistle pointing out a row of books here and there, then naming a time period, as if this would explain something to Julian. Something like, "That row, just there? 1630."

Finally, they came to an ordinary door. It had a pane of glass in the middle not unlike something an elementary classroom would have. Marcus Birdwhistle reached a long arm into his forest green trouser pockets and produced a large gold key that looked much too grand for such a door. But when the key touched the lock, the door soared in height and burst out in ornate carvings of vines and roses done in gold leaf. Without a backward glance or word of explanation, Marcus Birdwhistle stepped into a room that only could be described as part oval office and Louis XIV's study. A large imposing desk adorned with a stylized open book wrought in gold carved on the front of it. Tapestries, a scattering of faberge eggs, and two paintings that Julian could swear were Rembrandt's "Storm of the Sea of Galilee" and Vermeer's "The Concert" hung from the walls. Paintings that Julian knew his art professor had lamented as stolen and "lost forever". Where in the world was he?

Seeing the direction of Julian's gaze, Mr. Birdwhistle gestured toward the paintings and spoke.

"Oh, that's right. You're an artist yourself. The creators of these pieces left them here with me in their travels between worlds. I'm more of a impressionist man, myself, but you can hardly argue with a master, eh?"

Julian's mouth fell open, and he felt faint. This was certainly shaping up to be a very surprising day.

Marcus invited him to take a seat, and then wandered out another door before returning a few minutes later with a tea service complete with chocolate biscuits. A large, orange cat followed him out from what must have been a kitchen, and after circling around several times, settled itself resolutely on Julian's lap.

They each took a few sips, Julian still hopelessly overwhelmed, while Marcus Birdwhistle appeared almost bored. Finally, he set his cup down and fixed Julian with a kindly look, and cleared his throat before speaking.

"I don't know how much you know already, but your Aunt, no doubt, has informed you of what you are?"

"A...a reader, sir?" Julian answered uncertainly.

"Well, yes. Obviously. But you are the only reader of your generation, my boy. Not enough people interested in books anymore and all that. You were selected early, of course, but all of the varied books' attempts to get to you were thwarted by your mother, who for a while we feared was a Tenebrae...but I digress.

"I'm sorry, you thought my mother was what?"

"Tenebrae. My boy, this is elementary Latin. It means 'concealment' or 'dark corner'"

"It also means 'ignorance', Mr. Birdwhistle"

"Quite. I thought your aunt would have told you, but it seems that she has been negligent. The Tenebrae is our name for the group that has hounded us, The Lectors, from the very beginning. From the first time that words were put to paper, the first history. The first story that was written, our kind has been able to move through the papyrus, through the parchment, through the vellum, and into the world of the story. And ever since then, the Tenebrae has been fearful of the power of words, and jealous, too. At least I think so."

"So, what does this all mean?" Julian was puzzled, but with the same fervent confusion that kept one reading to the next part of an unfolding plot on the page. There really was a whole other world here. Not just the past with Lively, but this whole other reality where one could read and become the story.

"It means you have a great gift, Julian. But it also means that using this magic has its own dangers. Now, I am very busy maintaining all of these books. I will answer three questions today."

Julian was taken aback. He was sitting in a golden room with stolen, or rather, stored, paintings on the walls from some of the greatest artists of all time. He had traveled to this place via a blank book that was a gift from an aunt he'd never met until a few weeks ago. And he couldn't stop thinking about a girl that was mathematically, long dead. Three questions, *really*?

His eyes widened and the old man sat leaning back on the sofa that had probably come out of a palace somewhere. The cat shifted in his lap, angry that Julian's body wasn't built for her maximum comfort. He exhaled and leaned forward, further upsetting the cat.

"Three questions. Well, first, what is this place?"

Marcus Birdwhistle smiled and looked Julian full in the eyes.

"An excellent place to begin. This is what we call the Panopticon. But it isn't like other libraries. The only books here are the accounts of other Readers or Léctors in the world. Some of the Reader's accounts are finished, meaning, they are now deceased. Others are ongoing, moving between times, or fictional realities, or between times *in* fictional realities. As the Reader travels, it is recorded invisibly on the pages in their manual automatically for our files. It is important that I can locate a Lector at any time. For each manual that is presented to a Reader, its sister is housed here, which provides each of our people the ability to retreat here for rest, or answers, or advice at any time. It's also the way we return here, if say, we have a gathering. The Liber Libri is essentially your lifeline, your history and your ticket here. Obviously you can understand why it must be kept safe, as there are many who would desire to find this place and destroy everything we have built and every Reader along with it. As far as the Panopticon goes, it has always existed as far as I know. It was here before the first keeper, shelves ready and prepared to be filled with the lives of books. Because it is the guide of our world, we call it "Panopticon" or All-Seeing Eye, as it sees each reader as they travel. Next question."

Julian sat back, digesting the information. He felt a little like laughing out loud, or perhaps sobbing into the satin pillow beside him. Ridiculous, all of it. But, so absolutely tantalizing to someone with an adventurer's heart, a true bibliophile. The gift of living within your favorite stories, to move through time.

"I can travel into any book then?"

Marcus Birdwhistle poured himself another cup of tea and tilted his head to the side.

"It's not common anymore. Most Readers can usually disappear into no more than five books, excepting their manual. Although, your aunt seems to think you are an exceptionally gifted Lector, like your great-grandfather, Domenico. If you are wondering why you've never traveled before now, well, it is because you never had the right book. Not every book works for every reader, and for a time, it did seem that the books had despaired of you and had stopped seeking you out. We're not sure about this diary business, by the by. Especially since the girl on the other end doesn't seem to have the gift. It is very strange for one of the Caeca, our word for non-readers, to even be able to see our world. Most troubling, and of course it means that the book you are using for transport is not really your own. Most distressing. Another thing you must understand, is that the Libri is a special kind of book, anyone can use it to come here—Lector, Caeca or Tenebrae. This is why it must be kept safe, at all costs. Final question."

Julian didn't understand why the book being Lively's diary was such a problem, but he didn't want to waste his last question on clarification. Especially as it seemed that Mr. Birdwhistle had been purposefully vague.

"What's the purpose? Not that I'm not completely humbled to have been chosen for this honor, but what is the point of it all?"

Marcus Birdwhistle's smile turned into a full toothy grin. He smoothed his white whiskers and bit into a biscuit.

"With your usual discernment, Mr. Cole, you have hit upon the precise question. It will be up to you to leave your own story, fiction or biographical, though it will seem as fiction in either case, for others. So that future readers will have another book to journey through when you are gone. You are free to write more than one, of course, but only one is required. And your manual doesn't count, obviously. I believe your aunt may have travelled into the future to find your book, but when you return to 1900 you will find it is empty, as you have not written it yet."

Julian's face was utter confusion.

"No time to explain time travel, my dear boy, and now you must return to your own time to make your plans for your new life within books."

Julian thanked him, and grabbing a biscuit followed him out the door, which shrank to its smaller proportions, and back through the rows of books. Marcus Birdwhistle seemed to be in more of a hurry this time, and so moved quickly through the stacks, his long strides causing Julian to do a kind of undignified jog to keep up. He was sweating under his cotton oxford shirt and his tailored dress pants were too restrictive to allow for running. They were silent this time, except for Julian's breath and the whir of thoughts in his mind. He heard a sound and looked up to find the cat, running along the tops of the shelves, following them from above.

Finally they reached the blank space on the glossy wooden floor where he had first arrived, and Mr. Birdwhistle grabbed his hand for a ruddy shake.

"Glad to have met you, Mr. Cole. A pleasure. I am sure I will see you sooner than you think. You're certain to think of more questions."

"Thank you, Mr. Birdwhistle."

The old man gestured toward the black leather book that Julian had kept tucked under his arm during their meeting, and Julian understood that to return he would need only to open it. He stared at the cover for a moment, running his hand over it reverently. He felt suddenly, a warm belonging. The search for his purpose accomplished somewhat. He looked back at Mr. Birdwhistle, who again had taken on a look of impatient boredom, and then up to the orange cat peering down at him from the shelf.

"What's the cat's name, sir?"

Marcus Birdwhistle reached out and opened Julian's Liber Libri, and as the whiteness began to envelop him, he heard the man's muffled voice.

"I distinctly said three questions, Mr. Cole. But, her name is Marmalade."

The sound of rustling pages ceased, and the muted white of the pages faded into the angles and colors of his own study, where he sat awkwardly in his chair staring at the black leather book. Looking down, he saw the snoozing figure of Marmalade, who opened a sleepy yellow eye in his direction, before resuming her slumber.

CHAPTER THE NINTH
Comings And Goings

Julian had never owned a cat. There was something terrifying about it, and at the same time, spectacular. At first he had thought that the cat herself was imbued with magical powers, but soon began to think that a cat's enchantment had more to do with her nature than any supernatural additions to this specific feline. It would explain a witch's affinity for them, surely. It was possible to be alone when a cat was your companion. Never with a dog, a dog was like a baby or another person, a cat…well, a cat was different somehow. Sort of *with* you, but not with you, as if it already lived in another world, and the cat's owner was merely glimpsing a shade of its existence. Having a cat was experiencing solitude together, in a way that no other creature could replicate. It wasn't loneliness any more, it was being alone. A subtle difference for some, but for Julian it was wildly opposite. He hated loneliness, he ached to be alone. But, there was also that part of him, that growing piece of himself that called out for that other life, that other place that had been promised him. And so, Marmalade was a perfect introduction to Julian, to the space between loneliness and love.

After his journey into Mr. Birdwhistle's peculiar library, he had exhausted his mind thinking of the wonders he had glimpsed in that place. It was an explosion of fantasy, a labyrinth of imagination. As he understood it, his mission was to produce his own work of fiction or non-fiction, which didn't seem daunting as he had seen the copy of his book, published, in his aunt's home in 1900. But he didn't bother with figuring out how she'd managed to add a book printed in 2085 to her 1900 collection, because Julian had decided that time ran very differently than he had supposed previously. And so, he was better off without trying to make sense of it. He'd had an anarchist friend in Vienna that had waxed poetic for an entire summer about the time travel paradox, a subject that had never seemed to bore Karl, but had exhausted Julian after the first afternoon. If it was a subject that scientists and philosophers couldn't agree on, nor understand properly, then it was nothing for Julian to plague himself with. He had an excellent brain, and he'd like to keep it in working order instead of tying it up in knots.

Graduation had come and gone, and with it, Patrick. His roommate, his friend, had extended another invitation to New York, even half-jokingly asked Julian if he wanted to room together in the Big Apple. When Julian walked the stage, Patrick's mother had very sweetly served as an odd stand-in for his own parents at the ceremonies. She had then invited Julian along with Patrick's family to a celebratory dinner where both boys' names had appeared on the blue and yellow themed cake.

Oddly enough, it had been the cat that had finally convinced Patrick that Julian wasn't coming. Julian had spent the morning helping Pat load up his pickup truck with new clothes and a few canvases, finished and unfinished. They embraced awkwardly, purely because it was something people did when saying goodbye. Patrick had smiled, and then without meeting his eyes, said,

"I guess I got to leave you to your mysterious dream girl from the paintings, your weird books and this mangy ass cat. You're planning on making a life here after all."

When Julian had looked confused, Patrick had laughed and continued,

"People don't buy pets when they're about to start traveling, or moving to a different country, Jules."

He hopped in the car and started the engine, and Julian couldn't help but call out to the retreating truck,

"You never know, I might just have wanted a traveling companion." He could hear Patrick's laughter as he pulled away, waving.

What does someone do when he knows he is seeing a person for the last time? Even if he ever came back to this time period, if he moved between worlds and times as his aunt or Mr. Birdwhistle said, he hated to think that Patrick was not part of that future. No matter where it lay. It wasn't quite like losing his parents, but it was heartbreaking in a different way. They had never been close, not really, but they had needed one another somehow. They had been a surrogate family to each other when both boys were in a moment of their lives when something about them had to be hidden to everyone else. Patrick wouldn't just be gone he would be out, learning, exploring, creating, building a future for himself. Julian hated that he would never see that future, and would never share in it. They would never be old men, reminiscing about the days they had shared. The days they had become men together.

But, he had made a choice, and for the most part it was the most exciting thing he could imagine. Or perhaps couldn't imagine, because his mind could barely perceive the wonders of the world that had been opened to him. Julian had begun packing as well, though he could take far less with him than a pickup truck crammed full. His aunt had left other notes scattered around his apartment for him to find in the past few weeks. Requests for his measurements, so that she could order his clothes, dates and times for his arrival, and ideas on what was appropriate to bring to his home in the past. Just that morning Julian had awoken to find a vested waistcoat, a suit with trousers and a jaunty bowler hat laid out on his dining room table. He was glad Patrick had already vacated the apartment, or he would think Julian had taken a part in a local production of Mary Poppins. Packed already was the Liber Libri, which he had stuffed into his favorite leather satchel with his sketchbook, and a few novels that hadn't been written yet in 1900, that he didn't think he could live without. He had also packed a leather duffel as near to full with his own modern clothing, his parent's picture and knick-knacks from his childhood. Julian had purchased a few choice antique pieces of jewelry as well, thinking he could either give them to Lively, which was preferable, or liquidate it to cash if his aunt insisted. If his aunt had planned it all out as perfectly as she claimed, he would be arriving three days before the ball, to which she had secured him an invitation. So, he would have three days to master the waltz, and three days to temper his speech with a convincing accent and try to lose any slang or modern mannerisms that would make him appear even more strange than he already would. The night of his departure was upon him, and though there was still a hesitation in him to leave, still a part of him that believed his parents might return for him, he knew that what his aunt had said was true.

But lately, he had wondered why. Why had they died? A growing coldness had taken over his thoughts, wondering, was it his fault? Was it this Tenebrae that Mr. Birdwhistle had told him of, searching for him? Would he always be looking over his shoulder?

When the thoughts pushed forward in his mind he tried to push them back, thinking instead of pleasant things, the life that waited. Soon, tonight, the time for anxious wondering would end, and it would be replaced with exploration, travel, and a future of word-wandering, maybe with Lively.

As the all-important moment grew nearer, he sent another e-mail to a storage company to come and pack up his belongings the next day. He triple-checked all his other arrangements, preparations that would allow him to effectively disappear. The last message sent, the last document faxed, and then darkness began to fall over Ann Arbor. Julian had scattered his parents ashes over the Detroit River late that afternoon, thinking that he would leave them where they had left him. The last part of this phase of his life joined forever to their memory.

He opened the window in his bedroom and listened for the sounds of girls chatting on cell-phones and students heading home from summer classes. He looked down the street to see people lined up at a small, popular local deli, and he could feel the balm of Michigan summer in the air. He wished momentarily that he'd driven north, just once, to sit on the beach and look at one of the Great Lakes. Maybe to greet the day in Tawas on the eastern side of the state, and then drive across to Traverse City on the western side and say goodbye to the retreating sun.

He steeled himself, and closed the window, clearing his mind of everything as he changed into his new clothes. He was surprised by how well everything fit him. The clothing was well-made, and constructed from high-quality fabrics, a trait in fashion that his father had taught him to admire. Craftsmanship, his father said, is a rare form of passion. When he peered into the full length mirror in the hall, he thought he looked very much the part. His hair was cut strangely for the time period, but it would grow. It was his face more than anything that seemed strange in the reflection. It was a modern face, a face that had seen the world and thought nothing of it. A face that had spent time in front of computer screens and smart phones, a face that had seen war and death unfold on a television set. A face that had kissed many girls, had been shaved with an electric razor. He was a modern man, with modern memories and reliant on technology. Julian was almost ashamed of his own good fortune, of the beautiful life he had lived. Why hadn't he seen before how incredibly lucky he was? It was then that Julian realized that he was grieving. Grief brought on by the idea of his own death, for that's what this choice meant. To sentence himself gladly to a world that was foreign in every way to him, to surrender to magic and dreams. To face head on the dangers of the path that he had been chosen for, and that he had, in turn, chosen.

He placed the bowler hat on his head, and pulled the front slightly down, giving him a somewhat rakish look, he put the duffel on one shoulder, and the satchel on the other. Undoing the clasp on his satchel, he brought out the book his aunt had lent him, wondering again if it would really work. It was Morocco leather and very fine, though he still wasn't certain why it would be sure to bring him to her. He hadn't dared open it yet, in fear that it would work too well and bring him to the past before he was ready. He inhaled deeply and cast a parting glance around the place that had been his home for four years, recalling moments and memories fleetingly as his eyes skimmed the walls. It already seemed alien to him, and so, exhaling, he brought the book up and opened the cover. He realized it was a book his aunt had written, with her name proudly glaring off the title page, just before the pages enveloped him.

The off-whiteness of the consuming pages dissipated, and he was standing again in the unused bedroom of the second floor of his aunt's home. The chamber was now much more friendly, gone was the stale smell of non-use and instead the scent of clean lemon and washed linens greeted him. The bed looked to have a new quilt spread upon it, and the room was properly dusted. He placed the Morocco leather book on the desk, and then took out the others he had brought in the satchel, arranging them on the little shelf above. He pulled out the silver frame that contained his parent's picture, and though it was too modern, and he shouldn't have brought it, he placed it reverently on the escritoire, just as it had sat on his desk in the future. He walked to the wardrobe to hang up the empty satchel and stash the duffel, and found clothes hanging smartly within. It appeared to house a few pair of everyday trousers, all as fine as the ones he was wearing, along with some starched white shirts, and a few evening suits. His aunt had certainly taken care of her part of the deal. And though most men his age wouldn't be pleased to move back in with family after graduating from university, Julian found that he couldn't be happier. Time enough to be his own man, time enough yet to take on the loneliness and responsibility of adulthood.

Aunt Isadora's voice rang merrily up the staircase, followed by her light tread.

"Julian, is that you?"

He heard her muttering to herself about the wardrobe and the room and wondered if she always talked aloud to herself. Something he would learn soon, no doubt.

"Yes, Aunt, I'm here. It worked!"

"Of course it worked. Why in heaven's name would you doubt that? It's magic my dear pet, it would be stranger if it did *not* work."

His head throbbed even considering this statement, and so pushing her words out of his mind he stepped from the bedroom and came face to face with Isadora.

"Well, let me have a look at you. My, you do look handsome indeed. Your mother's eyes and your father's shoulders. They'd be very proud to see you right now. Very fine."

"Thank you, aunt. But I think they would be mostly confused to see me in duds such as these. Unusual garb for a man of the 21st century."

"Pish-posh, I won't argue with you tonight. We must have champagne, and then your studies must begin in earnest."

Julian followed her quick steps down the stairs, thinking again of the difference in electric lighting, and cursing himself for not realizing how amazing electricity truly was. Odd the things one takes completely for granted.

Down the hallway toward the library, they passed a series of beautifully framed portraits. Distinguished looking gentlemen reading books, ladies posed in striking ballgowns, and a woman astride a unicorn. Julian paused, and looked again. Yes, this woman was very clearly riding a mythical animal, smiling into the camera. Julian searched the image for doctoring, having learned the different techniques in one of his art history classes. Sensing that he was no longer following her, his aunt turned around and came back, glimpsing the photograph that had so arrested his attention.

"Aunt, my apologies. I know there is much to do, and very little time to do it, but this photo is very well done. The fakery is imperceptible."

His aunt laughed, covering her mouth coquettishly and looking at him oddly.

"Julian, I assure you that this print is as real as you and I."

She continued her steps toward the library, leaving Julian to scramble to follow.

"What do you mean, 'real'?"

His mind was spinning in circles, an activity that seemed to be his constant lately. An idea occurred to him, an explanation and he tried it out, feeling foolish that he hadn't thought of it beforehand.

"Oh, it was taken in a different world then, where such things exist?"

His aunt had pointed to a seat and then left the room, returning with the champagne and its accompanying flutes. She popped the cork and then poured the golden bubbles, overflowing into each glass. They raised their glasses and clinked them together ceremoniously. She drank down the glass in its entirety and then re-filled it before meeting his eyes to answer.

"Well, yes and no, pet."

"What do you mean?"

"Well, *this* is a different world. Unicorns exist here. Not that I've seen one of course, but there was a Mr. Branning, the druggist who had quite an interesting story about one that was eating his turnips. Or perhaps it was tulips. I can't remember now. Charming man, Branning. "

Julian laughed and sipped his own champagne not understanding her words. He must be tired, or perhaps she *was* insane. Living alone in a past time would work crazy into anyone. It could be the chemicals they used in this time period, leeching into her brain, maybe.

"I think I would have heard if there were unicorns in 1900, aunt. It would be a hard fact to leave out of the history books."

He laughed again, taking another sip, unnerved by the intensity of her eyes on his face.

"Julian, perhaps I should have made it clearer before, but I wasn't sure how much you understood. Let me be plain, you have not gone back in time, well, you have, but not in the way you think. You have gone back in time, using writings that exist within a fictional book. You've gone to 1900 *in someone's novel.* And in this novel, some things are different than in the world you came from."

He opened his eyes wider and then shut them tightly together several times, his mouth opening widely, jaw slackened in utter confusion.

"Yes, pet. I had a feeling you thought you were going back in time, as if you are using a book as a time machine. Of course, that can be done, but only with non-fiction books. A history textbook perhaps or an autobiography that hasn't been over embellished. Although, good luck finding one of those, in my opinion. Practically everything is a subtle fiction."

"But…but I came using Lively's diary, and your book. Those are books that belonged to people in real time, in actual history."

"Well, that would be true, but, you see, unfortunately, Lively is a character in a book."

"A book about unicorns in Detroit?" Julian asked incredulously.

"No, not about unicorns, but, see, the author never wrote that they didn't exist, so, in the world of this book, they do. It's all confusing, pet, but know that you are inside of a book, and reading the diary of a minor character within that book."

Seeing the look of perplexity and disappointment linger on his face she tried another tack,
"But, you're a strong reader, even Marcus thinks so. Which is quite a compliment…you will have many marvelous journeys no doubt"

"What does that mean?"

"Well, for one it means that you should be able to travel through almost any book you'd like, once you practice more. But, you should understand that she will never be able to go with you. She isn't a reader, she can't be, because she is an expression of another writer's imagination. True, the characters once created, become much larger and more complex than any writer dreams, but she is a figment. A dream. Lively will be real when you are here, as real as any person you've ever met, but if she were to try and leave the confines of the world of this book, she would simply disappear." Aunt Isadora paused, weighing his reaction before finishing,

"I have given a lot of thought to your reaction to her before, and your stories of how the diary appeared to you, and just thought it was best that you understood this all from the beginning. "

She searched his face, measuring his reaction.

"Well, that's enough about that for tonight. We need to begin your studies."

The words she had spoken had passed through him like a chilly wind in winter. It made him think of standing too close to the canals in Amsterdam in December. Cold, everywhere. Wondrous and hypnotizing, but freezing. What could she mean? How could Lively not be real? He felt slightly ashamed, like being in love with an actress playing a part on the television. The person didn't exist. And yet... Lively did. He had felt her warmth and heard her laughter. Aunt Isadora was right though, he hadn't the luxury of considering any of this, it was time to learn to dance.

Julian stood up straight and assumed what he thought was the correct starting position for a waltz. His aunt shook her head and passed him a book, a meaningful look on her face. She flipped through the pages, read a few words and passed it over to him. It was a gilded-age romance novel, and the page she had passed to him was a ball scene within the tale. His eyes ran over the words, drinking in the descriptions of chandeliers and ice-sculptures, ladies filling their dance cards and gentlemen jostling for a dance with the black-haired beauty across the room.

And suddenly her hand was in his own, he noticed how creamy pale her skin was, the blue of her eyes. She was a tiny thing, coming only to his shoulder, but the music began and around and around the floor they moved. He didn't think of his feet, or the dance, he thought only of her eyes. She was smiling and saying something about the weather, but he had only the whir of color from the gowns around him and the cloying smell of too much rosewater and the closeness of too many bodies in one room, and her eyes, always her eyes. The music ended and they were returned to the spot that their dance had begun. He raised her hand to kiss it, and looked into those eyes again, entranced by the dance they had shared. But when Julian looked into the icy blue eyes of the black-haired girl, all he could see was that they weren't grey and her face wasn't framed by a riot of cinnamon waves. This girl was a lovely dancer, but she wasn't Lively. He gave her a bow, and backed away as the music began once again.

Julian blinked his eyes and he was staring at the escaping honey colored bubbles of the champagne, fleeing to the air at the top of the glass. His aunt's golden eyes flashed a more vibrant hue, and the electric lights winked on the wall.

Whatever in the world had just happened, it seemed that learning to waltz was no longer one of his worries. His aunt's eyes greedily drank in his reaction, and he rewarded her with yet another dropped jaw and shrugged shoulders, hands raised open palmed in confusion.

"What *was* that?"

"*That,* my pet, was the waltz."

"Clearly, aunt. But, I'm afraid I don't understand."

"Do not always seek to understand. Some things just simply are, and you are dragged along with the tide of them. It is better when these currents come to just allow yourself to float along, taking in the view."

As she spoke her hands had unclasped and her arms had spread wider and wider, in league with the smile on her face. Drawing her hands back to the table she pushed another stack of books toward him vigorously. Each had red ribbon sticking out from between the pages, marking them to be opened at a specific place. A few of the books looked as though they were just recently printed, and others were well worn, the edges blunted and spines cracked. Aunt Isadora offered him a meaningful look and nodded her chin toward the stack, before standing up and walking crisply out of the room. Julian heard a gramophone start up in the library and the tinkling keys of Scott Joplin's *Swipesy Cakewalk* played murkily on a faraway piano. He played the piano quite well himself, and had been to many music festivals and concerts of all kinds over the years. But, there was something enchanting about the music from the gramophone. He had never heard music fill a room like that, the very walls danced to the beat of the new century. Even if it was simply one author's imagining of the new century, Julian was still thrilled to be a part of it.

He turned his attention back to the books, and sighing, pulled the top one off the stack. This was a newly published work, in this time and place, and it was a guide of gentleman's comportment. Julian was hesitant to move to the place his aunt had marked for him to read, excited and afraid to be sucked into the book, but after a few minutes of boring reading about tying a cravat and appropriate dance conversations, he was mostly irritated. He realized that not every book would call to him the way the diary or the romance novel had…but non-fiction like this was downright dull.

After reading the chapters his aunt had marked and draining the champagne in his glass, he moved on to the next. This too was a recently published work, but he found to his great delight that it was familiar to him. The yellow and green cover featured a rather pedantic-looking lion wearing spectacles. *The Wizard of Oz*, in it's original edition was a gorgeous piece of fantasy. He opened the book and thumbed through the pages, thinking of yellow brick roads and Good Witches named Glinda. And then he watched as a little girl with braided pig-tails like an Indian Princess, entered into his Emerald City brave-faced and resolute. Her strange friends, one, an automaton made from tin, the other a large looming lion with a bashful expression walked alongside of her and an obnoxious little dog trotted behind. He was just one of many citizens in the Emerald City, and he wondered what the Great and Powerful Oz would have to say to these visitors.

And then in a moment, he was staring lazily at the open page of the yellow and green book, which he closed firmly. Obviously the lesson had merely been to acquaint him with the popular culture of the time. If he was to be the 20th century man, he needed to act the part, but he hardly had the time or desire to reread *The Wizard of Oz*. The next work was a few years older, and it too offered scenes of dancing and romance. Scenes that Julian read fondly, but did not engage in. And so he sat as the light outside his aunt's house deepened from startling blue to smoky grey and finally the unbroken black of night. He read the books where she had left the ribbons, some swallowing him into the world of the story, and others he read as he always had, eyes skimming pages, consuming the words.

He finally came to the end, and his back ached, his legs surprisingly tired from waltzing in worlds shut between leather covers. The final book was Sigmund Freud's *Interpretation of Dreams*. It was written in the original German, and if Julian's memory served, it wouldn't be translated into English for over a decade. His German reading was far from fluent, his spoken German too, was rusty. He had always been more adept at the romance languages, excepting French which he could never get his mouth around properly, and he struggled to read the paragraphs his aunt had indicated. Julian couldn't help but wonder why his aunt would include this book. He couldn't think of anyone but others engaged in the field of psychology that would have heard much about it. He soldiered on translating as best he could until he came to a section that his aunt had underlined, and in reading it, found his own doubts.

"... dream's evanescence, the way in which, on awakening, our thoughts thrust it aside as something bizarre, and our reminiscences mutilating or rejecting it— all these and many other problems have for many hundred years demanded answers..."

Yes, he had thrust this dreamworld aside as bizarre, he did seek to question and uncover and disbelieve all the new truths that had been presented to him. Perhaps his aunt was right, Julian needed to float along on the waves of his destiny, and admire the sights the traveling tides could show him.

Just then his aunt bustled back into the library, with two small crystal Madeira glasses half-filled with the sweet swirling amber liquid. He stood up and faced her, taking one of the glasses from her long graceful fingers. She stood back in order to take a better look at the effect the reading had on him, and her shoulders lowered in relief.

"Yes, I think a little more reading, and some practice dressing...perhaps a trip to the bank, and you're ready. You have the look of your father, you know. Ready to take on the world."

Julian smiled in reply, sipping his madeira, but his mind was walking the halls of his memory, searching for the girl with the honey and spice hair, and a flash of her dove-grey eyes, smiling into his.

CHAPTER THE TENTH
Dancing With Destiny, Or; The Missteps

Her thoughts kept reaching back to the conversation she'd had with Mr. Chasseur on Belle Isle. Her memory grabbed fiercely for the ideas he had poured into her ears. He had spoken to her of Ransom Olds and Henry Ford and their ability to see potential. He was especially taken with Mr. Ford's ability to see the potential in automation. Of the possibilities of the motor car and the freedom it would present to any who owned one. Mr. Chasseur described cities packed like sardines with horseless carriages, each citizen reveling in infinite possibility. Something of this optimism had captured Lively completely. What, after all, wasn't possible? Dreams were being achieved in this new century that many in years past could never have conceived. Impossible, magical fantasies of man and machine and time and fashion. Her ancestors would never have believed in the power of the changing world around her.

She hardly believed the world around her, come to think of it.

Take today for instance. Here it was, sprung upon her suddenly even though she had been eagerly counting down the days, a prize hothouse rose that had finally bloomed. The ball, the gala, the birthday, whatever the name everyone chose to call it, it was *here*. Parties such as this were happening nightly in the ballrooms of London and Vienna, a never-ending production of frivolity and splendor. In New York or Boston, even Chicago, an entertainment of tonight's proportions wouldn't be the long awaited event that it was in Detroit. Detroit was different though, not a city of debutantes and dandies, it was a place lit vibrantly; but with innovation and change. A place that almost mocked the idea of European ritual, a new breed of man altogether reigned here. But, on the other side of the disdain for all that was old and traditional, was the fascination of it, the desire to create a ballroom fantasy even grander than anything a baron of industry or lordly duke could imagine. Hard to believe, indeed, but delicious to consider.

Her little satin shoes glistened in the electric light, and the color of her dress shimmered and rippled in the glow. Sometimes appearing as light as a spring pear and then in another moment it was deep bottle green. The light caught the ruby strands of her hair when she turned one way, and then in another, golden butterscotch tones shone brightly. Lively felt like a princess with her heavy waves curled and piled on top of her head, though she wondered if it would succeed in breaking it off her slender neck by the time the night was through. Victoria had dropped by her room to borrow some cosmetic, and Lively saw that she was resplendent in a bittersweet chocolate gown that was tightly corseted and heavy skirted, the brown of the dress the exact color of her large doe eyes. James had knocked on Lively's door just after his sister had floated out, looking actually quite dashing in his coat and tails, the trouser legs cut slightly larger than had been fashionable previously. He had teased her liberally and then offered to write his name on all the spaces of her dance card. She had forcefully pulled the small mother of pearl case, complete with a chain for her wrist, away from his grasping fingers, but she had allowed him the first dance anyway. He was very capable of imbecility and could be quite a nuisance, but in his heart he was dear. But for now, Lively was dressed, properly rouged and her toilette completed impeccably, unfortunately all that was left was to wait. She'd had to exhaust all of her own dubious beauty tricks, as Clara had all but disappeared.

Their house on Woodward was very large in comparison to some of their neighbors, and because of this and their frequent entertaining of guests, the Maxon's had need of more hired help than was usual in the city. If one added Aunt Charlotte's unwieldy size and general distaste for activity, over the years they had accumulated an impressive staff. It was Lively that had first noticed Clara missing, and had asked after her to her aunt's lady's maid and Victoria's. She had been disappearing since before their recent falling out, and a few days after their tearful embrace, she'd not shown up for work at all. After a full day with no news, Lively had realized with alarm, that she didn't know her friend's address. It was shocking to think how little she knew about Clara. More surprising still was to hear the other ladies' opinions of her. They assumed she'd gotten married to a beau, or had found work elsewhere. They spoke of her as if she was a soiled gypsy woman, as if the taste of her name in their mouth was sour milk.

And so Lively was alone in her bedroom, staring at the diary, wondering why it felt limp and dead within her hands. She had given him a sign, but had heard nothing since. She did not feel his presence in her bedchamber, could not feel the vitality of his person surrounding her as she once had. Lively had casually asked if anyone had heard of a young man arrived in town with Mme. Isadora Bellevie, but it was a delicate subject to bring up in company. Besides, she had no idea if it was merely coincidence that Mme. Isadora's nephew shared a given name with her mysterious Mr. Cole.

The clock ticked endlessly on the dresser and she found herself looking searchingly at her reflection in the looking glass. When she turned a certain way or tilted her head just so, she could see her mother. Not that they had looked very much alike, or did even now, but there was the ghost of her mother's face within her own. The lines of her smile, the dance of her eyes lived within Lively's. It wasn't just a likeness in their expressions, it was something deeper, more resilient. She remembered a night when her mother and father had come home late from a ball of their own. She didn't recall precisely where they had been living at the time…perhaps Prague or maybe Florence? Lively had hidden in her mother's dressing room, little hands gently touching strands of pearls and scarves so soft that they felt like the lightness of a breeze. She had heard her mother in the hallway, knew she would be caught, but it didn't matter. The sight of her mother in her gown and gloves, her rubies and dripping garnets, was well worth it. There was a faint humming in the hallway, her mother's voice reliving the melody of a dance, the sound filling the hallway and the dressing room sweetly, thought it was hummed quietly. Her mother had opened the door to see Lively's eyes peeking up from the spot where she'd buried her chin against her chest, and she had wrapped herself sloppily in one of her mother's kimonos. Even now, sitting in this foreign room thousands of miles away from that memory, she saw her mother's smile reflected back in the mirror. That was it, a wink and a strange sad smile, and she had continued humming the same sweet tune. It was a kind of confidence, both of them knowing she wasn't supposed to be there, but her mother had said nothing. As if it were perfectly natural to find Lively waiting in her private boudoir. Her mother knew how to keep secrets, everything about her seemed to be quiet whispers.

And it was then as a little girl that she first understood the power of a beautiful woman. The allure of the illusion, the performance that a woman puts on when dressing or applying cosmetics. Without her mother saying a word she saw her floating around the dance floor on her father's arm and felt the heat of twirling and the vibrance of the celebration. Touching her own cheeks she recalled the rouge on her mother's, twirling a stray curl from her coiffure she saw the intricate pinnings of her mother's glossy hair. She wished her mother were here, she wished she could repeat time and have her presence standing behind her, wrapped in a kimono watching her own daughter prepare for a night of amusement, just as she had watched her mother pack away the mysteries of her own beauty, so many years ago.

But her mother was not there, nor Clara, and Lively was alone. It wasn't the being alone that she minded, it was the loneliness. It was that ship lost in a storm feeling, that anything could happen and no one would hear her cry out that she was drowning. She hoped that tonight, something magic would happen. She hoped tonight that the splendor of her life would be once again revived into something vibrant and enchanting and worth living for. It was silly to fold so much expectation into one night that was largely out of her control, but she had felt for a long time as if she was on the precipice of something, the pinnacle, and that just around the next turn she would find the meaning she was longing for. If only.

In the meantime, she could hear her Aunt Charlotte's nasal voice, sounding like so many pigs in a pen fighting over a cool patch of mud. She was yelling about a sash, and then a missing ribbon, shouting because her broach clashed with her scarf. Her voice was everywhere, surrounding Lively like a raging rainfall. It didn't matter where she tried to hide herself, she would inevitably get wet. She straightened her shoulders and looked down at her dance card, James' name staring back at her on the first line. The cards had been delivered earlier that day, an odd idea, but it had served its purpose. Lively and Victoria had spent the afternoon memorizing in what order which dances would come, and who they would like to partner for each. Lively looked up from the card to her clock, and saw that it was now time to begin putting on her velvet coat, time to make her way toward the front door, the carriage, and finally, the ball. She made to stand up and slip the mother of pearl case and dance card into the pocket of her coat, when her hand was stayed by an idea. It was mischievous, and a bit of a gamble, but she'd been much too docile and submissive lately for her taste anyway. She reached for her favorite fountain pen, and hurriedly dashed,

Julian

on the line for her last dance of the evening, before she could change her mind or give her self time to think it through.

Bringing the dance card closer to her face, she blew on the wet ink to dry it, not wanting it to smudge when she closed it in the case. A hundred thoughts flew through her mind, what if Mme. Bellevie's nephew was boorish? What if Julian was a heel? But mostly, what if the Julian that lived in her thoughts and her diary wasn't this man at all? Tucking her doubts into the mother of pearl case along with the dance card for once and all, she stuffed it hurriedly into the pocket of her thick, velvet coat, and tied the sash briskly. One final glance in the mirror revealed a face that she saw every day, and yet did not recognize for the expression of excitement and anticipation it wore. She heard jaunty footsteps in the hall and opened the door to see James smirking in the corridor.

"Shall we, my dear?"

Lively rolled her eyes at him dramatically and linked her arm in the one he proffered, and then listened to him gossip and complain all the way down the stairs until he handed her into the coach. Her Aunt Charlotte, Uncle George and Victoria were all waiting within each lost in their own thoughts. Her aunt made a series of noises that could have been mistaken for grunting growls and the carriage set in motion. Only about a mile lay between the present moment and the answers to questions that Lively had only been brave enough to ask in her own mind.

The house, upon entering, was a glittering dazzle. A splendid performance of everything that was beautiful and expensive. It was December the 31st and the eve of 1901. The night before Detroit's centennial, though the celebration for that wouldn't be until the summer. But still, the year was significant and the new century was on everyone's mind, even if it wasn't on their lips. There were dozens of tables laid out in the opulent ballroom. The tudor revival home, only recently built, had been cunningly added-on and rebuilt in order to accommodate the party. Anton LeBlanc was an only child, after all, and he would only have one 20th birthday. Striking chandeliers lit with hundreds of tiny candles, like so many fireflies gathered together, glowing with a sensuality that electricity could not capture. The walls were white with gilded details, the floors a pale white marble flecked with grey and touches of pale rose. A ballroom this size in a private home seemed almost impossible, a brag, a boast. But one look into Mr. Charles LeBlanc's eyes and anyone could see it was not. It was a celebration, and he owed it to his friends, his colleagues, his family and most of all, his son, to offer the most delicious evening one could dream of.

Her initial feeling was one of warmth—and too much of it. Too many bodies, too many candles, too much food and drink. It was overwhelming heat, but the windows along the wall overlooking the garden were opened, and the freshness of the night air drifted in, swirling around the revelers. The Misses Fitzgerald found their way to Victoria, and James found his way toward a group of his own friends, all overindulged, indolent boors. Lively shot him a look and waved her dance card, he wasn't going to get away with leaving her unpartnered.

Her eyes scanned the crowd, appraising gowns and the younger men dressed resplendently. She was standing near Victoria, Ellen and Lucy, who were tittering and preening like poodles. Aunt Charlotte had already settled on a settee with the other matrons, her Uncle George off smoking a ghastly cigar in another room, no doubt. Her eyes searched for Madame Bellevie, or if she was being honest, they looked for the deep coffee-brown hair and olive skin of her own Mr. Cole, his image imprinted on her eyes like a tattoo. But, no matter where she looked, or how carefully she scrutinized, they were not to be be found. Her cousin James appeared promptly with the first chords of the Campus Dream Waltz ringing merrily from the keys. And so the night went, she spent every dance searching for a man that wasn't there, a man that may not even exist. Her card had been full from almost the beginning, and she was beginning to feel foolish for so boldly adding his name. Most of her partners danced well, if a little hesitantly, though she was not one to judge, her own dancing being less than expert. They were polite, and flirtatious, complimentary and many were handsome. Mr. Chasseur had secured her for the cakewalk, and looked put out indeed that her card had been sought after. But, no matter the conversation or the flattery, her eyes were always faraway, her thoughts hovering somewhere above the crush and crowd.

Until, it was the last dance, and each couple was taking the floor. Lively's throat was tight, her hair felt unbelievably heavy on her head. Traitor tears of disappointment threatened to bathe her cheeks with their salty sadness. She forced a smile onto her face and squared her shoulders. She raised her eyes and was met with the dark features and glistening black hair of Anton LeBlanc. Everything about LeBlanc was flash. The shine of his hair, the gleam of his white teeth, the twinkle in his too-blue eyes. He laughed loudly, spoke brilliantly and danced beautifully. He extended a hand, murmuring words about the dance that she couldn't understand, such a cacophony of sound and light in her brain. Other ladies were unleashing a quiver of angry arrowed looks in her direction, the handsome birthday boy himself had selected Lively as his last dance. There was something insistent, almost brusque in his manner, and for some reason it frightened her. Before she could be drawn out onto the dance floor, her other hand, clutching the card came forward under his perfect aquiline nose.

"Oh, Miss Lindenwood, my apologies, I didn't think you were partnered for this dance. Where is this "Julian"? I have not heard of the man, nor made his acquaintance."

His voice was casual, his remark off-hand. Lively cleared her throat to answer but instead a deep voice spoke from behind her, a voice she recognized although she had only heard it once before.

"That can be quickly remedied, I should think. Mr. Anton LeBlanc, many returns of the day."

The men shook hands, a strange look appearing on Mr. LeBlanc's features. The two men continued staring at each other for a few awkward moments. Julian's face never relaxed, his eyes lit with the same smile on his lips. There was no trace of awkwardness or hesitation. He was a man who was confident anywhere, an easy grace that he wore as close as his white tie. As she stood next to him, she found her body almost aching to be connected to his, just his hand in her own, his eyes on her face. Lively's eyes missed nothing on his person. The way the coat fit perfectly, just a suggestion beneath a well-muscled physique. His stance was as she remembered it, a tiger about to pounce, or an athlete waiting for the whistle. He blinked and then continued speaking.

"My apologies, I am Julian Cole, nephew of Madame Isadora Bellevie. It was too good of you to invite me, I'm sure."

Anton LeBlanc sniffed, and arched an annoyed eyebrow.

"Yes, I'm sure."

Ignoring the slight, Julian turned his head to face Lively, a wide grin on his face, Anton LeBlanc completely forgotten.

"Now, if you'll excuse me, I believe I have the last dance with this angel. Lively, shall we dance?"

And they were off, spinning around the parqueted dance floor, honeyed and shining beneath them. His eyes, his eyes, she was trapped inside them. Gold and green and earthy brown, they were the color of springtime and they held her in their thrall. He was speaking, but she could not hear. The other dancers were speaking, she could feel the buzzing of gossip. The girl who had turned down Anton LeBlanc, the girl who was dancing with a strange man whom nobody knew. A strange man that smiled too big, and spoke too boldly. A man that was only a few inches taller than herself, but seemed to fill the room. He hadn't been there earlier in the evening. Lively knew because if he had, she couldn't have missed him. No, he would have been impossible to over look. The final notes were being trilled over the piano, the violins were singing their last, but still he held her close, unspeaking, as if the words he had first attempted had fallen apart somewhere between his mouth and her ears.

Too soon, so quickly, the music stopped, and he tucked her hand into his arm, walking her back to her family. They still didn't speak, but instead stared into one another's eyes, eyes that asked questions their voices couldn't be trusted with. Questions that didn't need answers any longer. Are you real? How did you find me? How long have you waited?

He released her to Aunt Charlotte, kissing her hand much too long, and looking at her far too soulfully. He melted back into the crowd, leaving Lively colder than she had been all night. After that everything moved so swiftly, the whole night before that last dance had been a casual stroll, and every moment after a desperate dash. Her aunt looked at her strangely, and then bundled her into her coat, and shooed her and Victoria into the carriage where James was waiting petulantly. Lively turned back and looked out the window, hoping to catch one last look at Julian. She had waited months to see his face, to ask him a thousand things, and when given the opportunity she had said nothing. A flash of dark hair and her face lit with happiness, but it was not Julian, it was Anton walking purposefully toward their waiting carriage. He knocked on the carriage door and opened it quickly apologizing to everyone inside.

"I just wanted to thank you all for coming. Father is always speaking of the wonders of Mr. Maxon's mathematical mind and its seamless running of the bank. 'A better partner couldn't be found' he always says."

Uncle George beamed proudly and nodded his head acknowledging the compliment. Victoria flashed him her most winning smile of tiny white teeth and wished him a happy birthday and James shook his hand heartily, saying the same. Anton LeBlanc now turned full on to Lively, as if all his other words up until that moment had been only uttered so that he might speak to her. His face took on a less sincere cast, and a slight arrogant smirk played upon his lips.

"Miss Olivia, I was most wretched at not having the opportunity to dance with you. I would very much like to call on you this week."

Before Lively could answer, her Aunt Charlotte's mouth was already open and agreeing, her jowls flapping her speedy acquiescence. Anton wished them all a good night, and closed their carriage door firmly before waving their driver on.

Lively bristled at her aunt accepting an invitation on her behalf, and disappointment settled once again heavily in her heart. She had so wanted one more smile from Julian. Just one more minute of his arms about her waist, his eyes living within hers.

Her aunt was speaking now, a running narrative of the night, which Lively ignored by staring out the window. Soon, Aunt Charlotte got to the last dance though, and Lively could tell she was scandalized by Julian's behavior.

"Who was this Mr. Cole? Where does he come from?

Madame Bellevie has plenty of money and clout in this town, but I wouldn't call her exactly respectable, and this nephew seems a good deal worse. Barging in like that in front of Mr. LeBlanc. He should have allowed the man to dance with you, it was his home *and* his party after all."

Lively couldn't help herself. "Yes, Aunt, but Mr. Cole was on my card. He was in the right."

Her Aunt gave a grunt of irritation and began mumbling about manners and propriety under her breath. They arrived back shortly, her Uncle George handing her out. He winked at her conspiratorially, which she took to mean he either approved of Mr. Cole, or of her standing up to Aunt Charlotte, or perhaps both. She was tired, her legs ached from dancing and her little feet were probably no better than a collection of blisters from her pretty shoes. She undressed quickly, missing Clara's ready fingers for letting down her hair, and found herself eager to write down the events of the night. Perhaps there was a message from Julian in her little book, maybe he had a profession of feelings waiting for her.

She sat down at the desk and grabbed the ball point, easier for writing with when she had too many thoughts on her mind, and then paused, looking at the photograph of her parents. Or rather, where the photograph of her parents should have been. The frame was gone. A maid must have moved it, or perhaps it had been knocked under the bed. Her brow wrinkled in confusion and she turned her attention to the book. Lively turned the pages slowly, making sure to miss nothing. The very first few leaves felt different, and she stopped looking at the writing within. She realized that the first few pages had held her father's writing, and those had been ripped out. Her brow furrowed more deeply now in anger. Someone had been in her things, someone had ripped her father's words, ripped her last memories of him from the world. She was turning the pages again, thinking of who to accuse and how. She came to the end and her face brightened slightly seeing the crisp even printing that she knew to belong to Julian. As her eyes scanned his words, though, the storms and shadows returned to her features.

> *Lively,*
> *You must be a witch, for you have enchanted me. You are everywhere. When I close my eyes, I see yours. I can smell your hair and feel the warmth of your palm in my own. You surround me, and yet, I am alone.*
> *My angel, you are in danger. I can say no more. Do not be frightened. All will be well, I swear it. Meet me at Campus Martius, noon tomorrow. Come alone.*

> *Yours, truly,*
> *Julian Cole.*

Lively glowed and shuddered at the same time, half full of incandescent happiness and half full of foreboding dread. A paradox of opposites, light and dark, sun and shadow, looming over her at her little desk. She looked back at the place the photograph should be, and flipped back to the front of the book and the torn pages. She bit her lip, and furrowed her brow.

Something was coming, she could feel it.

CHAPTER THE ELEVENTH
In Which Something Splendid Is Revealed

He'd climbed into the carriage to find his aunt waiting, her foot tapping impatiently on the floor. She was grinding her teeth, the expression on her face reminding him of a similar look his mother would make when his father asked her about shopping charges on the credit card. He frowned and settled in opposite her.

"What is it, Aunt?"

She didn't snap back to the moment immediately, but continued tapping her foot, her leg vibrating crazily on the seat, like the movement was powering her brain. Finally she stopped and covered a yawn, before meeting his eyes.

"Oh, dear. There is a problem. We have a real predicament here, pet. I don't know how I didn't see it before. But I see it now."

Julian loosened his bowtie and rolled up his cuffs, leaning forward in his seat. A few moments before he had been twirling effortlessly around the dance floor with a fairy princess made flesh, the woman he had longed to hold for months, and now he was having to twist his mind around this. His brain was too soft this moment, his heart beating too fast, he felt giddy and buzzing with happiness. Adjusting to his aunt's sudden seriousness was like trying to swallow pills without water.

"I'm sorry, what's the problem? This is all so new to me, I'm afraid I didn't notice anything but Lively tonight."

She rolled her eyes and grabbed his hand, the fingers holding his so tightly that it hurt.

"Olivia is precisely the problem. And she's surrounded by even larger difficulties."

Julian shook his head and shrugged expressively at her. She knitted her fingers together in her lap and then leaned closer.

"Oh, Julian. I was wrong. Dreadfully. She isn't a character in this book. She's human. And worse yet...she's surrounded by Tenebrae. We must get out of this book, and quickly."

He stared at his aunt in disbelief. He'd only just arrived. This was supposed to be his future. He'd met *her*. Finally. Of course he couldn't just leave— not now, not her.

"I know what you are thinking, dearest, but it must be a trap. How did they get inside this book? This *particular* book? Why is she here if she's not working for them?"

She shook her head back and forth, as if in the shaking of it the pieces would fall into place and become understandable. Her foot resumed its restless tapping, her eyes focused on nothing. The carriage stopped outside her house and she was up and out before he could even offer assistance. He followed her into the foyer and inside the library, where she took a seat by the fireplace, somehow still lit and stoked brightly. She gestured absently toward the Madeira on the table, and Julian hurriedly poured them both a glass. She sipped it primly, and then sat up, meeting his eyes.

"What is it, Aunt? Did I do something wrong? It *is* her diary that called me here, you can hardly fault me for my interest. And I *did* tell you that she was real."

"Nothing, no, no. And yes. I don't fault you in the

slightest, but you must understand, it is not usual, nay, it is almost unheard of for a Caeca, a non-reader, to be moved within a book. Your Olivia, she is not supposed to be here. I cannot impress on you enough the seriousness of this."

She paused and her eyes grew larger.

"No, *I* cannot impress it on you, but Marcus can. Grab your black book Julian, we're off to The Panopticon."

She stood up and whirred out of the room like a spinning top, her urgency inspiring the same rush in Julian. He took the stairs two, three, at a time and walked through his bedroom door. He shook his head. He'd had three days to grow used to this being his new home, but it still felt like a foreign hotel room. Quickly, he changed from his finery into the jeans and hooded sweatshirt he had stuffed into the bottom of his leather bag. His aunt had not been pleased when she had seen it, but this was exactly why he'd brought it. Mr. Birdwhistle's Library had no dress code.

He spun around to the desk to grab his Liber Libri, and settled right beneath it he found Lively's diary. His initial feeling was elation. It had been so long since he had seen the little book that he had almost forgotten the feeling of the old leather and the scent of its spicy sweetness. The combination of them together almost overwhelmed him with longing. Just a few minutes before….ah, but he couldn't think about that now. Things were happening, and fast.

Julian walked over to the door, and listened for his aunt. He did not hear her tread on the stair, nor her voice urging him to hurry. Smiling to himself, he turned back to the desk and opened the diary, turning pages feverishly until he got to her message.

His fingers went to the page, feeling each word as he read it, trying to absorb any latent warmth from her fingers, to sense the expression on her face as she had written it. He came to the end of her message to him, and he could feel his heart beat harder in his chest.

But, stay. Please, do not leave me, no matter what you may be. I would know you better if I could as well.

So strange, this connection between them. How strong a force her words were, how captivating the message beneath those words. He felt that he had known her his whole life, like she was a shadow that had always been standing next to him, and she had finally taken shape. On the page, and now tonight, in the flesh. Of course she was real.

But why was that such a calamity?

He heard his aunt's steps on the stairs, and he grabbed his fountain pen, swiftly jotting down a message for her to read, before slamming the book shut and stashing it underneath his Liber Libri. Strange, he hadn't noticed before that the books were precisely the same size.

Aunt Isadora knocked briskly and then walked into the room, carrying her own eggplant colored Libri. He stood up, palming his, and walked over to the door. She made a clucking noise as she surveyed his clothing, and then shrugged, as they both opened the book and disappeared into the pages. Marmalade, lying on the bed, opened one golden eye, stretched and then resumed her snoozing as the little gold and black book on the desk faded and then disappeared too.

Julian and Isadora arrived right back on the smooth wooden floor of the Panopticon. Both books snapped shut, and were tucked under their owner's arms. A smiling Mr. Birdwhistle appeared from a row of books, along with a small mousey-haired, bespectacled gentleman.

"Dearest Izzie! What a wonderful surprise! I see far too little of you. You know our dear Mr. Relish, of course. And young Julian! I did tell you that I would see you soon."

The smaller man with Mr. Birdwhistle had spent the entire exchange bobbing his head alarmingly, as if he could not agree more with Marcus, but was trying to do so with all of his body. Aunt Isadora stepped forward shaking both men by the hand and gestured for Julian to join her.

"Marcus, yes, it is always the height of joy to resume our friendship. However, I am afraid today's visit comes under very regrettable circumstances."

Marcus Birdwhistle's face grew stern suddenly and he began walking toward his office without delay, followed by Isadora, Julian and the odd Mr. Relish who was waddling quickly on two insubstantial legs after them. Julian's eyes were caught again by the books on the shelves, the gold lettering on the sides and the way the light hit them, creating the effect of so many stars winking in the sky. He noticed that on a few shelves the books were moving, one was leaving a stack and floating over to a different row, re-shelving itself. After he saw four additional books re-arrange themselves, he tugged on his aunt's sleeve, pointing toward the sight.

"Oh, don't be silly, pet. It's only Lectors moving between books or times. The rows are set up by year or by realities, and when a Reader moves from one to the other, the books move to show Marcus where they are. I'm sure I don't understand the system at all, but Marcus does. Do try to pay attention, darling. We've a serious difficulty! No time for lollygagging."

They stepped outside the office door, which today looked more like the glass door of a shopping mall, and when Marcus took out his key, the glass turned dark and twisted itself into an enormous wrought iron gate, which seemed to be guarding an expansive estate with fountains and white horses beyond the drive. Upon opening the gate however, the room inside was the same gilded wonder Julian had glimpsed his first time at The Panopticon.

Marcus gestured them all to take a seat, Aunt Isadora opting to recline dramatically on the chaise, and Julian resuming his spot on the sofa from last time. Mr. Relish gave them a little bow and then followed Mr. Birdwhistle into the kitchen. Julian's aunt tapped his knee motioning toward the retreating Mr. Relish.

"Unusual man, Relish. Had a bit of an accident in a safari-adventure story a few years back, and has been a bit peaky ever since. Constantly writing, thinks he's a book himself, I think. Takes to children's stories mostly now."

Julian nodded as his eyes widened wondering about what kind of accident had occurred to the mild Mr. Relish. He leaned back into the couch, resting his head on the top, eyes gazing into a mural on the ceiling. It looked like winged orange cats chasing winged purple mice, and in the corner, inexplicably, a banana suspended by a rope from a zeppelin. He tilted his head back to his aunt, who smiled at him warmly, as if nothing at all was out of the ordinary. Which again, to her, nothing probably was.

Mr. Birdwhistle and Mr. Relish emerged, carrying trays with port, golden-glass goblets, chocolate covered strawberries and a large slice of pizza, which was handed unceremoniously to Julian, who shrugged and ate it. Mr. Relish poured the glasses, bobbing his head hazardously every time someone thanked him. When all were settled, he then walked over to a chair in the corner of the room, and pulled a large sheaf of papers from his waistcoat, which he began savagely scribbling on. Julian stood up, his expression caught by the interesting little man, and stepped to the corner to see what exactly he was writing so furiously and to speak to him briefly. Mr. Birdwhistle cleared his throat, loudly, and Julian plopped back down on the sofa, half-eaten slice of pizza in hand.

"Now, Madame, I hope those strawberries are to your liking. What my dear, seems to be the problem?"

His aunt sipped her port for a long moment, bit into the strawberry, leaving a small smudge of chocolate on her lip, and then fixed Mr. Birdwhistle with a piercing stare. And with no preamble, launched right into the issue.

"They've found Julian. Already. And what's more, they are using a Caeca as bait."

Marcus spit out his port, and became visibly ruffled, looking between Julian and Isadora, and slipped backward in his own chaise. His aunt stood up, a look of anxiety on her face, before Marcus gestured for her to resume her seat. He tapped a long index finger on his wrinkled forehead before speaking.

"This is most concerning. Are you certain? And is the bait the young lady then?"

"Yes, Marcus. Yes. And I know she is not a reader herself, I've spent much time with her. But she is most definitely, *not* a written character."

Julian's gaze shifted between the two of them, the tall, old man with his long flowing silver hair, and his aunt, the ghost of his own mother in her eyes. He only half understood what they were saying, but their tone spoke volumes. They were both badly shaken. He realized for the first time that night, that his aunt was actually terrified.

Mr. Birdwhistle sat back in the chaise for a moment, placing a hand over his mouth, his eyes closed. They all waited silently, the only sounds were the sip from a glass, the chomping of the pizza and the maniacal writing from Mr. Relish in the corner. Mr. Birdwhistle's eyes popped open and his hand left his mouth, slapping his knee heartily. Aunt Isadora and Julian looked to him, surprised by the sudden change in his attitude.

"I've got it! Can't believe I didn't see it before. Madame, can you please tell me the name of the book you and your nephew are visiting?"

His aunt's eyes narrowed, not understanding the significance.

"It's called 'The Paper Serenade'. You know that, Marcus, you're the one who recommended it after what happened."

"Yes, yes. But as you recall, it was the first work of a teenage Lector. A person you knew *very* well. One of our prodigies, if you remember. Now what was his name?"

Mr. Birdwhistle pretended to be thinking very deeply, though it was obvious that he already had the whole of it figured out. Julian watched as his aunt's eyes opened wide in comprehension. Her whole face went slack as realization bloomed on her cheeks. Her expression though, quickly turned to despair.

"Alistair Lindenwood."

Julian's mouth fell open as he too, thought that he was beginning to understand. Marcus' smile deepened into the same awkward yet deeply creased lines, satisfied with his memory.

"Alistair Lindenwood. Deceased. Father of one Olivia Lindenwood. Husband to Alice Shoesmith Lindenwood, Tenebrae." Mr. Birdwhistle finished.

His aunt's eyes were downcast, staring at her hands in her lap. Julian had never seen her so downtrodden, she was always one to be bright and cheerful, on top of any obstacle before it had even come in their short acquaintance. Marcus reached over and took one of her hands, petting it gently as if it were a cat, and then spoke quietly to her.

"Yes, I see. You assumed he, as an author, had simply given a character his own last name and then, later, named his own child after that character. She arrived so suddenly in the text though, and I remembered at the time being fuddled about where she had come from. I didn't remember her from the first time I had read the novel. But she is such a minor character and I do read so many books."

He drew his palms up near his face expressively, a kind of defensive shrug. He snatched back the slowly retreating hand of Isadora's, and then turned to Julian, who was still pitifully in the dark.

"You must be hopelessly confused, young Julian. Let us remedy your discombobulation. It seems that your Lively, whose diary you've been reading to access your aunt's world, is more than two dimensional. This girl, she is real, as your aunt says. She's a human girl who I believe has been hidden within books for almost the whole of her entire life. Her father, Alistair, had been hunted for many years by our enemy, and was killed last year by the Tenebrae. He was a very prolific writer and at one time, long ago, was betrothed to your aunt...."

Marcus squeezed Isadora's hand gently, searching for a reaction. When he found none, he cleared his throat and looked back to Julian.

"Well, my boy, as I said, Alistair Lindenwood was an extremely prolific writer. He used all kinds of pseudonyms and had his books published all through the decades. He was...a bit secretive too, though, I'll admit. We knew for a long time he was being tailed, and we wondered if he was hiding his family in different stories. He was a strong reader, you see, and writer. A writer can store whomever he likes in his own books, even Caeca, and apparently, even Tenebrae."

He paused, and looked to Julian whose mind was tumbling all over itself.

"So, sir, I'm afraid I don't understand. If he was in hiding, and so adept at concealing himself from the

Tenebrae, how did they find him?"

Marcus Birdwhistle released his aunt's hand, which floated back toward the other, her eyes still cast down upon it. He inhaled deeply and closed his eyes once again, before opening them and fixing Julian with a hard stare.

"They always found him, because they never left him, Mr. Cole. I am sorry to say that Alistair's wife, Olivia's mother, was herself, a Tenebrae, though he didn't know it until she killed him, I'm afraid. Every book he brought her into, every story they lived in together, she left the pages open on the other side and helped the others through. They meant to catch Alistair, and his Liber Libri, and then to destroy everything the Lectors have built. A sad business. A most distressing tragedy, indeed."

"Oh, Julian, please do shut your mouth. You'll ruin your looks by stretching your jaw so."

Two sets of eyes came to rest on the newly poised Isadora. Her golden eyes were glowing with intensity. She carefully picked the strawberry with the most chocolate and brought it toward her red lips. She smacked them heartily before picking up the narrative.

"I chose 'The Paper Serenade' because *I* am the star of the book. Alistair had written it for me when we were young, but that's a tale for another day. I think now that Alistair later placed his daughter in the book for a reason. He had already written two perfect guardians, her aunt and uncle, who are stupid, but loyal. He knew also that I was in the story to watch out for her, and he gave her a book that enabled her to communicate to the outside world, which is of course, how Julian found her."

Isadora's smile grew as she turned toward Julian, all traces of her former misery swept away by the sunlight on her face. But Julian had something important to add.

141

"Mr. Birdwhistle, Aunt, I do not think he wrote her a special book to communicate with the outside world. I believe the book that she is writing in, well, I believe it's his Liber Libri. I think he hid his daughter and his guide in his own book, because he *knew* his wife was Tenebrae."

The smile disappeared from Isadora's face and a look of horror settled on Mr. Birdwhistle's countenance. Each of their minds running over the ramifications of such a scenario.

"This girl, then, this Caeca, is in possession of one of our Libri, writing her own personal thoughts and experiences in it…without any knowledge of what it is."

Mr. Birdwhistle shook his head, back and forth, a metronome of disbelief. Aunt Isadora clapped her hands gleefully, her whole face re-lit.

"Oh, but that is marvelous. He protected her and the book against the Tenebrae. He must have known what was happening and couldn't chance traveling back here to tell you, Marcus. Especially if the Tenebrae were on his heels. So he stashed Olivia in my book, and then arranged all the rest. And the book, his Liber Libri, was seeking out a Reader strong enough to complete his mission. Brilliant. He always was brilliant."

Inclining her head toward Julian she asked, "Pet, when was the first time you ever saw the gold and black book? Not read it, saw it. Glimpsed it."

He thought for a moment, running his mind back on every time he'd ignored it or noticed the corner of it sticking out of a drawer or a flash of the gold winking on his living room sofa.

"I'm not sure, perhaps a year and half ago. It was very

sporadic in the beginning, I only caught peeks at it, until last fall...then it came more urgently."

Mr. Birdwhistle and Aunt Isadora exchanged a knowing look.

"Precisely when he went missing, and when the sister book travelled to the deceased section of the Panopticon. Well, Izzie, I must say, between the two of you, you've fairly sorted it out."

Marcus stood up and the motion triggered Mr. Relish who jumped up from his chair, stuffing his papers heedlessly back into his waistcoat and began to clear the trays. He eyed Julian's cast-off pizza crust strangely, before popping it into his mouth and chewing on it as if it were a foreign chewing gum.

Mr. Birdwhistle was whisking them out of the office, congratulating them both, and walking them back toward the space on the floor of the Panopticon. From where they would reopen their guides and vanish. They were walking briskly again, and Julian was only nominally better at jogging with jeans on. Mr. Birdwhistle was mumbling something to his aunt about Julian being the key, and him finishing what was started, when finally he couldn't help but yell out.

"STOP! What in the world am I supposed to do? I'm not a powerful anything! I don't even understand what this is all about!"

They turned around slowly, confused at his sudden outburst. A small, rusty voice sounded from behind them.

"Too true, I'm afraid. The lot of you haven't told the boy a thing."

Julian turned around to find a sheepish looking Mr. Relish, staring intently at his mis-matched loafers. Turning back to his aunt and Mr. Birdwhistle, he saw Marcus check his watch, and then reach into his pocket for a handkerchief cheerfully embroidered with orange cats. Replacing it in his pocket, the old man stared up at the shelves of books, hundreds of feet high, once in a while a book changing shelves, floating past them, in a hurry to get to its rightful place. He gazed back down at Julian from his incredible height, and smiled benignly. Resting a hand on his rounded stomach, he wiped his other hand over his mouth, and spoke.

"Mr. Cole, you are the only reader of your generation. It has been…difficult. There were a few others, you understand, your age, but, they have died, or relinquished the gift for the ordinary world. The Tenebrae have celebrated heartily over the decline of readership in general. Reading books is dangerous. It allows a person to depart from their present reality. To visit places and times they never could, to make friends and see perspectives of the world that are foreign to them. It is…an expansion of the mind in a way that is uniquely important. Reading makes every life larger. But for us, Lectors, Readers…we are able to take a step beyond. To fully participate in a book. To gain actual life experiences from an author's ideas. It is this broadening of the mind, this involvement with stories that scares the Tenebrae. A thoughtful, imaginative people are a danger. Much easier to keep them controlled with long hours and new technology to keep them from creating their own stories."

Marcus paused, and fixed his face with what he must have thought was the correct amount of gravity, and shot a look at Isadora before continuing.

"If the Tenebrae get to you, then the future of our kind is uncertain. If the Tenebrae get to the Panopticon, our future and our past is lost forever. Alistair, in his way, chose you. We don't have a plan yet, but I am sorry to say, that any plan we do have, starts with you."

He felt three sets of eyes pleading with him somehow. He could sense Mr. Relish behind him fidgeting with emotion, and his aunt's eyes poured a thousand words unsaid into his own.

"Well, what do I do?"

The whole room exhaled with his response, and his aunt stepped toward him.

"We don't know yet, Julian. But we know that the enemy is within the pages, we know that Lively is a vital part of this too...and we know where the Liber Libri is. Our goal for now, is to protect Olivia and the book at all costs." She stepped closer still, and kissed his cheek. She brought her own Liber out in front of her, preparing to open it.

Isadora looked back to Marcus and nodded, "Right then, have Theophilus Bythesea and Waylon Fernsby here as soon as they can be fetched. Unless you can think of anyone else who'd be of more assistance?"

Mr. Birdwhistle scratched his temple for a moment and then shook his head no. After assuring her it would all be done and prepared in time for their return, he kissed her on both cheeks, and she opened her book, vanishing in an instant. Marcus then turned to Julian, who was still stunned by the events of the night.

Sensing this, the old man asked for his thoughts. Julian exhaled, bringing his hands to both sides of his head, elbows akimbo and squeezed his skull lightly before answering.

"You see, sir, earlier this evening, it was like...like I was inside of a daydream. This...this girl. Who I have been thinking of for months...we were together. And

145

everything was light, and happiness and….and…well. Now, everything is topsy-turvy, and I've got to basically drop a bomb on this girl's life and defeat an army of people I can't even begin to understand. And if I don't, I will ruin the legacy of a group of book-explorers that I only just realized existed. And I am supposed to do this with powers I don't know, inside of a book I've never read. It's…crazy."

Marcus stared at him for a moment, his silver hair blowing slightly in an imagined breeze. The sound of hundreds of rustling papers, jostling and crinkling and the same shrill voice spoke from behind Julian, clearer now, less coated with the tarnish of disuse.

"Yes, that all sounds quite marvelous, doesn't it?"

Marcus' face broke into a smile, as he grabbed Julian's book from the crook in his arm, and opened it. As the pages surrounded Julian he heard Mr. Birdwhistle's voice, "Yes, quite."

The angles and lines of his bedroom in his aunt's house came into focus, and he placed the book back on the desk. He noted that Lively's diary, her father's Liber Libri, had flown off, once again, to deliver his message, a message that was even more important now.

He thought about his description of his task to Mr. Birdwhistle, and Mr. Relish's response. He drummed his fingers on the desk, and his mind emptied. He was clearer now than he had been in years. He knew exactly what to do, and precisely how to accomplish it. Julian sat down at his desk and began the first phase of his plan. Picking up his fountain pen, and pressing it deeply into the paper, he bled the ink all over the page, like the blood of his enemies.

Yes, he was the key. And yes, it *was* marvelous.

CHAPTER THE TWELFTH
A Rendezvous On The Avenue

It had been easier than she'd expected. Much.

She had thought that coming up with an excuse to go to Campus Martius, not that they were to know where she was going, would be quite an obstacle. But, instead it seemed that everyone was really in a titter to have her out of the way. Which was fine by Lively, she only wished she had tried to escape before.

Mr. LeBlanc, Anton, was visiting in the afternoon. Aunt Charlotte had managed to arrange all of it sometime in the interim between the ball and this morning, which was an admirable feat for someone who usually was too busy eyeing the breakfast rolls to plot much of anything. But, as a result, Lively had simply plead the need for fresh air, and her aunt had barely looked up from the LeBlanc household reply as her chubby fingers shooed her out of the room. Only the reminder to be home and dressed before 2 o'clock accompanied Lively out onto the front stoop and through the crackle of the frost in the grass.

They lived in an enviable part of town. Just far enough away from the real hub and bustle of things, yet so intimately close. Connected by the tramway, the world of the city was a short ride or pleasant walk from their doorstep. She walked a few houses down and paused, realizing the stillness of the afternoon. It was eerie almost, she was so used to the sounds of a growing metropolis, of children outside and people hurrying to work, or back to their snug houses. Of course she knew that there were many others, on the other side of town, that had no comfortable place to warm themselves. Those that slowly froze their icy fingers, hardening up into stony expressions, praying for summertime and warmth. She shuddered involuntarily, and a weight descended in her chest. Sometimes she was ashamed of herself, embarrassed at her own good fortune.

But, the city around her was lazy today, it was New Years Day and so she knew many of the businessmen and their families were tucked near the fire, dozing or reading a new novel. Many were probably recovering from last night's celebration, but not Lively. She was out, and striding comfortably down the frosted white avenue, patiently pacing toward her destiny. Perhaps she was being a touch melodramatic, but, it honestly didn't feel that way. She wanted to see Julian. She wanted to see him in the glaring light of a new day, in a new century, in a new world. She wanted to observe his features, and measure them against the man highlighted by candlelight and the life-drunk world of the gala. To her, he was perfection, but not because he was perfect. He seemed ideal instead because he was so obviously flawed, because he was so like her. Because she could feel his loneliness, his insecurity, and his excitement as she felt her own. The feelings scared her in a way she couldn't verbalize, not even to herself.

It wasn't love exactly, not yet, not that she'd ever felt that emotion for anyone excepting her parents. It was something, indefinable. A recognition, perhaps. Through his eyes she saw herself as she wished she could with her own. Through his words on the page her own passions seemed more vibrant, life seemed magic. It was the dawning of herself, the darkness being chased away finally by the light he shined on her.

Stray snowflakes danced and twirled around the streets, landing and vanishing on sugared roofs or catching on barren branches, that were grasping and reaching for the flakes like children in the snow. The Campus Martius wasn't far from her Uncle's house and soon, she was standing in the middle of it, feeling suddenly very exposed.

Lively looked up into the sky, the white cotton puffs of snow drifting leisurely toward the streets. She saw an American flag waving bravely atop the building closest to the square, flapping and snapping in the robust winds. Above the quiet sounds of the world around her, she heard the sure clop of a horse's hoof. There were only a few horses about, pulling carriages indolently, as if they too knew today was a holiday. But this sound rang louder in her ears. The same clop-clop of this horse came on quicker, the rider urging this steed with heightened enthusiasm. And then she saw him, and the rest of the city was invisible. His dark hair, and the shine of his leather shoes, reflected in the warmth of those green eyes. Green as a serpent, and just as deadly, she couldn't help but think. And then he was nearer to her, and she descended the portico.

Lively expected to feel as her favorite unlikely heroines did in romance novels. She knew she ought to be clumsy and to think of herself as ox-like and awkward, bumbling her way to him. But, it was not at all like a novel. It was like greeting an old friend, or walking toward her own reflection. It was, natural, as if the rest of her life was a graceless floundering in comparison.

In one movement he was off the horse, and he looked back at it peculiarly, one would almost think he'd never sat a horse before. If Lively was counting on the wordlessness of their last meeting, this illusion was shattered immediately. He stepped close to her, too close for propriety, and opened his mouth into a wide grin, revealing very straight, white teeth.

"Lively, you've come. You're here. In front of me."

His eyes were bright as he spoke, and she couldn't remember ever being looked at that way.

"Of course I came. Though, you will have to explain how you came to be breaking into my room and scribbling graffiti into my private diary. And of course you need to explain this 'great danger'."

Her eyes were teasing, and she was amazed by her own bravado. But, to her dismay, his expression was one of disappointment.

"This is going to be a troubling conversation. You will find it very difficult to believe anything I tell you. I don't even know where to begin."

They had walked a pace, and then stopped, his face filled with indecision. She could almost feel him pulling himself away, rethinking this rendezvous.

"Well, my papa used to always say that there is 'no place like the beginning for commencing a tale'."

Julian laughed, the tension broken like the surface of a pond and he grabbed her hand, impulsively. Her first reaction was to snatch it away and to admonish him for his forwardness, but Lively found that her body would not obey her. So instead she widened her eyes and left the hand where it was. Half praying no one of her acquaintance would see her, and the other half hoping someone would.

"The beginning, yes. I guess that's the place to start. This may sound strange, but, well, your journal kept hounding me. I would find it on my desk, in my backpack, on my nightstand near my alarm clock. It was everywhere. At first, I didn't even give it a second look, you know? But after a while, I guess I got curious. So I opened it, and... it was your writing. And the more I read, the more I felt like I was falling into your life. Until soon, I was literally traveling through the book, and into your world. Seeing you at tea, watching you write in your diary. And it made me feel like like I needed to be where you were, like there was a connection between us that had been stretched too much for too long. So I left my own...reality. My own life, and came here to live with my aunt. And now, I'm finally here with you. But, I'm afraid that this is only the beginning of my journey, for I have some news. I need to tell you some things, about yourself. About your parents."

She had gone cold all over. Julian Cole was clearly a lunatic, perhaps even a dangerous one. Sneaking into her rooms and watching her! With his devil-may-care admission and loopy explanation of himself! Astonishing, especially when combined with his odd manner of speaking and diction. Who was this man who was holding her hand so tenderly? And how had he found her? Her heart had settled into a slow and trudging thud, like her blood had turned to sludge in her veins. This man that she thought was so like her as to be her shadow...he was no more. And yet...and yet...she could not sense madness, other than from his words.

He was staring at her as they strolled around the Campus Martius, trying to read her expression. Lively, never a talented actress, was doing her best to conceal her true feelings. Of course the man who made her heart flip in her chest would be insane. Of course.

"Well, Mr. Cole, I will take care to shield myself from any imminent hazards and thank you for your concern. I had best be heading back home now, though....before I am missed."

She smiled her sweetest smile, but something in his eyes gave her pause. As much as she knew she should be running as fast as she could, away from this man, she found that she couldn't. Or rather, she didn't want to. She realized that some part of her...believed his words, and that the way they were spoken, in a curious accent she couldn't place only made her trust him more. Julian was nothing if not true, even if she couldn't understand it.

He looked defeated and a bit rattled, and seeing this, she went on.

"Or, mayhap I am being too hasty. I haven't even let you describe these terrors that may plague me."

Julian nodded, his eyes focused out in front of him, his other hand came to his mouth like he was trying to pull the right words from it. He looked at her again and his brow creased in concentration.

"You are beautiful, you know. You have this, I don't know...presence. A beauty that knows no time and has no passing fancy. It's impossible to capture. It is a shade of something that wouldn't show in a photo, and can't be painted."

He laughed and mumbled under his breath, something that sounded like "believe me, I've tried" though she couldn't be sure. He shook his head and went on.

"Anyway, yes, danger. Terribly precarious situation you're in." He looked around, turning every which way, seemingly looking for others who may be listening. "I don't think I can explain all of it here, I don't want to put you at any more risk. But I will say this, your parents... they are involved in this. Your father, he tried to keep you safe, but the same forces that took his life are now hunting you. But, I promise, I will take care of you. I swear it." His face was earnest, almost pleading. He had become suddenly very serious. Julian turned around to face her, and was holding both of her hands, almost too forcefully, but she hardly noticed such was the intensity of his gaze.

"If I asked you to go somewhere with me, somewhere I couldn't explain, would you go?" The expression on his face became almost a challenge and Lively pulled back a little, overwhelmed with the conversation. She had assumed she was coming for some kind of romantic assignation in the park, that the danger he had alluded to had something to do with the attentions of Anton LeBlanc. She had thought he was simply being romantic and dramatic. And now, while both romantic and dramatic, she felt foreboding by the implications of his speech.

"I...I don't know. That is, I couldn't possibly say. I don't understand any of this, Mr. Cole. What do you know of my parents? Their death was an unfortunate accident, a trial that I am only recently recovering from. I can't begin to fathom what you are saying."

Julian sighed and paused, hunching his shoulders. He looked up to the sky, searching for inspiration, and then seeing none, looked back to her quivering lips and bright grey eyes. Gently, he reached over and wiped a tear that had broken free from the cage of her eyelashes, and ran rebel down her cheek.

"Oh, damn. This isn't the place. Can you come to my aunt's house? Later this week? We will explain all of it to you. But, know this, you must be on your guard. Do not answer questions about your parents, do not discuss where you come from. Do not explain my presence at the ball to anyone."

"But why?"

"Come on Thursday, the day after tomorrow. I will have my aunt send round an invitation. But please, guard your words, and your person. For, I do not know why, nor can I explain it even to myself, but you have grown most precious to me."

His face came closer to hers, and she held her breath. Her stomach fluttered and her pulse raced, and smiling, he bent and kissed her, full and hard on the mouth. His arms were around her waist and moving up her back, as the kiss deepened. She was breathless, the fluttering in her stomach becoming warm, and desire crashing over her like a wave. And then, he released her, planting a kiss on the tip of her nose, and on her forehead.

"I know I am not supposed to do that. I think there's a law about it here or something. But where I come from, when you want to kiss a girl, and she wants to kiss you too, then there is nothing for either of you but to pucker up."

Lively laughed, a breathy, shaky thing. "Well, I must admit I'd rather live where you come from. It seems very pleasant, indeed."

He raised both of her hands to his mouth, his eyes never leaving hers, and bestowed two more kisses. He approached his horse slowly, and swung himself on top of it, a bit awkwardly. She began walking away, or, perhaps floating if her feelings could be trusted, when she heard his voice.

"Be sure to write to me. In the journal. Tonight and tomorrow. I will be looking to be sure you are unharmed."

"I will write" she called to him, "but at some point you must tell me how it is possible that you read my journal from miles away!"

Lively thought that she heard him laugh, though she couldn't be sure. Looking up at the clock in the square, she realized she would have to rush to change and prepare herself for their visitor at home. She hastened back, her thoughts lingering on the warmth of his olive skin, the burn of his ardent kiss. The tingling of it on her lips glowing, making her feel horribly wanton in the way that her aunt always warned her about.

CHAPTER THE THIRTEENTH
In Which Danger Is Avoided Unpleasantly

She arrived home to a general uproar. Aunt Charlotte and Victoria were in a tizzy resulting from James not having felt the need to emerge from his bedchamber yet that day. And all attempts to rouse him were met with tired yawns and refusals. He had drank too much at the ball and smoked far too many cigars and wouldn't they all just leave a poor man alone?

Downstairs the maids were cleaning invisible dust from tables and shining silver that had been cleaned too recently to need polish. Cook was singing an Irish song at full volume and Clara was, apparently, returned. The good news of her friend caused Lively to brighten immediately, and she dashed past her red-faced aunt and bewildered cousin to her room. She burst through the door without knocking, it was her chamber after all, and found Clara sitting calmly at her desk. She was brazenly pawing through Lively's diary, without even the sense to look ashamed, though Lively knew she'd made enough noise on her arrival to have alerted Clara. Lively stepped over to the desk, the smile disappearing from her face, like the sun behind the clouds, just as Clara was in the process of ripping out a page of Julian's writing.

"Clara! What are you about?! Stop that immediately, those are my things!" Her eyes blazed for a moment before she went on, an idea occurring to her.

"It was you! You ripped out my father's notes in the front of my diary! How could you?"

Her friend's face looked up at her, angelic and sweet, a small smile tugging on the corners of her pink mouth. It was the same face she had shown to Lively countless times, and it was only now that she saw with a shiver the disingenuousness of the expression.

"Oh, Lively dear. How wonderful to see you. You misunderstand. I am trying to *protect you*. If your aunt or cousins saw your father's crazy scribbles you'd never hear the end of it. The same thing with this strange man who has obviously, *scandalously*, been in your bedroom. You'd be labeled a common harlot, and that's the truth. I just want the best for you, darling. Think of how the news would affect dear Mr. LeBlanc…and after you made such an impression on him at the gala."

She simpered briefly and made to stuff the pages she had torn into the pocket of her skirt. Lively, however was neither cowed, nor charmed.

"Not so quick, missy. You seem to have all of the answers sitting prettily on the tip of your razor tongue, don't you? Well, I'm not fooled for a minute. You disappear for days at a time, and yet you seem to be very knowledgeable about my private life, and my dance partners. It was you, after all, who made sure I went to the dance in the first place. You who beguiled me with stories of Detroit and teased me out of this house by whatever means you could set your wits to. If I'm not mistaken, I'd say you had questionable motives. I think I will look after my own character and choices, if *you* please."

Lively snatched the precious note from Julian out of Clara's hand, tearing it a bit, and pressed it into the pocket of her blouse. Clara's face had gone red, her eyes hard with anger. Lively met her expression with her own icy glare.

"I don't know who you really are, or what you think you are doing here. You are a stranger to me. You need to get out. Now."

Lively flicked her eyes toward the door meaningfully, standing her ground in a way that she never would have imagined before. Something about her meeting with Julian had made her bold, uncaring about niceties that she had always abhorred but still had observed unquestioningly.

Clara stood up, fists clenched and jaw trembling with rage and backed toward the door, as if Lively would pounce on her and tear her to shreds if she turned her back. Which Lively might have done, truth be told. The mood in the little room had blackened and was beginning to smolder. She reached the door and still did not turn around. Clara spoke softly but her words were hard as steel and bit at Lively's ears as she heard them uttered.

"You're making a mistake, Olivia Lindenwood. *They* are looking for you, and *they* will find you. You are helpless here, and no one can save you. I don't know what you've done to that book…but it doesn't work as it should. We will find you out in the end."

Lively's anger turned suddenly to utter confusion, and she laughed uncontrollably, shooing the crazed girl out of her bedroom.

"Oh heavens, get out. You are obviously demented."

Clara left in a huff, the door clicking shut, and Lively fell into her chair, smoothing the torn page back where it belonged in the diary, fretting over its almost destruction. She exhaled long and heavily, one hand coming up to hold the heavy burden of her hair, allowing her scalp a moment of respite. Her heart was breaking in her chest, the splinters of it pricking and bleeding. She had felt something strange in Clara since the first time she had disappeared, something off about the suddenness of it. Something odd in her urging Lively to go to the ball. To make Lively believe she was so eager for her to go, in order that she might tell her of it, and then to disappear right as she was going to attend… it hadn't added up. There was something broken in their last disagreement. Clara had been about to tell her something that day, something that she now sensed Clara had been struggling against, and had since let take her over. If only she had listened, begged her to reveal her secrets. In her heart, Lively had wanted to be wrong. She had wanted so badly for there to be a mistake, an explanation. But now, seeing her face, watching her tear apart the one thing that Clara had known was sacred, had known contained her past, and her future hopes. She had seen the leopard's spots, as it were. The realization still broke her though.

She would not weep. She had cried out all of her tears, emptied out the ocean of her sorrows when her parents had died. She would not bawl for someone less, someone who did not deserve the honor of her tears. If she had learned anything on this unusual day, it was to trust herself. Even though Julian's explanations may have seemed deluded, she knew to her core that he was true. And no matter how much she had wanted to believe Clara, she knew the account she had given of her own behavior was a web of falsehoods, knew it to her bones. She may only be a woman, and a young one at that, but it was time she began using her mind a little more in the service of her own decisions. The mind her father had so ceaselessly encouraged her to cultivate. She wouldn't disappoint him. Or herself.

She heard Aunt Charlotte's voice, a cross between a bark and a whine, and she knew Clara had left the house. Her voice carried irritatingly up the staircase and Lively could hear the maids upstairs scurrying to answer the summons. She turned toward her mirror and saw that her hair needed re-pinning and that the hem of her dress was soaked with the wet of melting snow. She turned to her wardrobe, opened it, and strangely, her cousin Victoria popped into her room without knocking. Lively turned her face toward her cousin, who pressed her index finger to her own lips in a sign of silence. She came close, looking over the skirts and gowns, every-day dresses in neutral colors and passed over the mourning blacks Lively had cast off a few months past. Her small fingers paused at an aubergine colored dress in a heavy silk that hugged in the waist and set her figure off at its best. She appraised it for a moment and then, looking Lively in the eyes, pulled it out, placing it gently in her arms.

"I always think purple looks so wonderful with grey eyes. I can't wear it myself, I always think it makes me deathly pale." She said it so quietly that it was almost a whisper.

It was a small type of kindness, but she saw it for what it was. An extension of friendship. Lively smiled her thanks, though still confused at her cousin's behavior. Victoria stepped back, allowing Lively a look at her choice for Mr. LeBlanc's visit. She was in a sky blue frock with a high collar that made her appear taller and smoothed her figure. Victoria was striking this afternoon, her cheeks blushing sweetly under Lively's gaze. She had never noticed anything about her cousin except that she seemed pathetically daft and as interesting as a millpond. But, today continued to be a day of surprises, because she saw a glimpse of the same complexity and character she had noted in Mr. Chasseur's company. A brightness in her cousin that Lively had shrugged off before.

"Thank you, Victoria. It was very kind of you to come to my aid. I am never very talented at putting myself together, I'm afraid."

"What a bunch of bunk! You always look marvelous, like the ladies in Harper's Bazar."

Lively started to dismiss the compliment, but Victoria waved her off.

"No, there's no time for that. Listen, do you want Mr. LeBlanc's attentions? Because mama is dead set on one of the two of us catching him."

"Oh, Victoria, no. He's all yours, I…I couldn't possibly…" Victoria rolled her eyes and then spoke again in the same feather soft voice as before.

"You misunderstand, Olivia. I don't want Mr. LeBlanc any more than you do. He's a miserable louse. James and I just wanted to be sure you weren't in love with him. But, if we're all in accord, then don't worry, James has it in the bag."

Lively placed a hand on her cousin's shoulder, floored by this information, and by her cousin's liberal use of slang.

"Wait, what exactly do you have planned? And I thought you were wild for Anton?"

"Hardly. There is *someone* I'm mad for, and I think you also have a somebody…if my instincts aren't failing." She giggled girlishly. "Don't fret a minute. Everyone thinks James has been recovering from the bash last night, but instead he's been avoiding mama, in case she sniffs out the plan. We'll send the goopy bonehead packing, just you see."

They exchanged a conspiratorial look, one that Lively still didn't understand, and Victoria stayed to help Lively with her dress, the lady's maids being too busy with Aunt Charlotte. Lively's head was spinning, her cousin spoke hardly better than a common merchant, and her wild behavior was uncouth. She liked her better for it.

At the stroke of two, both girls were walking side by side down the staircase, trembling slightly, unsure of what would happen next.

A knock on the door, and Uncle George appeared from nowhere sending Victoria a wink, before opening the door to the slick backed hair and smug expression on Anton LeBlanc's visage. It was an expression that wouldn't last the afternoon.

Dear Diary,

When I was young, I had a dream that felt like a memory. A gossamer-thin, breakable dream, that shivers and crumbles the more I reach for it. In the dream, we were in a house, but it is not a house I remember from any real time. Everything is odd to me in my mind, nonsensical. There are objects in the room that I can't describe, there are sounds I have never heard, some noisy and irritating, some soft and soothing. I am walking toward father on my chubby legs, arms stretched out in front of me, grasping at a book he is reading. He looks at me, and smiles, and just as I am about to reach him, he is gone. The book has vanished, and his whole person, leaving nothing but the chair and the warmth of the body that had been sitting upon it. Then I feel mother's arms, rocking me gently, cooing away the tears. Her face though, her face is so angry. It is filled with hatred that I cannot fathom.

That is all. Ridiculous, I know. Silly that I should poke about for meaning in a child's dream. But the potency of the moment has stuck with me. And sometimes, when everything seems confusing, and I cannot see my way out of the web of my life, I come back to this dream. It gives my mind something impossible to mull over, something to help me forget the mundane frustrations of my existence.

I had the dream again last night, but instead of father, it was Julian. The same smile, the same book, the same vanishing. What does it mean? Will I lose Julian as I lost father? Is it a warning? Or is an overworked mind seeking release in fantasy?

After these past few days, I can hardly tell what is real anymore.

Yesterday's visit was no exception. Two of the people I had considered the greatest clods in the world turned out to be helpful allies. Aunt Charlotte was in her full glory, dominating conversation, her ample and tumbling bosom coming uncomfortably close to falling out of her corset. Her voice coming out in sharp wheezes owing to the tightness of her lacing. If Victoria or I spoke, she sent squinty-eyed warnings in our direction, daring us to make fools of ourselves. For myself, at first, it was a relief to not have to speak to Mr. LeBlanc. Something in his expression is troublingly wolfish, and the way his tongue runs over his lips between his sentences makes my skin crawl.

But, he was not to be deterred. He was a man on a mission, his inquiry into my tastes, my opinions and my past was alarming, his focus on my person, unsettling. His gaze ran over my figure and my face, and every time I felt his eyes on my body it was like a sharp burn of pain, the scrutiny was unbearable. He wanted to know all about papa, and our life abroad, and asked if I happened to have any likeness of his. His line of questions, though posed in a deceivingly harmless fashion, reminded me of Julian's warnings. I was as evasive as possible, but I admit I was growing exasperated. Between Aunt Charlotte's dagger-looks and the relentless nature of his interest, my mind was not as sharp as I had always thought it to be.

Luckily, James, dear man, came to my rescue. He had not joined us in the parlor for some time, and I confess I had forgotten about Victoria's hints at a plan to sabotage this visit. But suddenly, in the middle of my inquisition, James walked blithely through the door. Aunt Charlotte's face could have soured milk, but Victoria grinned unabashedly. His face was red, and his hair was mussed, still wearing his coat from last night's gala. He hullo-ed Mr. LeBlanc and clapped him firmly on the back, before bowing exaggeratedly in front of his mother. She looked as though she would breathe fire. He turned toward us, half-bowing and then turned back to Mr. LeBlanc. He made a frightening retching noise, and Victoria and I sat as far back as we were able on the settee.

I could hardly believe it, and even now I cannot credit what I saw. Mr. LeBlanc only realized himself as it was happening. James stepped forward in a kind of swoon and released the contents of his stomach all over the immaculately pressed trousers of Anton LeBlanc. The sudden intake of breath in the room, and the ensuing pandemonium has rung out over this house ever since, and I am only just recovered from the hilarity to make an entry in my diary. Mr. LeBlanc had grabbed for his hat, as a drowning man would reach for a life-ring, and Aunt Charlotte and her team of maids almost succeeded in embarrassing the man even further with their unwanted ministrations to his soiled clothing.

Still questions linger in my mind, coiling and twisting about themselves, creating knots and puzzles that frustrate my thoughts to exhaustion. I am endlessly wondering why this is all happening now, and seemingly so quickly. Not that my life was so ordinary before, that is to say, before I came here to Detroit our lives were an endless caravan through places and cultures. But, the now that I live in, these past few months has been so quiet. It feels as though all of these present events have been like a tiger hunched down in the leaves, hidden in the grasses, waiting to pounce. I will not pretend to understand Julian's warnings, or how he knew what form of attack they would take, but I have done my best to heed them, especially as the caution was given in so convincing a manner.

Which leaves me here, curled up in bed still, though it is late in the morning and I should rise. My mind drifts again and again to my encounter with Julian Cole, the fervor of his lips on mine, and the deep feeling within me that he and I are connected. That our hearts beat the same rhythm, that our souls, if examined closely would

be made up of the same fears and passions and secrets. His lips on mine, the warmth of his breath…and then the dream. The dream I've had so many times, but that changed so strangely last night. Changed to something that both frightened and fascinated me. What can it mean? What can any of it mean?

Tomorrow he has promised me answers. And so I will wait until then to see his face. Unless, of course, the dream comes to me again tonight. A dream where I watch a mysterious man vanish as suddenly from my life as he appeared.

CHAPTER THE FOURTEENTH
A Brief History Of Charles VI

It was early for Julian to be home. She heard the soft patter of his little leather shoes, coming up the stairs from the Paris street, the sound of her own child's steps unmistakable for a mother. Though, why Finnegan insisted in dressing the boy in smaller replicas of his own clothing, she would never understand. He looked like a miniature Clark Gable in his polished shoes and pressed trousers. But he was early today, which meant that he'd run home after school as quickly as he could, not stopping to talk with other students, or even lingering on the streets to peek into the shop windows as he might have done. She had been guiltily listening to American pop music which she now turned off. She wanted Julian to think she was always surrounding herself with the more 'sophisticated' music she usually listened to. The Edith Piaf or Cole Porter that she normally played while writing, and mothers are allowed to have secrets, aren't they? Sometimes she missed the bubblegum commercialism of the States. Europe was beautiful, but often so serious.

Julian had trouble adjusting to the new school here in Paris. French was his worst language, and she knew he felt self-conscious speaking it. Kids were so cruel at 12. Though she had trouble imagining he was very worried about other children's opinions. He wasn't the type, usually too lost in thought about something he read or something he wanted to draw. He had always been different that way, and she and Finnegan had always appreciated the things that made their child stand out.

When he finally pushed open the door, it was done very carefully, as if he was being gentle on purpose, as if he was worried he would break the door if he pushed it too hard.

"What's up, Jule-bug?"

He raised his head suddenly, like he had forgotten she would be home, or perhaps because he had forgotten how human interaction worked. The child really was strange, having a way of drawing people in, while easily absenting himself from those same people.

"You're home early, Julesy. Did something happen?"

He considered her a moment, and a strange expression came over his features. She had seen the look before, and knew she was in for a very unusual conversation.

"Can a person be...made of glass?"

Mia sighed and exhaled, relieved. She was always arming herself for the big questions, the ones about himself that she didn't want to answer. This, though odd, was interesting and she and Finnegan encouraged him to ponder strange questions like this.

"No, sweetheart. Not that I have ever known. How did you think of that?"

He stared at his shoes for a moment, trying to decide if she was wrong or not. Between his mother and his father, he felt the entirety of human knowledge was contained. But perhaps this was more of a father type of question, and his mother had been the wrong parent to ask. He raised his eyes to answer her, and couldn't help but smile.

Most boys do not think about their mother's looks. But Julian did. He liked having a pretty mother, more so, because his father seemed to feel lucky for it. His mother's attractiveness wasn't in her looks only though, but in her eyes when she spoke to you. An intelligence that many women shied away from owning. He liked that his mother was beautiful, because he knew that she had made him, and that it probably meant he was somehow beautiful too.

"It was in class today. We were learning about Charles VI of France, and I thought perhaps I had misheard the maîtresse when she said he believed himself to be made of glass. You know French is not my strength, and so I had asked her to repeat it. But it seems that yes, he spent years thinking he was made of glass. And it made me wonder, if perhaps he could have been, and everyone else was maybe too stupid to even consider the possibility."

She marveled at this boy, her son. That his mind could leap immediately to a different perspective of the story, discounting at once what conventional wisdom said. She wondered for the millionth time if she had done right in keeping those magic, dangerous books away from him. His was a mind wasted in this reality, where only one truth was accepted. She nodded at him, being sure to keep her expression thoughtful and serious.

"I had never thought of it quite that way, Julian. Perhaps it *is* possible. There is a disease, you know, people call it 'Brittle Bone Disease' and it is very much like being made from glass. You remember in the movie *Amelie*…"

'Non, maman. Not a disease. Is it possible he was actually made from glass, and that no one even thought to check?"

She sighed, sometimes he was quite stubborn. Mia considered another tack.

"Do you know the yellow cat, the one that Mme. LaChance is always shooing away, but then feeding anyway?"

"Yes, Franz."

Mia's brow furrowed and then she shook her head clearing it. She did not know the cat had a name, and suspected that it did not. Julian had probably decided the cat's name on his own and now believed it common knowledge. As if reading her thoughts he frowned and interrupted.

"It *is* his name. He told me himself. You see, he was left here by an Austrian family, and prefers to be called Franzi…"

She waved her hands in the air, shushing him. Sometimes his imagination, as brilliant as it was, was too much for her to follow.

"Yes, well, you know *Franz*…"

"Franzi."

"Fine, *Franzi*. Does he seem very much like a cat to you?"

Julian considered a moment, weighing each of his mother's words in his mind, trying to get at the marrow of what his mother was driving at.

"No, I suppose not."

"What does he seem more like to you?"

Thinking he understood where she was going with her questions, Julian answered confidently.
"A dog."

"Precisely, and why do you think that?"
Julian tilted his head toward the ceiling and scratched his chin. He looked back at her with his half smile, the one he gave when he was truly happy.

"Because he is only always around dogs. No one else here in the building has a cat, except the orange one that howls on our balcony. Franzi *thinks he is a dog!*"

The smile disappeared a moment after solving his mother's puzzle though, and a confused frown took its place.

"I'm afraid I don't understand, Maman. What does that have to do with poor glassy Charles VI?"

This time Mia couldn't hold the laughter in. She giggled and gasped for a few moments, the frown on Julian's face becoming angry storm clouds. He, of course, did not see anything humorous about this. Acquiring knowledge was a serious business.

"Oh, Jules. My point is that one can convince themselves of almost anything. If you think long and hard and often enough about anything, making sense of the insensible in your mind, you can be tricked into believing anything. Now, consider how much easier it would be to convince someone of something if many people seemed to think the same."

One eyebrow was arched, and she almost felt that she could see the thoughts swirling about his mind, trying to latch onto the truth of them.

"Think, darling. If when you were very small, you decided you were made of glass. Convinced yourself of it, perhaps broken a bone in a fall, and saw how delicate your body is. If you thought about it constantly, what do you think would happen?"

He closed his eyes, imagining this alternate reality where he believed he was glass. How frightened he would be of heavy objects, or to sit down and shatter his legs.

"Now, what if your father and I had told you the same. Had agreed with you that you were made of glass, and covered your body in pillows and never allowed you to get out of bed for fear that you'd break?"

Julian nodded his head, all the pieces coming together.

"Yes, and no one disagrees with the King. If he says he is made of glass, everyone will agree and treat him that way. And so his own idea would be proved to him, and he would believe it all the more."

Mia smiled. "Yes, exactly."

This seemed to convince him and he kissed her cheek and asked for her to read what she was writing. It was an article about Versailles, in fact, for a travel magazine in the United States, and they both laughed as she read how one trip to the palace would make anyone understand why the peasants wanted the monarchy dead. That any one family should be allowed a home like that for something as silly as having the right blood, well, it would turn anyone rebel. He loved her writing, and always told her to put all of her articles into a book. He'd told her once that if she did, he would buy it, and she could sign it, and then he'd travel around with her words all the time.

He kissed her cheek again and wandered into the kitchen. Julian snapped up a few Normandy strawberries, the sweetest Mia could find, from the counter and started walking to his room. She wouldn't see him again until Finnegan came home, and there was no telling if he'd do his homework or not. Some days he just read, and because she could not see the books, those days frightened her. Much better for him to read in the living room near where she was working. Before she could ask, he grabbed the cleaned paint brushes from the windowsill, and headed for his room. She sighed, again. Relief. He was painting then, nothing to worry about.

She had just settled into her article, proofing it for the numerous errors she made in the thrall of writing, when the sound of his bedroom door opening softly captured her attention.

"Yes, Jule-bug? What is it?"

"But is it *possible*, Maman?"

"Is what possible?"

"Could he have been made of glass, and no one knew it?"

She sighed and shook her head, hiding her smile. She looked back at his eager face, and nodded.

"I suppose *anything* is possible, Julian."

CHAPTER THE FIFTEENTH
Wherein A New Story Is Written

His bedroom door had been closed fast the last two days. Isadora only heard him sneaking out briefly for a tepid bath or for a hunk of bread and cheese before locking himself back in. His aunt had knocked lightly a few times, eyebrows knitted, worrying over the activities in her nephew's room. He had returned from his rendezvous in a fever, eyes blazing crazily as if he was a different person altogether. She knew he had lit upon some kind of idea, she only wished he had discussed it with her before throwing himself into it so completely.

But then again, she was his aunt, not his mother. And even if she had been his mother, he was far too old to be consulting his parents on his life choices. He had simply announced that Lively would be coming round on Thursday, and could she please send the invitation. He had pointedly requested that it was clear from the wording on said invitation that Lively was to come alone, and that she was to be sure to bring her diary. But after that, he hadn't said a word more.

The relationship between the two young people was puzzling to Isadora. She had thought that her nephew was infatuated with Gibson-esque beauty, the curving hips and full lips of the girl with enough hair for three young ladies. But, what she had seen at the gala was something very different. He had seemed to not even see the girl he was dancing with, instead he was seeing deep, deep inside of her. As if he were allowed a glimpse into her very soul. The depth of their contact had unsettled her, and she had a mind to mention it to Marcus, but found she couldn't bear to do it in front of Julian. It felt like a betrayal, and so she had kept silent. After all, they had enough to agonize over just now, didn't they?

It was coming on evening that Thursday, and Isadora paced, waiting for the knock on the front door. She only kept one woman-of-all-work to help around the house, but had given her the night off. She had a feeling that Julian would want everything to be kept confidential. He had taken quite easily to life here, slipping into the identity of Julian, the 20th century man of innovation, with gusto. Before all this trouble she'd had a mind to take him round to Ford and perhaps slip him some ideas. It could be rather wild to pretend one was impacting history, instead of living within the performance of the novel's storyline.

She had always liked living within the pages of books, and had been glad when her mother had deemed her old enough to choose a story to reside in. But really, it wasn't too much different than living in the world Julian had come from, the real world. Most of the same rules applied, depending on the book, and the people within the pages were roughly the same as any human she'd met on the outside. Characters and people had their eccentricities, and fears, friendliness and generosity. And as time moved on after an author finished a book, the characters that he or she had created seemed to change on their own. So that on a second or third encounter when reading them, one saw different aspects of their personalities, behaviors that changed or became more pronounced. It had made her feel like she was reading a brand new book every time she cracked open the cover of a well-loved volume and disappeared inside. One couldn't grow too close to the characters within the pages, though. Contact with a human would change their personalities just as surely as writing the characters creates their behavior. She'd be willing to bet that Miss Lindenwood had altered the Maxon family beyond Alistair's recognition. But a Tenebrae in a book, that did far more damage. She cursed herself for not noticing earlier the tweaks and changes in these characters she had known so well.

She had lived here peacefully, in this book, "The Paper Serenade" that Alistair had written for her, so many years ago. It was when they both had come of age, both able to choose a book or books to make their home in, to do their work, to fulfill their writing mission. He had presented this volume to her, on her birthday. Quietly published, not many copies of it existing. It was to be their home together, it was to be their hideaway, their escape. In the novel, she was the belle of the ball, the talk of the town, and the character of Anton LeBlanc had been Alistair's to vanquish for her affections. But, then it all had changed. He grew tired of this, his first novel. He began re-writing, tweaking the characters himself. He wrote more and more, authoring book after book, tome after dusty tome. She could see that his heart had been bursting for adventure. That he longed for swashbuckling and fantasy places that never existed, worlds upside down, places that only he could explore. Until one day, he had finally left. He had re-written the story, allowing her to re-buff the attentions of an unwanted suitor herself, and an ending in which she lived out her days happily and prominently in the burgeoning city of Detroit. And so here she had lived, and grown older, only popping back to the world she was born into in order to visit her mother and sister. And then later, after the accident, she only returned because of Julian. Julian who had now shaken off the dust and grime of her own half-lived life, shining a light on her loneliness here in this book that had become her prison.

She heard the scrape of his chair push back from the desk upstairs, and heard his steps over to the upstairs tap. She sighed, it was times like this she was glad she had chosen this version of 1901 to live in, was glad that when Alistair had written this book for her, at least he had been clever enough to include the copper pipes and tap water. His soft steps went back into his bedroom, and a few moments later his leather shoes could be heard on the stairs. She turned from her pacing-post near the front door to observe him, and her mouth fell open in horror. Was he *trying* to scare the poor girl?

Julian looked down at his clothing and knew his aunt wouldn't approve. Once again, he had opted for the grey sweatshirt and his favorite pair of jeans, and besides the fact that his choice of fashion was decades too early, he didn't see anything in his appearance that was so shocking. He shrugged and flashed the leather portfolio, bursting with papers, in her direction.

"They're just clothes, aunt. I figured they would help support my story."

"Yes, well, I do wish you'd consult me first, my dear. You've probably already managed to scare her off. It doesn't look as if she's coming."

Just as the words left her mouth she heard a faint knock on the door, a sound so hushed that any other time she would never have heard it at all, or her mind would have dismissed it as wind. She stepped forward to open the door, and almost tripped over the cat, who was completing figure-eights through her ankles. Stooping to pick the needy creature up, she turned the knob on the door and opened it, revealing a shivering and anxious girl, whose pompadour seemed to be acting as a very ineffectual hat in the winter winds.

Julian's face lit when he saw Lively, and in one motion he scooped her toward him, holding her tenderly in his arms. Her first reaction was to sink completely into his embrace, an audible sigh escaping her lips. But then, as if remembering her manners she backed away quickly, blushing so prettily that Isadora couldn't help but be charmed. Julian watched as his aunt took Lively's hand and led her into the library, and he remembered his first time in that room, just a few short weeks ago. He couldn't believe how completely his life had changed in that short amount of time. He also was at a loss how he possibly could be face to face with Lively, the girl who had started out as a dream, then a vision, and now was flesh and blood and pink cheeks and sitting beside him.

He didn't realize that he was staring until he heard his aunt audibly clear her throat. One of her eyebrows was cocked expressively and she was handing two crystal glasses of Madeira over to him and Lively. They both accepted and sipped for a moment, their eyes now staring shamefacedly at the floor.

"Alright Julian, out with it. I've had enough secrecy in this house for the past two days. It's driving me mad."

Lively tittered nervously, obviously unsure of why she was there or what was going on.

"I suppose you're right, aunt. But, before we start, you need to know that I've already told her. I don't think she really believed me, but I've already told her."

Isadora's jaw fell and a sound escaped from her throat.
"Julian! But...but that was rash! I'm surprised she even came after hearing what she could only have thought of as nonsense."

Up to this point Lively's face had burned crimson, her eyes studying the whorls of the wooden floorboards beneath her little beige boots. Aunt and nephew alike were surprised to hear her voice, not small and coquettish, but clear and bold, ring over their bickering in the room.

"You are correct, Madame Bellevie, I did think it a terrible heap of malarkey when he first told me. But certain...events of my life these past days have not only convinced me that he thinks he is speaking the truth, but have also revealed that the two of you are more real than any other part of my life since I came here. I cannot pretend to understand it all, except to say it must be as Julian said. This all must be related to my father somehow."

She turned to face him, her hands linking within his own, and then she turned back toward Isadora. The physical connection was a statement. To herself, to Julian and to Isadora. A declaration of her loyalties and her trust. Though Isadora was still inwardly shaking at the way the evening was playing out, quivering with all of the sudden changes brought about by the Tenebrae here in her book, by her nephew's entrance into this world, and now this. This girl, the daughter of the man she had loved her whole life. The girl she now knew he'd hidden here for her to protect.

She looked at both of them and knew whatever her nephew's plan was, it was the best chance they had. And so she told them, explained the world of the Readers and the Tenebrae to Lively. Explained why Alistair had written the book for her, and how he had changed it subtly through the years. She explained that after Lively was born, Alistair had written her into all of his novels. She bled her heart dry discussing her self-imposed exile here, in these pages, the safety she felt knowing that someone who had loved her, though he no longer did, had inked the words for her alone. Finally, Isadora came to her meeting with Julian in her tale. She told her how she had brought him into the book from a reality in the future, and that because of him and Lively, the Tenebrae were here, hunting them. That they were looking for a way to destroy the world of the Lectors, and all of the knowledge they held sacred.

When she came up for air, she saw two shining sets of eyes fixed on her face. Julian's hand reached for his aunt's and he held it tightly, squeezing it gently every few moments.

"You are no longer alone, aunt. We're together on this. And I have a plan. You see, what I've done these past few days…"

Lively interrupted him suddenly, holding her hand in front of his mouth.

"Stop. Stop. Stop. I need a moment. I need a few moments, actually. The tale that I have just heard is absolutely fantastic nonsense. And while I believe every word, I need to at least finish this wine before I can hear any more. My father and the both of you are some kind of mystical book travelers, and the world I have been living in is, in reality, made up of the thoughts of my father's mind. You said this was related to my parents, Julian, and I understand that he was one of you, but then, how did they die? Or are my parents simply living within another of his stories?"

Her face did not look hopeful, as if she knew that the answer to her question was simply a few details that the pair of them had avoided telling her. Julian squeezed his aunt's hand again once more, meaningfully, and released it. He turned fully toward the woman he had waited months to look at, but now his eyes couldn't meet hers without wincing.

"We did gloss over that, and I'm sorry. I just…don't even know how to tell it."

"Like papa said… 'there is no place like the beginning…'"

"Yes, but, I'm afraid we've come to the end, and so I must pick up from there, my angel. You see, your father's death was not an accident. Your father was killed by your mother. Your mother… she was, well, she was a Tenebrae. She was one of them."

Isadora stood and moved to stand behind Lively, placing both hands protectively on the girl's shaking shoulders.

"Yes, child, I know, it is terrible to hear, and your dear heart is bursting with loss anew. But she was not always one of them, before she was just a woman, a woman your father fell in love with. No different than Julian's mother, or any of the ordinary-extraordinary women beyond these pages. But, the more your father disappeared into his books, I suppose her heart grew hard. And the Tenebrae can be very convincing."

Lively's grey eyes were angry storm clouds, raining down hot pain from deep within the tempest of her heart. She turned her head slowly and inclined her neck, looking into the kind eyes and sadly smiling red lips of Madame Bellevie.

"It was real, then. It was a memory. Not a dream, but real. And my own mind knew the truth about Julian too, before he even really explained any of this."

Julian and Isadora exchanged looks of bewilderment. Julian ran a hand through his dark hair, already mussed with the tousle of the repeated gesture.

"What dreams, Lively?"

She explained to them the recurring dream, or memory and it became clear that not only did she have her father's secret locked within her all these years, she had also had her mother's. They all sat back a moment, Isadora pouring a much needed refill into the delicate crystal glasses. All were silent, Lively still weeping silently, the wound of her loss reopened and fresh. Julian appeared to be dazed, staring at nothing, then fully engrossed in the wisps of hair framing Lively's face. Then he turned back to his leather portfolio, fingering the papers within timidly.

Breaking the hush that had descended on the company, he stood up, holding the sheaf of papers.

"There will be more time for contemplation and grieving later. Now, we do not have the luxury of time. I feel a disturbance in the world of this book. More characters gather outside this house. The gala was... hostile, as if waiting for a spark, a signal from someone to ignite their plan. I believe that my appearing in this book hasn't hastened their plans, rather, I think it stayed them temporarily. I think something was meant to happen to you that night, Lively. Something awful. I don't know who or how many were involved, but, I think my showing up disrupted whatever schemes the Tenebrae had."

"Who do you suspect is involved, what characters have they recruited to their side?" Isadora asked anxiously.

"Well, Anton LeBlanc for one thing. It must have been a tough game for him here, existing only to be vanquished or rebuffed? An author writing a character odious enough that anyone who reads knows that he is undesirable? Him, definitely. But someone else, someone closer to Lively, but I don't know who."

Julian puzzled for a few minutes, and then stuck his finger up into the air, a eureka moment shooting into his mind, then he lost it, placing his fingertips to his lips. He motioned toward his portfolio, and Lively interrupted once again.

"It was Clara. My lady's maid. She stole my father's writing from the front of my diary, I found it gone a few days ago. I caught her attempting to steal a note Julian had left me too. She was the one who encouraged me to go to the gala. I...I had thought she was my friend."

Hot tears broke anew on her face and Isadora perched beside her placing a protective arm around her sobbing body.

"Oh, Julian, we've broken her heart. Perhaps you'd better explain this plan of yours."

He took a step toward Lively, his aunt waving him off, gesturing toward the papers in his hands.

"Yes, well, I guess I had better. There's nothing else to tell now, is there? I'm not sure if it will work, honestly, but I have been writing these past days. I have been plotting out stories, for us to escape into. I have written us into them, along with whatever we might need. I tried to think of everything, and so, I believe I have found the way to banish the Tenebrae. I simply…"

His voice was cut off by the front door slamming recklessly, followed by several sets of angry footsteps coming toward the room. Julian sat down next to Lively, taking her hand in his own, his eyes telling his aunt to keep close.

The door to the library swung open with a bang, revealing Anton LeBlanc with another man Julian didn't recognize, followed by a vivacious young woman, who Julian sensed was Clara due to Lively's stiffening next to him. Her eyes were stone as she looked at her former friend, and LeBlanc's mouth turned into a twisted sneer.

"Well, well, we have all of you here. Gathered together, each of your precious Liber Libris either on your person or 'safely' tucked in one of your bedchambers. That's right," He went on smugly, "I know all of your smart little secrets. So much easier, having you all in one place."

The man with Anton was shifting uncomfortably, his light blue eyes darting around the room as if looking for a place to escape. He appeared neither young nor old, was neither especially handsome or terribly ugly. Instead, he was a thoroughly forgettable kind of person, a face that one has seen a thousand times with very little variation. So it was strange to Julian that Isadora was searching the man's face, a flicker of recognition registering on her carefully schooled features. But she didn't act too interested, and none of them would show Anton LeBlanc fear. They wouldn't give him the satisfaction.

The room had grown quiet, the cat jumping up in Julian's lap, the only sound the vibration of her constant purr. Anton looked to his companions, the fire in Clara's eyes urging him to commit whatever foul deed of distraction he had planned for them.

He looked back at Lively and winked, reached into his pocket. Julian shouted, "READ!" his hand clamping like iron on Lively's. The first page he was holding came out in front of their little group, and he and Isadora's eyes frantically came to the paper. Anton was laughing loud and cruel, obviously not understanding he had lost the upper hand. Then, only the sound of pages flipping in a high wind, the blankness of paper and then, blinding light.

CHAPTER THE SIXTEENTH
A Quick Respite

The light had softened and branches swung lazily overhead. Julian looked around at the clearing they had landed in beneath a single beech tree, its sprawling branches reaching far over them, a hovering blanket of green. The sun filtered in between the leaves and the only sound was a far off whippoorwill and wind skimming through the nooks of the tree. They were all supine, and still none had made a sound. Julian raised himself on his elbows and looked around him.

It was all as he had written. Every blade of grass, every feature of the surroundings. The weather, the time of day, everything reproduced just as he had described with the clumsy etchings of his pen. He breathed in the clear late-spring air of his own creation and smelled the faintest hint of peppermints, the scent of his mother. He invented this paradise, and so he wondered if its beauty was more pronounced to him. Like a new father, he couldn't help but wonder if this place was somehow *more* to him because it grew from his mind.

He looked over at his aunt who was now sitting with her body propped against the trunk of the tree, sunshine spotting through the leaves and glittering on her arms. Lively was still laying down, and so he worried for a moment that she was hurt, or that the magic hadn't worked as he'd thought. But leaning over near her, he realized she was softly dozing, just as he had written. She blinked open a grey eye, clear and bright, and the corner of her mouth pulled slightly as she too sat up and stretched her arms languidly, like a child awake from nap.

His aunt's voice broke the preternatural silence, shaking him from his introspection.

"Well done, pet."

"Thank you, aunt. It's not a book, just a scene. I've written dozens of them, places we can hide in, move through."

Lively looked around, admiring the world he'd built around her. She fixed him with a questioning stare.

"Why not just take us back into the world outside of books? Or the Panopticon your aunt spoke of?"

"Because those are the two most dangerous places we can go. From what I understand, Lectors are much easier to kill when they are not within pages, and to take them to the Panopticon is nonsense. It would be leading them right to where they want most to go. Madness."

She nodded her head, digesting this information, and then both women leaned heavily against the solid bulk of the trunk of the beech tree, allowing the sunbeams' gentle warmth to soak into their skin. Silence descended again, it seemed to Julian that the scene he had written was conducive to introspection and quiet, even though he had written it in a fever of inspiration. For a few minutes he thought his aunt had fallen asleep, but her voice broke into his thoughts.

"Let me tell you what I know of the Tenebrae. They do not have a hierarchy, and they are are not a united force as one would normally suppose an enemy to be. Instead, they seem to be invested with the same spirit, a similar anger coursing through them. Throughout time, one of their number always emerges, a sort of figurehead for their general purpose. This figurehead can be either human or character, though, for obvious reasons the threat is more serious when it is a human. Characters are more restricted to their respective books, and cause havoc on a smaller scale. But when a human and a character are working together....it can be very troubling indeed. Characters, as I told you before, Julian, *should* disappear when they leave the book they are written into. But, sometimes, they are able to temporarily exist outside, a shade of themselves, to be sure, but existing nonetheless. The only other place a character can dwell is the Panopticon itself, which is another reason a character tuned Tenebrae cannot be allowed to reach our great library. If a rogue character can inflict so much damage...only imagine what a human Tenebrae could do. What we do, as Lectors, living within the pages of books, traveling through them like ships in the sea, seems impossible. We are fueled by adventure and imagination. The Tenebrae do not understand this. They rebel against it. They are willing to kill to rid the world of it."

Julian had scooted closer to Lively, so that their bodies were touching. Her head was using his shoulder as a rest, and he gently ran his hand down her lower arm, marveling at the smoothness of her skin. He had held hands with many girls, been close to his share of beauty, and so it amazed him how the innocent touch of her skin thrilled him. Even so, he could not fully enjoy this moment, his aunt's words nestling into his brain painfully.

"So, it could be anyone? Is that what you are saying?"

His aunt frowned and shrugged, picking a fallen leaf off the collar of her dress.

"Yes, I'm afraid so. There is no evil lord, or monster in charge with which to vanquish all Tenebrae forever. It is made up of many, nameless people who would tear our world apart. Those who linger, hunting for one of us to attack. They are endlessly searching or a way into our Library, in order to destroy our world."

"But surely, demolishing our world would impact theirs as well?"

"Yes, pet. But that is how ignorance and anger works. It destroys everything."

Julian pondered for a moment, plucking a question from his mind and offering it to his aunt for her examination.

"How is it that the Tenebrae can travel through the books as well? I had thought it was a gift enjoyed only by Lectors. Why then can those who hate us the most grasp our same magic?"

Isadora breathed out heavily, her hand coming to her forehead. So much to explain. She felt a sting of sadness that her nephew had so few happy moments as a reader thus far.

"It is complicated. Though they abhor our power, and would seek to destroy it, the Tenebrae are often...*one of us*. Or had been Lectors previously. Something happens in their story, or they realize they are unhappy in whatever world they have chosen to live in, and they become bitter. Or...sometimes they are those who are close to one of our number, traveling alongside a Lector into a story, and allowing others to slip in with them. It is the same as hating anything, really. When one obsesses over their hatred, they focus so much on the thing that they hate that they seek to know everything about it. What does it eat? Where does it sleep? What are its dreams? And in a sense, from collecting so much information about the thing that is repulsive, the one who hates becomes like the very thing they would destroy. And so, sometimes they find they are endowed with the very powers they seek to rid the world of."

Julian's brow furrowed, partially understanding this explanation, but bubbling over with further questions. His aunt continued.

"Just know that usually when an attack becomes this serious, it is because one of our own number has turn their coat, as it were. I would bet my life a former Lector was behind this...but who? Even with our Libris, we can be difficult to track."

Lively's voice, clear and bold as it had been in his aunt's library rang out now, stronger and recovered from her sorrow.

"There may be no central organization for this group, but it seems, for now, that dealing with Anton LeBlanc will lead us to the puppet-master. That through him, we can trace back to the man holding the strings."

"You may be right, my dear. Or he could also be a distraction to confuse us. The man that was with him...he could also be behind this. Though I had not thought to see the man again after our last parting. Like seeing a ghost. This is how it always begins, a swelling somewhere that erupts into our world, and that cancer at the moment, is one of these men."

"How do you know him, aunt? Your face looked peculiar when he came in through the door."

Isadora's mouth pursed, her eyes narrowing. He could see she was making a decision, whether it was the right time to reveal what she knew. Her face cleared and warmed, he knew she had decided to hold back whatever truth she had been on the edge of sharing.

"I'm not sure if I remember just now. I will...tell you when I think of his name. All we need know right at the moment is that he is surely someone to avoid. At all costs." Her expression grew sharper, the angles of her face showing more prominently in the fading light of day.

They sat for a few moments longer, enjoying the late afternoon sunshine that was slowly moving toward gloaming. Julian stood up and dusted himself off, taking out his portfolio. His aunt looked at him, questioningly, before she too, stood up and joined him.

"We can't sleep here tonight, we must move on. This place is not well-sketched out, and I fear that the Tenebrae will find their way in. We must move on."

"But what about our things? And my book! I didn't grab my Liber Libri!" Isadora's face took on a new expression of panic.

"Not to worry, aunt. I took care of all of it."

He opened the leather case and brought out both of their books, handing his aunt the eggplant colored leather tome, which she hugged to her breast. His own black leather book he kept tucked under his arm. Julian gestured toward Lively, and pointed toward her lap. Isadora stepped forward, picking the little gold and black book up gently, as though it were the new bud of a rose.

"I never thought to see this again. His Liber. This was Alistair's most prized possession, until his daughter, you, Lively, were born. I should have known he would find a way to preserve both of his treasures."

"I am sorry I defaced it by writing in it..." Lively began.

"No, it was exactly the correct thing to do. If you hadn't, Julian would never have discovered his gift, and he would never have found you."

Julian glowed and the same shine was reflected on Lively's face.

"Now Julian, what is the next stage of the plan?"

Julian shifted his weight, and brought out the different

papers and stories he had written for them. His eyes studied the pages for a minute and then he looked up, ready to meet his aunt's glance.

"Aunt, the next stage of our plan is to split up. You will take these papers, and give them to Marcus. I will take Lively into the next scene that I have written."

Isadora took the papers he was holding toward her, her face filled with incredulousness.

"Split up? But you can't be serious!"

He didn't answer. Only looked at the grass at his feet, praying that she would understand, when suddenly, she did.

"Oh, Julian, I see. You are trying to keep me safe, and you must also get this message to Marcus. Very well, I had already accepted that whatever plan you thought of was our best hope, and I will not veer from that decision. Do take care of the girl, won't you? She is dear."

Isadora walked over to Lively, and raising her up to standing, hugged her fiercely, whispering something in her ear that Julian couldn't make out. She approached Julian, and looked into his eyes for a moment, trying to say with an expression what her voice could not be trusted with. Julian saw his mother, and his aunt. He saw his past and his future. This had all changed so quickly, he was still catching his breath, and yet. He wouldn't have it any other way. She kissed his cheek quickly, opened her Libri, smiled, and was gone.

Julian took one more look around this beautiful scene he had laid out, was awed by the simple beauty of the place, and the girl who was now under his protection, and who was in turn, his protector. He selected from his sheaf the next scene for them to journey into, and she stepped close beside him.

"You know, I spent my life wandering the world with my parents. Or at least the world of books, whatever it was, that my father created. So these past few months, I felt that I was stuck in Detroit. That I had been trapped. It is wonderful that my ticket out was through a book, through words that reached across worlds and touched you."

Julian shook his head, unable to express just how similarly they had been trapped. How long he had yearned for the same ticket out, and how it had come from the same book. So instead he smiled, and took her in his arms again, putting into the kiss every kind of gratitude and feeling he could, hoping she would be able to translate.

Night fell on the little scene, and holding tightly to Lively, he drew out the next page he had written, and they vanished.

CHAPTER THE SEVENTEENTH
Meanwhile, Back In The Panopticon

Strangely, there was no one there to meet her when she arrived. Isadora was used to the long strides and familiar gruff throat-clearing voice of Marcus Birdwhistle greeting her enthusiastically. But instead, the only sound was the tap of her own feet on the well polished wooden floor of the Panopticon. Softly, softly, another noise sounded from above, and she looked up to see the lithe form of the orange cat, jumping from bookcase to bookcase, matching her progress from above. She had never understood the way the cat moved through the books, as obviously she wasn't able to read them, and besides, Marmalade was far too old for a cat. Marcus had always simply shrugged his shoulders, saying that the mystery of any feline was too much for even him to try and unravel.

She was growing closer now, and she could hear voices behind the door. From the outside, it looked like the front door of her childhood home, the one she had shared with her mother and dear Mia. The same buttercup yellow cheerful door with a brass knocker and doorknob that she'd seen so many times, and yet had forgotten until now. As she approached the door, the voices were clearer, some she hadn't heard for many years. She felt an immediate rush of pleasure, and was glad that Julian had sent her here, back with the other Lectors of her youth. As she turned the knob on the door, it transformed before her into an enormous bank vault, the knob becoming a shiny metal wheel attached to the round vault door. She shook her head, Marcus was forever changing the doors of his study, for no reason other than it seemed to amuse those who visited him. She stopped briefly to pinch her cheeks, before stepping through the door, and into the gilded room Marcus called home.

When her eyes adjusted to the light, she spied familiar

faces, sitting around the table, enjoying their host's hospitality. Marcus Birdwhistle was sitting in a straight backed chair with golden upholstery and twin lion heads perched on the top. She had seen the chair before, but couldn't place it, when suddenly, it came to her.

"But Marcus, those are from my book! They normally reside in the Maxon's parlor!"

Shining clear blue eyes looked to her, and the light playfully lit his silver mane of hair. He stood swiftly, his tall form dwarfing every other feature of the room. In one step he was at the door, ushering Isadora in, taking her coat, and the papers from Julian, before placing her on the end of the settee next to Waylon Fernsby.

"So they are, so they are. Don't you fret, they are only replicas. I had to have them for my own, you see. Exquisite workmanship, to be sure. Izzie, you remember Waylon and Theophilus, of course? And our dear Mr. Relish."

Waylon had been one of the first Lectors that Isadora had ever met. Older now, near to Marcus' age, with hair that had at one time been a brilliant shade of red, but had now mellowed into a yellowy-white. His face too, had been perpetually red, as if he was always out of breath, and she was glad to see that in this case, the red had remained. His body was uncomfortably square, not able to decide whether to give into the comforts of roundness or to hold fast to the slimness of his youth. He stood graciously, effusively expressing his gladness to see her. He had a tendency to spit while he spoke, which, while disgusting, was also somehow endearing. She wasn't sure why she had requested him specifically to aid in the plan, but he was trustworthy and loyal, and there were few others she regarded so highly. Turning from the enthusiastic welcome of Mr. Fernsby, she felt the hot gaze of the other man nearby, the long-time heartthrob of the Lector world,

Theophilus Bythesea. The Bythesea family had been prominent Lectors for generations, and Theophilus was the paragon of their stock. He walked in measured strides to her now, having been speaking privately with Mr. Relish in his untidy corner of the room when she walked in. His long auburn hair was tied into a small queue with a black ribbon. For whatever reason, Theophilus wrote mostly Sci-Fi thriller novels himself, but preferred to live in regency romances, where he of course, stole hearts as was his wont. He was perhaps 35 and the youngest Lector, save Julian. Isadora thought her nephew was more handsome with his olive skin and inky hair, something boyish and sincere that Theo couldn't replicate. But, looking into his honey-brown eyes, his charm oozing from his perfect white-toothed smile, his every gesture designed to swoon, Isadora also saw how he did quite well with women— whether they were characters or otherwise.

Marcus waited until they had exchanged their greetings, and then without even so much as glancing at the papers from Julian, was clearly ready to begin their discourse, on this, their most important conversation. Each of the Lectors had poured themselves tea, and Mr. Relish in the corner had even slowed his vicious scribbling in order to hear what Marcus would say. Mr. Fernsby quietly took out a gleaming silver cigarette case, popping it open without observing his actions, so usual were they for him. He generally smoked during discussion, feeling it fueled his mind. Indeed, Isadora could hardly picture him at all in her mind without a pipe, a cigar or one of his hand-rolled cigarettes. But, a warning gesture from Marcus sent the little white stick back into its case and returned to his pocket. Mr. Relish in the corner had flattened himself to the wall, shaking with fear. She'd forgotten, as he believed himself to be a book, made from paper, he was deathly afraid of stray sparks or nearby flames. Poor, strange little man.

But now was time to begin, Marcus was silently summoning their attention. His face took on a grayish cast, his eyes became hard, and he stood up theatrically. It was clear that he had a difficult message to share.

"My fellow Adventurers, Lectors All, welcome. Thank you Bythesea, Fernsby, for traveling here from whatever place or book that you had been residing in. You are some of our most active members, and I believe that your participation is paramount to the success of our efforts. Now, without further ado, we must consider some of the beliefs we hold as Lectors. For some of you, what I have to say is no surprise, for others, it will be a great shock. Please, I beg you hear me to the end."

He peered about the room, looking into every set of eyes surrounding him, weighing and measuring the effect his words would have.

"You have been told that the Tenebrae are a disorganized force. A loose group, comprised of those humans, creatures and characters that oppose us." He paused again, and everyone in the study nodded, the very paintings on the wall seemingly in total approval of what was being said. Isadora even risked a look at the unusual Mr. Relish, whose head nodded so violently in approbation that she feared he'd finally succeeded in addling his brain completely. Marcus looked around, and went on.

"You have been told this, but it is not *precisely* true. That is to say, in one sense, that is exactly what the Tenebrae are. But the complete truth is infinitely more complex."

Isadora, Theo and Waylon exchanged bewildered expressions, brows furrowed and eyes narrowed.

"As you all well know, Tenebrae is Latin for 'ignorance'. It is a term used by us, the Lectors, for they have given themselves no name, random confederation of individuals that they are…"

Waylon cut in, his spit spraying in a disturbing mist with each word.

"What are you saying, Marcus? That they *do* have a leader, then? Is that the marrow of this bone?"

"Patience, Fernsby. I am coming to it. Not a leader precisely, but rather, they are infected by the same spirit."

"A demon!" The shrill voice of Mr. Relish cried out from the corner, his head nodding in the same metronome approval of Marcus' speech.

Isadora dragged her eyes from the strange figure of Mr. Relish coming to stand next to Marcus, his disheveled hair only coming to the top of the tall man's trousers.

"What do you mean by 'spirit'?" Isadora asked primly.

Marcus bent his grey head, his hair falling like a veil over his features, and he sank like a stone into the lion-tipped chair. The room was silent for a moment besides the incessant rustling of papers that always seemed to emanate from Relish's person.

Waylon Fernsby settled in comfortably, a man who appreciated a fine storyteller and was making himself ready for a tale. Conversely, Theophilus shifted stiffly, and Isadora picked up waves of anxiety rolling off the young man. His usually smooth and charismatic visage was now creased into folds of apprehension. She could not but think that he knew something relating to whatever events Marcus was about to relate.

His silver veil never raised, his face hidden beneath the shining strands. He cracked his knuckles one at a time, and his gruff voice became suddenly clear and melodic.

"Many years ago, throughout our time on Earth, back to the beginning, back to the first written words, and the first men and women who could travel within them we begin our tale. Into the myths, into the stories that people wished to keep sacred, into the very coarsest lines of the reed pen or ancient words carved into rock. Many of these first Lectors, were descended from tribal storytellers, from the poets, from the keepers of a nomadic history. These were the people that would take hold of the imaginations of their weary families, brothers, sisters, cousins, all members of a tribe. This keeper of stories, lodged legends within their brain in a special way, recalling the details that made the story come to life for their listeners, the exact cadence in which the tales must be told. And so, these people were living two lives. One as a member of a family group, or tribe; and the other as a person who lived outside of the realm of the present reality, and instead had one foot in the land where stories live. From the moment that these tales were put to paper, the reader and writer of these fables, these legends, these allegories, was able to leave behind completely the reality of their time and escape into the narrative itself. And almost at the same time, there were members of these same tribes, same families, same societies, that disapproved of this practice. That saw no gain to be found by a physical body leaving their share of the work to be divided among their own kindred. A spirit of discord was then born, or perhaps it had always been there, waiting in the shadows for a body to live in and take hold of. Some believe it to be a physical being, others believe it to be an apparition. For myself, I believe it is like the stories themselves that the Lectors travel into, invisible to anyone who is blind to them, but visible to all those who would give in to its power. The spirit has no name, but he is the root of all of Tenebrae. This being sows hatred, confusion, dissatisfaction. He infects people in the world, and the creatures and characters within the story. He is not a leader, but instead…more like a virus that leeches onto the fears and doubts of its host, and drives them mad by feeding those feelings."

The metallic, screeching voice of Mr. Relish began speaking, but quieter and more subdued than Isadora had ever remembered. Strangely, he had also stopped his incessant nodding, a preternatural calm overtaking his features, movements and voice.

"I had some signs of them in my regular life…I do not know if any of you know about me, or who I was before, but, I was a schoolteacher. I…I taught history. I had limited my travels in books to summer vacations and winter breaks. I liked teaching, lecturing, being around young minds. I had planned so long…so long. For the adventure. It was a book, you see, a book that had been given to me by a colleague and fellow Lector, and it was exactly what I wanted to experience. A safari, native people, a woman to save, animals to protect from poachers…it was…my dream. I was going to be my own animal-loving Theodore Roosevelt, a rough rider of the Serengeti, as the case may be. But of course, I should have seen that it was too perfect. Too perfect. My colleague from the school was there, waiting for me, and…and…"

The poor man began shaking his head again, vigorously, his arms stretched around his body in a kind of self-embrace. If the arms reached any harder, Isadora had the impression he would succeed in pulling himself apart, the idea of which seemed almost appealing to his tormented face. Marcus easily picked up the narrative where Relish had left off.

"Yes, it was one of our more unfortunate cases. This colleague, an unpopular Lector with little imagination was…inhabited by the spirit and was convinced quite easily to dupe and then torture Randall. It was actually Alistair that found him. And though he had been subjected to terrible agonies, he never did reveal the path to our library, or give up the secrets of his Libri" He looked to Relish with pride. Pride that was not echoed in the distressed man's features. Marcus looked around to the group meaningfully, all of them thinking that saving poor Randall Relish had probably made Alistair Lindenwood the next mark for the spirit.

Isadora interrupted quietly, news that she knew would not be welcome to the men in the room.

"I knew the man who did this to Randall, and I thought I should never see him again after he turned. But, I saw him earlier, with LeBlanc...he is part of this new terror too."

The pronouncement encouraged further shaking and rustling of papers in the corner.

Theophilus shifted awkwardly once more beside Isadora, and hesitantly opened his mouth to speak, his characteristically smooth tenor voice coming out in fits and bursts, like a child with a speech impediment giving a presentation to his class.

"My father, rest his soul. Suffered the same. But... many do not know this. Silas Bythesea was...he was killed by his own hand." He paused, placing his hand over his usually warm eyes that had instantly lost their fire. "The creature, feeding doubts into his mind... got deep inside of him. He could feel it asking questions, searching his brain for answers about the Lectors, the Panopticon. It was...angry. My father suffered greatly, but could not seek help, because of his concern that he would bring the monster here, and in so doing, ruin our brotherhood. He ended his own life rather than give away the secrets of the Lectors."

He exhaled heavily, the story slipping off of him like a heavy cloak unclasping from his shoulders. Isadora grasped his hand and held it gently, and his once-splendid head came to hang in sorrowed shame, shame for a problem he couldn't have solved, an affliction he could not control but wished he could have helped his father bear. Marcus looked pained at seeing those he cared about so cast down, but he rallied, eager to continue.

"There are many stories like this. It is a great gift, an important power that we have inherited, but it does not come without its own risks and terrors. Down the annals of our history many of the Lectors have suffered such, but it is with this last attack, the attack of Alistair Lindenwood by his own wife that we have felt a stronger evil in the spirit than we have in centuries. Alistair was our hero, our greatest hope. And he died by a hand that he loved, a hand that he trusted. But not before he set events in place to bring about the destruction of the spirit through the efforts of Julian Cole."

"Will he be annihilated for once and all? And this Julian then, he is the chosen one?" Fernsby demanded.

Marcus laughed heartily, surprising all assembled. Mr. Relish even gave off his nodding again, momentarily.

"Good heavens. You all *do* read too much. No, evil cannot be vanquished forever. This spirit will always find a way to attack the minds and fears of those who leave themselves vulnerable to hatred and ignorance. And there is no 'chosen one'. Of course, there is a hero for every story…a savior for all calamities, if he or she should choose to rise and accept the challenge. Julian has done that, as many before him in fiction and in life have chosen to do. He is in no way more or less remarkable than any of these preceding him. Let us just say, that I believe Alistair chose wisely, and that perhaps when the boy sees fit to tell us his plan of action, we may judge whether or not he is the hero of the hour. It should be noted, however, that he has already found his way into over a dozen different books. Quite prolific for one our kind, and not to be dismissed. But heroism is another matter, and his valor will be revealed, no doubt, in time."

He stopped speaking, his head rising quickly, his hand grabbing for the glass before him that had sometime in his narrative, changed from a tepid teacup into a wide goblet filled with scarlet wine. He drank heartily and looked around at the Readers before him, each murmuring to themselves or deep in thought about all that they had heard. Excepting Isadora. Her gaze was fixed on his own, her eyes full of impatience. She was gesturing toward his lap, and he looked down to find the sheets of paper, hastily scrawled with words. He brought the papers to his face and read them, once, twice, over and over again, not believing what he was seeing. He laughed loud and earnestly, the flat of his hand smacking against his thigh in his hilarity. He laughed until tears came from the creases of his ancient eyes. The company was looking at him, aghast. All, again, except Isadora who merely looked bored, having already read it all herself. Marcus howled and cackled before finally exclaiming his thoughts between snorts.

"300 hundred years I have been the proud Librarian for the Lectors. 300 years! My father served faithfully as Librarian for 500 years before that, and back and back and back it goes. Never in all of that time, has any reader, no matter how clever, no matter how learned, ever suggested something like this. It's so...simple. Julian's suggestion is almost painful to read. If it succeeds, it will be the craziest, most foolhardy plan we have enacted. But, goodness, quite simple. Quite. Brilliant, but barking!"

He laughed again, his giggles shaking the painting on the walls, his guffaws plainly annoying the figures on the ceiling.

Theophilus and Waylon waited silently, perplexed most dreadfully by their Librarian's behavior.

"Dammit, Marcus! Are you going to reveal the plan or not? What is it that the boy will have us do?"

Now Isadora laughed too, not because it was especially funny, but because it was so uncomprehendingly simple. In a world that could be controlled with the stroke of a pen, the punch of a key, the Lectors had forgotten their own power over the stories they lived in, had lost track of their upperhand. They were the masters of storytelling, and the story could not be told without their imaginations, could it?

The three of them, four counting a subdued Mr. Relish, leaned in close, as Marcus told each of them what to do, in between chortles and snickerings of laughter, at which, his explanation would begin anew.

The plan *could* work. It had to.

CHAPTER THE EIGHTEENTH
A Sabbatical By The Seashore

Her neck hurt. The strain and sorrow of the day had melted together with the burden of the heaviness of her hair to create cricks and aches that Lively had never experienced before. But the physical ache was nothing to the anguish she felt at the knowledge she had so recently learned. Her mother. Her own mother.

She was alone on this stretch of beachfront, made up of small rocks interspersed between patches of sand. Above the beach were terraced cliffs leading up to a green summit she could not see the top of, so far was it from the sand. It went on and on into the blue of the sky as if there were two seas, one kissing at her feet and one hovering above. She could not see Julian, but she felt his presence nearby.

The waves lazily lapped at the shore, farther out they tumbled and somersaulted like children at play. She looked down at herself, realizing that her clothing was very changed. She was wearing something that was nearly inappropriate, even as an undergarment. It was just a thin, simple cotton gown, ending at the knee. It was tighter around the waist, and then fanned out prettily. She knew she should feel naked, exposed, but here in this place it felt natural. In fact, she fairly wished that she were nude so that she could jump into the waves. She longed to feel the water wrap around her completely, the fullest embrace imaginable. An embrace that she needed in order to understand what she had heard of her parents. Who they were, the life she had been living with them and the life she had lived after their death, was too fantastic to comprehend. The truth of it weighed on her, as if she were covered in chains. And in this moment, near the water, all she could think of was surrender.

Julian still had not come, and so she sat on the edge of the sea, looking out into the boundless blue. To think that as vast as this written, storied world was, the *real* world outside of the book was even larger. Billions of real stories happening to living people, reinvented in their minds over time in a myriad of versions to suit the narrative they wanted to tell themselves.

This ocean before her reminded her of that. She could see the attraction of living within a story, of course, moving from one tale to another like lily pads on a pond But, wasn't the outside world the same? The millions of years of history, the thousands of cities and billions of people? All living lives that were mostly unrecorded histories, unimaginable fantasies, unspeakable horrors, unbelievable adventures. In that way, Julian, her father and Isadora were no different than any human living a normal life. They were just better able to don the suit of another perspective, more inclined to change character as one would a pair of socks. Lively sat and she mused. She made sense of herself, her life, her family, and the different worlds that she could choose to live in. Would that she could remember the outside world, as her desires always came back around to that place she felt she should know, felt she should remember.

If she really thought about it, she had known her mother was unhappy in the life they shared. Not in a demonstrative way, but in a thousand silent sighs, exhaled into a void. She recalled the night her mother had returned home from whatever gala or ball she'd attended, the same night she'd remembered so fondly just a few days past. The same memory, when turned at an angle, in a different light, her mother's dissatisfaction became illumination. She realized that every day with her mother had been a dress rehearsal for the final goodbye. But no matter how she twisted it, she couldn't bring herself to understand why. Why had she done this terrible thing? Could she really see no other way?

A tear, a droplet containing the whole of her sadness, streamed silently down her cheek. With the edge of her finger, she captured it and leaned forward, enveloping her hand and the tear in the briny sea. The ocean was made from tears such as these, a billion sorrows collected, that were nothing but proof of pain on their own, but together, they could float you around the world.

Or drown you into oblivion.

It was then that she saw a figure, in white, his tell-tale crop of dark chocolate hair announcing his identity. She didn't stir from her seat on the rocky sand, though every part of her pulled toward him. Her hand came again to her neck, massaging the dull ache that had taken firm root.

His steps grew closer, and looking up she could see the bright sea-glass green of his eyes flash in the sun, and the sweat on his brow. He smiled his half smile, an expression of his that seemed to suggest more real happiness than a full one. He dropped down beside her, placing a leather bag containing papers and clothing, from what she could see, behind them on the beach. His shirt was white linen, his trousers a thin khaki. He looked so cool, so easily a part of this lonely beachfront. And then, suddenly, his face changed, and he looked so much like the American Indians she'd seen at a traveling circus that it fairly shocked her. Regal bearing, his features impassive, his gaze all-seeing and focused on the line of the horizon, considering the limits of his own creation. The effect was lost in a moment though, as he turned back toward her, offering the same half smile.

"Sorrento" he said, his head turned back to the rocky outcrop of cliffs and the green terracing above them.

"I beg your pardon?"

"Sorrento. In Italy. That's what I was thinking of when

I wrote this scene. I tweaked the details of course. Less humans and no houses, save one. I lived here as a child. The real Sorrento. Me and my parents. "

Her cheeks burned pink and her eyes came back to the easy mesmerism of the waves. His voice broke once again into her thoughts.

"How are you feeling, really? I tried to give you some time alone, though I wasn't sure if you were the type who wanted it. But, for some reason or another, it seemed to me that you would be."

"Yes, sometimes I need a few moments to let my thoughts battle one another back and forth in order to silence the war of my emotions."

His green eyes shone emerald now in the bright sun, and he leaned forward, slowly, allowing her time to pull back or meet him halfway. She was drawn to him, darkness to stars, and their lips met softly. Her body was heat. The light of the sun, the warmth of the rocks and the pleasant burning in her stomach, in her arms and legs and lips. They broke apart, a little breathless, their eyes swimming in the depths of the other. He had taken hold of her hand and held it like a precious treasure. She wanted only more, more of him. To crawl into his arms, his kiss, his heart, his soul, and when there, she would rest awhile. She would stay there inside of him and let him heal her. But the touch of his hand said differently. He wasn't there to be a fairytale hero, to protect her from any harm. But instead, a partner to wander out of the labyrinth alongside.

Julian looked at Lively, his heart finally slowing to a more manageable rhythm. A part of him was laughing at his newfound, old-school patience. He'd been kissing girls since the 6th grade, he'd had sex with a number of girls in high school and college. He was a millenial for chrissakes. But, this was different. It was special to him, and so he would treat it as such. He wanted Lively to be his only in all the ways that mattered most, in whatever ways she could. And so he wanted to savor all the firsts, knowing that for him, they would also be lasts. Julian wanted her to feel his love, and these were the first steps toward proving that. Something he knew he'd never be done proving. His father had always told him how real love worked, a job that was never finished, a project that was never really completed.

So instead of giving into the passion that twisted and tormented his emotions, he held her hand and told her of his parents. He spoke of his travels, his struggles, his pure love of books and art. Julian found himself speaking of his parent's magnetism, how they had so completely fit together, yet existed as individuals. Puzzle pieces that signified a full, brilliant picture on their own, but an even grander vision when joined.

They both discussed their loneliness and isolation. Lively spoke of the places she'd lived, even if they had been in her father's books. She told of Clara and her cousin Victoria, characters that had been as real as her father or Madame Bellevie. He told her of Patrick, the closest friend he didn't realize he'd ever had until he was gone. Never realizing how dear he was to Julian until they went their separate ways. They talked and talked, as if they didn't have enough words to say all that they wished, as if the very syllables did not exist to pour out all of the secrets of their lonely hearts.

Julian sat back, taking in the full picture of Lively, sitting so sweetly in this, the most beautiful place he could have conjured.

"What is it that you want to do with your life? What would you like to do? Where would you go? Think beyond your present circumstances, beyond this reality. What possibilities would you dream of, if you could populate your dreams with infinite opportunities?"

She saw that he was in earnest, and that he wanted so

much to give her something. Some kind of freedom or hope that she might be grasping for.

"The truth is, I've been swallowed by a constant tumbling of events, the one thing after-anothers of my life, that I have never really considered it. Will you give me a little time? Perhaps when this is finished, I will know better."

He nodded, shaking his head back and forth as if surprised at his own rushed words. Of course she was right, there would be time for wishing and hope when the present was settled. And so, for a long time they sat, just staring at the sea, lulling them into forgetting the tasks and dangers before them, like Alice and her poppy fields.

Eventually she slept. They had both been long without rest, but now it was time. He picked up her supine form, her face as innocent as a child's in repose. He slung the leather bag on his shoulder and carried her up the Roman steps (though why he hadn't written in an elevator, he couldn't imagine) and into the little white villa. He placed her on the bed and covered her sandy feet with white sheets. He bent to kiss her forehead, and decided to let down that glorious mass of chestnut and flame-colored waves. Each pin he removed seemed to erase a line of pain from her face, creases he hadn't noticed until that moment. And then stepping back, he marveled at the splendor of the sea of hair swimming over the pillow. He stepped to the other side of the large bed quietly, and then paused considering. He shrugged and kept all of his clothes on, laying on top of the sheets. Yes, this was best. Surely, she could not mistake his motives.

So it was a surprise to awaken in the night, the light of the moon beaming brightly through the window, winking his eyes open. He was now under the sheets, solidly tucked into the warmth of her pearly arms, made luminescent in the moonlight. The soft sound of sleep cooing from her slightly opened mouth. He made to move, to escape her embrace, but she only held him all the tighter.

"You looked cold. In the night. So I covered you and held you."

He could hear rather than see the smile on her face. And turning back to the gleaming moon, he slept again for a time, blissfully ignorant of anything outside this room, this villa, this beach, this story from his mind.

Julian blinked his eye open, looking to the window and found the first grey lights of day beginning to creep into the sky. Slipping from the safety of her arms he stepped to the bathroom, modern as he possibly could have written it after living in the 1900 copper-piped nightmare. Showered and dressed in five minutes, and then shaking Lively gently awake. He began the hilarious task of explaining the shower and all the modern accoutrement of bathing he had always taken for granted. He wondered, not for the first time, how her father could have given up technological conveniences so easily, but one look at her sweet face, staring at him so earnestly as he explained the hair-dryer, and he knew immediately. What wouldn't a man do to keep this woman safe?

He left her be, and found the kitchen, right where he'd written it. And inside the refrigerator found a selection of fruits and cheeses, juices and sparkling water and brought it out to the balcony. He was blown away breathless by the beauty of the bougainvillea edging the whitewashed walls of the villa, and lemons dripping like jewels from the grove beneath them. Looking out at the landscape, conjured from his own imagination mixed with faraway memories of the summer he'd spent with his family in southern Italy, and saw that as richly detailed as it was in some places, other pieces of walking daydream were quite vague. This worried him. It would have to be done just right, put into action *just so* if he was going to realize his plan. He hoped that it would work, prayed that Marcus approved of what he had written. In the meantime, he couldn't help think that this was a splendid place to spend a kind-of honeymoon. A wondrous trial run for him and

Lively. Yes, he could happily watch her sleep and see her hair splayed out on the pillow for the rest of his life. He wanted to sit beside every ocean with her and talk of their memories and make new ones. There was no story like a love story, after all. And he had never known a writer to be able to put into words the feeling he had when he saw her, or felt her beside him. Like a cool cloth to his brow, or an answer to a wish he hadn't known he'd made.

She joined him now at the wrought iron bistro table, an exact copy from his mind of the one they'd had in their flat in Paris. Or was it Madrid? He couldn't remember the place, just the al fresco breakfasts he'd shared with his mother, her long fingers scribbling words into a jumbled notebook. Loose papers flapping about, threatening to fly out and sail around the streets below. Women and words, this was an intoxicating mixture to Julian, the power and strength that women who wielded words possessed. It was through her written words that he'd met Lively, from her unguarded words that he had seen her soul. She sat carefully, hair blazing around her like spun copper and gold, towel-dried and lovely. Her movements were unsure, as he'd known they would be, in stovepipe jeans and a silk top he'd written for her. She had been so natural in corsets and long skirts, but this too, suited her. He wondered if the modern world would suit just as well. They sipped and chewed, but didn't speak, neither wanting to shatter these last few moments of unfettered bliss. Enjoying the last halcyon minutes of clear sky and sunshine, before willingly plunging themselves into the storm. But too soon, the time was upon them, despite their greatest efforts to stretch and cling to the moments.

Julian pulled the leather bag onto his shoulder, the soreness of the spot telling him that he had it in the same place as the day before. He pulled out his sheaf of papers, his tickets to places within his mind, and selected the correct one, exhaling through his teeth.

He leaned over and took her chin in his hands, pulling her to him roughly. Her body answered his longing with questions of her own, doubts that were cast aside by the force of his love. His emotions echoed back to him in the kiss.

"I promise you, when this is over, I will bring you back here. I promise to give you the beauty you deserve, the life your father would have given you."

She laughed and shook her head, she had never been one for dramatic romantic moments in novels. They seemed so impassioned on the page, but in real life, sentences uttered so tragically felt kind of embarrassing. But in this moment, he was not to be laughed at, he was serious, and he was scared.

"Julian, disaster would be beautiful beside you. My father gave me a world of beauty, and memories of a world that is long gone. Don't promise me beauty. Promise me truth and adventure. Beauty fades...I want something enduring, so that when I am old and disgusting that I will have imperfect memories to sustain me."

"I do not think you will be disgusting. For myself, I plan to be dashingly attractive until I'm 90."

They both smiled, the gravity of the moment lightened by laughter. He kissed her again and gritted his teeth, eyes on the page before him. No more interludes, no more blissful breaks. It was time to meet their enemies head on. He only hoped Marcus had acted quickly, and had thought his plan as brilliant as Julian hoped it was.

The page snapped in the sea wind, and the balcony was empty.

CHAPTER THE NINETEENTH
A Very Strange Place For A War

The wind smelled like rain. The surface beneath her feet was cracked and broken in places and the air was tinged with menace. Something about the place made her fearful, though she had no reason to feel that way, yet. Darkness alone couldn't be enough to invite fear into her heart, could it?

"What is this place?"

"This is my memory of the first time I ever went into Detroit." Julian replied, quietly.

She looked around, there were a few strange lights, or, there were many, but the majority of them were not functioning any longer. She didn't recognize the streets that she thought she had known so well.

"I do not think I have been to this part of the city before." Lively didn't know why she was still talking, she supposed it made her feel a little less frightened, the ongoing conversation keeping her mind off of the ominous surroundings. Julian tittered softly, almost so quietly that the laughter was lost back into his breath.

"I wouldn't imagine so. The first time I ever went to Detroit was when I was 16. I imagine it looks a bit different to you. We are 100 years in the future from a familiar part of town you would recognize."

"Oh." She said. And for once, she couldn't think of a reply. Was she ready to be in the real world? Especially if this version of the world, this future place she couldn't remember, or maybe had never experienced at all, was foreign to her. She was ashamed to admit that leaping forward to a world so far removed from her experiences terrified her. Keeping her head down, she counted their steps, not asking where they were going. She glanced at Julian and wondered how he always looked so cool. Calm, collected, and a little sad. Even when he smiled there was a sadness there, an expression that gave his true looks of joy a little more luster. He was boyish, and had the face of one who would always look that way. Never hardening into manhood, but the eternal beauty of a youth. A younger man's face that should not hold as much grief as it did. His movements were fluid and athletic, and something in his poise gave her strength. She tried to shake her fears off completely, like icy snowflakes in her hair, but only succeeded in making herself shiver.

Julian sensed her mood, and cursed himself for not putting her more at ease, but if his plan would work, he needed her to remain gloomily in the dark. She would need to be surprised when the time came, her reaction would need to be genuine. He steeled himself and let go of her hand, sticking his into his pocket, even though it was painful to see her expression when he did so.

The rain began to fall now, softly. Even though it was not a soaking downpour, the night felt ill-omened. But a few minutes later the showers fell more heavily, drowning the streets around them. When the first strike of lightning burst violently, Lively looked up to see the night sky, now as bright as the light of day, reveal the ghostly skyline. She was shocked to see soaring buildings, sharp as daggers, grazing the heavy storm clouds. Seemingly poking holes in their abundant rain-filled bellies, loosing the deluge from the sky. This world he wrote, this world from his mind challenged Lively, threatening her with its strangeness. The crack of thunder that boomed a few seconds after each bolt of lightning shook her to her bones. Her scalp tingled and the raindrops fell on her shoulders. The trench coat he'd pulled from his leather bag could hardly keep the rain out any longer. She wished he had held onto her hand, and another part of her wished she could crawl back into her faux family's house on Woodward Avenue, the new century waiting for her to make her mark. Lively was visibly shaking now, the rain seeping into her skin, the heavens sobbing all of its tears upon her head, burdening her with all of the anguish of this or any world.

And then she heard it. How she could hear something so soft, so seemingly insignificant when coupled with the jarring thunder and the constant hum of the rain was curious. She heard it over her own shivers and the racing of her own heart. Lively heard it over her hopes that Julian would reach for her. She had made out the sound despite the crushing crowd of her own thoughts.

Just a rock skidding on the pavement. A rock that the rain couldn't have moved. A rock that had to have been kicked by a human foot.

They had arrived. Julian had known that they would come, had known that the setup was too irresistible. The only question that lingered in his mind was if the plan would work. For some reason, he thought of Patrick, remembered something he had used to say on nights when they would hit up the bars on South University, 'It's easy to find girls out on a Friday night, Jules, but it's damn hard to convince them to give up their phone number'. He laughed under his breath remembering the way Patrick had said it, as if it were an important adage to live one's life by. He supposed in a way, it was true. He was most certainly putting his life on the line now. It was all too simple to set up a scenario for success, much more difficult to have it work out the way you wanted. Good old Patrick.

They were following, but not too close. He knew Lively had heard the sound of their trailing footsteps, could feel the waves of fear coming thick and hot off of her body. Julian looked over his shoulder, and in the next flash of lightning, he saw the cruel smile of LeBlanc, saw his stride pick up into a run. He pulled out the sheaf of papers and brought them toward his eyes, took firm hold of Lively's hand, and entered blinding light.

All was bright and garish colors. The dankness of bayou waters and too many bodies so recently in the vicinity greeted their noses. Their clothes were dry, and they were standing on a balcony looking out onto a debris-strewn Bourbon St, swirling with the ghosts of the madness from the night before. New Orleans after Mardi Gras had always seemed a trifle apocalyptic to Julian, and so it had seemed fitting for this portion of his trap. Lively, beside him, was shaking. He wondered again if he should have revealed the plan to her, if he should have walked her through how it would work. But her reaction was part of the key to this, and so he would wait, no matter how it frightened her. She looked to him now, biting her lower lip, eyes shrouded in worry. He could feel the beat of her heart in her chest, wondered how much she understood what it would mean if the Tenebrae caught them. Did she know that if you perished in the book that all lights of you were extinguished everywhere? Did she know the peril? Would she ever understand why he was willing to risk her? A sound swelled from the streets below, a sound he had not written, a sound that had not leapt from his pen and sprung from the page within his hands. This was a sound created by a new force, for he had left the last page behind, left it behind for the Tenebrae to come through.

He heard their shouts from the streets below the balcony, and listened to the march of the footsteps. Purple and green crepe paper jostled in the wind, hovering a few inches above the trash-filled streets. Bubblegum and cigarettes, spilled drinks and the contents of someone's stomach were below her, and the mingled stench rose up to invade Lively's senses. For a moment, she felt that she was going to be sick too, but then the memory, unbidden, sprang to her mind, of James, her one-time cousin, and his unwitting rescue of her from Anton LeBlanc. She felt as though she had somehow come around the corner of something, observing the same sight twice, and that this instance would end just as well as the other. She squeezed Julian's hand a little tighter and she laughed, a small, breathy giggle. It was replaced almost immediately by her former fears though, when the face of Anton LeBlanc appeared on the corner of the street in this strange, war-torn place, his eyes meeting hers with malice. And then they were off, northern Sweden in winter, sitting in the falling snow, only to hear the crunch of many shoes in the forest. From there the papers took them to the midst of an orchard, both of them held in the embrace of an apple tree, until the falling apples around them alerted them to the same menacing sound of approaching steps. He grabbed her hand countless times, through sand and water, fields and cities, castles real and imagined. And every time they emerged in a new place, the footsteps came sooner, so that everywhere that they tried to escape, there was less and less time to enact whatever plan Julian had hoped for. Lively wanted to ask if they were in trouble, wanted to demand he tell her what was going wrong. For very clearly, they were in peril. They were being found too quickly, Julian had no time to get his bearings, or put any schemes into action. The Tenebrae almost seemed to anticipate their movements, and Lively ran cold. She didn't understand all the rules of this place, or what his plan entailed. But she could tell by their movements, that they were harried, rushed, that Julian's design had no time to take hold.

Finally, in a room with a strange yellow chair, a cramped space with a writing desk and artist's easel, she felt Julian's shoulders relax. She didn't know the significance of this place, but it was obvious that it meant a great deal to Julian. He breathed in deeply, and the sound of footsteps in the hall sounded, heavy and quick. She could see a twitch in his mouth, a long blink, he was making a decision. He grabbed her hand tightly and raised the sheaf of papers. He then threw all the papers about the room scattering them like leaves from an autumn tree, save one, which he brought to his eyes. He read, read like a thirsting man drinking in the words of his own salvation, his face devoid of emotion, expressionless.

Their feet touched down on the familiar floorboards of the Panopticon. Every detail from his visits before, jumping back into focus in his mind. The stacks upon stacks of rainbow books, and even now, a violet colored tome was soaring from a stack far to the left, to a shelf that was nearby where they were standing. A shelf that was so full of books that Julian wasn't sure how it would fit. Lively's eyes were large and she turned slowly about, taking in the enormity of the stacks about her. Julian wished he had more time to admire her in this state of wonder, so like himself seeing this place for the first time. The shelves seemingly reaching into the sky, and higher, row upon row of never-ending shelves. The orange cat padded up to Julian playfully, completing figure-eights about his ankles, pausing to nip his calf when he didn't immediately bend down to stroke her fur. And then, footsteps.

Lively stiffened beside him, her body rigid, fear rolling off of her in waves. The figure of his aunt emerged from one of the rows, Marcus Birdwhistle behind her. From another row, two men Julian didn't recognize, their expressions inscrutable. His aunt gave an exasperated cry, and leapt towards him.

"Julian! What are you doing here? You will have led them right to us!"

Her face was contorted in misery, and Marcus Birdwhistle slumped, his spine curving in like a question mark, the unasked query all too clear. Why, why had Julian doomed them this way?

The other two men put their heads in their hands, and slunk backwards toward the books. Isadora gave her nephew a look that Lively didn't understand, a passing glance that she couldn't read. But she understood now. Understood that Julian had led them back here because he couldn't hold the Tenebrae back any longer, he had run out of ideas. He had brought them back here, hoping for help, too ashamed to admit to Lively that his plan had failed. She wept then, silently, unwanted tears that stung her eyes painfully, knowing that they did not aid her sorrow, but fell anyway, betraying her. She could feel the magic in the place darkening, the books becoming shadows of themselves. The Library. The Panopticon, the most important place in the Lector world. The place her father had died rather than betray, and Julian had led them right here, to the very spot he most needed to avoid. She was angry at Julian, and yet, she could not rouse her spirits to hatred. It wasn't his fault, really. He hadn't asked for this world, this life to be lifted onto his shoulders. His shoulders that were already weighed down, like her own, with a lifetime's worth of secrets.

She grasped his hand, and she heard the footsteps again, and although she was frightened, she felt light. *Not your fault, not my fault.*

Julian raised her hand to his lips, and kissed it tenderly. He was so sorry. So very sorry for what he had done. But he didn't know any other way. Anton LeBlanc emerged from one of the rows of books, his eyes blazing fury. Behind him, Clara, the sight of whom made the younger gentleman, who had arrived with Mr. Birdwhistle, gasp. Behind her, the other man who had broken into his aunt's house in 1900 Detroit. And then a dozen more, shadowy figures, eyes blazing, knocking books off the shelves as they passed, faces filled with triumph and hatred. Lively's figure seemed to crumble beside him. She was still standing bravely, but something inside her had crumbled and broken, though she would not give the Tenebrae the satisfaction to show it.

"Ah, Mr. Cole. Not the great white hope you were touted to be. Chin up, man, you may have failed in your mission, but you have provided an invaluable service to the completion of mine. Always a silver lining and all that, hmm?"

Anton LeBlanc laughed, down in his throat, an ugly guttural sound, and Lively wondered how this man could have ever been written as a romantic figure by anyone's imagination, especially a dreamer like her father.

The Lector who had gasped, from the row nearby stepped forward, fixing Clara with a look that spoke of broken devotion. The anguish in his voice so heart-wrenching it was almost too much to bear.

"Clara, it…it was you? You who led this wickedness into Isadora's book? You, who has corrupted the name of Lector with your falseness? How could you?"

Clara's face held an expression that Lively had never seen before, pure, blinding abhorrence for the man before her.

"You? Theophilus, you *dare* to speak to me of falseness? Of betrayal? You, a man who wears treachery and deceit like a new cloak? You weigh your own faithlessness much lighter than I do. The wrong you did me destroyed me. And now you and the Lector world will know the pricking pain of destruction as well. *This* is a reality where rogues like you may thrive and give in to the excesses and pleasures of women's affections. A world where a man like you has no consequences. For you and for anyone else who would bend the rules of reality to fit their designs. Life is not a fiction, and to live within one is the greatest treachery to reality. But now, it is at an end.

The Lectors are finished and the Panopticon will burn like so many sticks in a fire. "

Her hot anger chilled to ice, the pink of excitement in her cheeks dulled to a sallow grey. Julian realized that this was a woman who had eaten her own unhappiness for so long that she had made herself bitter and ill. A woman who had lived off vengeance for such a long time that it had burned away the part of her that could find pleasure in a happy ending. She was, unfortunately, wholly consumed by an evil spirit and beyond saving. He had been wrong about the source, wrong about their greatest enemy. So, *this* was the end.

Julian took out a small notebook from his leather satchel, and sat down on the wooden floorboards. Meanwhile, minions of the Tenebrae knocked down rows of books, papers flying this way and that, his aunt screamed and ducked down beside him. Marcus and the other two men had come to stand next to Julian, and Lively was softly crying. He heard her ask for him by name, begging him to hold her, to comfort her, here in the end. Here in the place where it had begun for Julian, with a book that vanished with a girl within its pages, a girl that had never disappeared from his thoughts. The Library that had shown him the possibilities of worlds springing to life within the words, and had given him a family he had thought he had lost forever. His hands danced across the pages of the notebook, and as much as he yearned to reach for Lively, to hold her close and kiss her pink-rose lips, he could not lift his pen from the page. It was almost over.

Anton took a step forward, a character whose use was over. He could only temporarily live in any other story beside his own, after all. The stacks of books fell like dominoes, the air above the Lectors was filled with paper, like fireflies in the night, a sky full of white, floating stars, the pages filled with a million mysteries that would never be read. Clara laughed, deep and hard, watching the figure of Anton LeBlanc sink into ashes, his death assured the moment he had left his own book. Around her, the other dissatisfied characters dissolved into nothing, each of their stories ended forever. Clara kicked over the ashes of paper that had once been Anton LeBlanc, and she stepped to the huddled mass of Lectors, men and women she hated for the powers she believed they used so callously, blinded by the hypocrisy of her own actions. She sent an expression of clear loathing toward Theophilus, the man who had broken her heart. Waylon Fernsby hid his head in his hands, obviously weeping. The great Marcus Birdwhistle bowed from the neck, even when sitting he stuck out among the others. Clara smiled, again, and her face became even grayer, as if she herself were turning into the blankness of a book page. She stalked closer and closer, watching this group of her former Lectors tremble and sway. Julian Cole was still writing, a maniacal expression of pure glee on his features. It was then that the building began to collapse. The Panopticon, indestructible, fantastical, the all-seeing eye of the Lector world, watching over the universe of stories as it crumbled all around.

But then suddenly, his pen stopped moving, and pure light filtered in from above. Sunshine so bright that it turned everything pure white. Waylon Fernsby raised his head and it wasn't tears that rocked his body, but laughter. Marcus Birdwhistle's grey strands blazed silver in the light, as one single book fell from above, whole and perfect, landing softly in Julian's arms. The leather was pink, with tooled rosettes. Clara blinked hard, uncomprehending. It was the sister copy of her Liber Libri, which she had destroyed. The boy, Julian Cole, was holding the husk of her former life in his hands. She stared up into the blinding light, and then her eyes went to Theophilus who had cast her aside, abused her heart and broken her spirit so carelessly. She looked at Lively, the foolish daughter of a man who had tried to convince her that there were many more stories to live in. Alistair Lindenwood, who gallivanted about his own tales, leaving his wife in a life of loneliness. And then to Julian, this boy. This boy who took the notebook he had been writing in, and calmly replaced it into his satchel.

Julian stared into the hard eyes of Clara and saw only blindness. He let out a low whistle and took his plain black Liber out of his bag, and handed Lively her father's black and golden one, the book that had brought him into this world, and with it, they would both be brought out again. On all sides of him the other Lectors brought out their own Liber Libris, and all at once, opened them, leaving Clara alone, in a Panopticon devoid of books, pen, or even the smallest scraps of paper. The kind of empty library she had created by her own design. A library with no escape, physical or mental. With no words to offer encouragement or succor or humor. A world without fantasy, fiction, or history.

She stood alone in the midst of the world of her own making, only now realizing what a life without stories looks like.

CHAPTER THE TWENTIETH
The Calm After The Storm

Once again, their feet touched down on the familiar floorboards of the Panopticon. The orange cat, sweet as her namesake, watched them arrive, perched on a nearby shelf. Before Lively could make sense of this place, this library she had just seen wrecked, burned and torn apart, the high-pitched squeal of Mr. Randall Relish descended upon them, as he jumped joyfully on his stubby little legs. Mr. Fernsby and Mr. Bythesea were clapping Julian on the shoulder, and Marcus Birdwhistle was shaking him by the hand. Isadora's eyes were filled with tears, but of happiness, and Lively felt as if she would swoon.

"What in the world is happening?!" She shouted, not angrily, but anxiously, her mind pulling in a hundred directions at once.

"A moment, my dear Miss Lindenwood. All in a moment. Let's get into the office for a nice cup of tea. Or, perhaps you would prefer something stronger, chaps? Oh, and no offense Izzy, of course I had not meant to insinuate anything of the kind. Women, of course, can handle any drink a man can. Of course. Forgive me."

Although his voice spoke of contrition, his face was all smiles, and Mr. Relish skipped and danced behind them all the way to the office. Julian held tightly to his aunt's hand, and squeezed Lively's longingly every few seconds. It was over. He had done it. He couldn't believe it had worked, yet, here he was. He looked to the books on the shelves with new appreciation and watched as a brown leather book flew gracefully above his head, finding its own way to its new position on a different shelf.

They approached the office door, which today appeared like the wooden door of a shed. Marcus stepped to unlatch it, and it stretched and shimmered into the golden gates of Kensington Palace, revealing a castle twice as large and shining with the colors of a new dawn. The gate swung open, and they found themselves in the gilded opulence of the Panopticon Keeper's office. The orange cats on the mural above them were still gliding noiselessly after the purple mice, a banana still hovered gracelessly from a zeppelin, and Rembrandt's *Storm of the Sea of Galilee* shimmered and waved as if it were a window to the water itself. The company arranged themselves on the chairs and settees, adopting different positions of relative comfort. Marmalade curled up on Julian's lap, falling asleep instantly. Champagne appeared magically on the table, uncorked and poured into glasses, the fizzy brightness of the drink echoing the lightness of the mood in the room.

Mr. Relish sniffed the champagne, and then opened his mouth wide, pouring it all in at one time. He smiled terrifyingly large, and hopped back to his corner, where he took out a few papers stuffed down his shirt front, and one or two plucked from his sleeves, but then instead of writing, he paused. Randall Relish, for the first time since he had become a book, did not know what to write. His eyes, like the rest of those within the room, came to pause on Julian.

Julian's cheeks warmed, not used to so much attention, and he sat up straight, bringing his champagne flute up for a silent toast. He looked into the eyes of everyone in the room in turn, and then sighed, placing his arm lovingly around Lively, drawing her close to him, he began to speak.

"Thank you. All of you. If you had not believed in me, and acted exactly as you did, I do not think I could have carried off the plan at all."

Marcus shook his head back and forth, captured in the delirium of disbelief.

"So simple. So infinitely simple. Can't believe it's never been tried. Marvelous."

His aunt raised her hand up, gesturing him to pause, and tilted her head a little to the left.

"Pet, we are infinitely proud of you, so proud in fact that we can never thank you enough. It seems we were wrong, there was a way to capture this specific meddling spirit, even if it is impossible to conquer all evil that would threaten our ranks. But, we must know, how exactly did this come to pass?"

Julian looked at the other happy faces around him, and noted the glimmer of confusion on each, especially Lively. All excepting, Marcus. Marcus, whom he'd known would understand.

"Well, it goes back to a story I heard, when I was a boy. A story about a king who believed he was made of glass..."

"Charles VI" cut in Mr. Bythesea.

"Yes, correct. Charles VI believed he was made from glass, and my mother once told me that a person could believe almost anything if enough people convinced them of it. Especially if a part of them wanted to believe it. And so, I wrote a story of the library. A story in which the Tenebrae would reveal their intentions and then would be defeated. I thought, if as a Lector I am able to write my own stories, my own worlds, why not simply write a story in which we win? We thought the ringleader was Anton LeBlanc, and so I thought it would end much more smoothly, with him believing his book was destroyed and thus falling into ashes. But, it seemed that the Tenebrae can only really operate when led by another Lector. Clara became such a Lector—a Reader that has defected to the enemy. When a Lector begins to find fault in their lives, grows discontent in the fantasy worlds of the books, a sinister bitterness can take root in their soul. An anger that festers and slithers deep inside them, a spirit that feeds off of the annihilation of happy endings forever and of the Lector world. Last time, sadly, it was Lively's mother, who used her husband's magic, which killed her too. And this time, it was Clara, a woman scorned."

Julian directed a look at Theophilus, who hung his head ashamed. Under his breath he murmured something to the effect of, "No idea, I'd hurt her so much. It was always such a lark to me, falling in love..."

Isadora scowled and shook her head, rolling her eyes at the foibles of men. "Yes, dear, but what does this have to do with men made from glass?"

"Well, everything."

Lively's expression of confusion had turned to interest as she began to understand the brilliance of Julian's plan. The threads picked up in her mind and began to weave together into the tapestry of his thoughts, so resplendently beautiful to consider.

"Oh, I think I see. By bringing me to so many places, allowing the Tenebrae to draw closer and closer each time, you convinced them that you were scared, that you were running out of options. The Panopticon you wrote was obviously not the true Library, but they believed it to be, because they wanted it to be, an idea that was supported by the appearance of the other Lectors. And then, in the end, you were writing in your notebook, because Clara changed the story. Now you needed to convince her that you were taking the only other copy of her Liber with you, and she would not be able to escape."

Lively turned to gaze at Julian, love and gratitude filling her eyes. "You made her believe, with your words, that she was stuck within her own book, just as Charles VI believed he was trapped within his own glass prison. Simply... fascinating."

Julian reddened. "No, it's just history. I knew there was a reason I studied it for four years."

A shifting sound in the corner drew everyone's attention. Mr. Relish had taken off his coat and was shedding layers and layers of papers, notes he had scribbled and chapters written. From his sleeves and his trousers, his socks and even a few pressed into his shoes. His voice was shaky and quiet, but filled with wonder.

"I...I can't help but be reminded of the day we met, young Mr. Cole. I told you that the Tenebrae had turned me into a book. You...you told me that although it was possible, you thought it 'highly unlikely'. Yes, 'highly unlikely', those were your very words. You...you suggested that I write myself back into being a man. And now, now that they are gone, I find...I find that I do not much feel like a book anymore. In fact, I...I do feel like a man. A small, meek man. But, a man nonetheless."

Marmalade jumped from Julian's lap and padded silently over to Mr. Relish. She settled onto his legs, pushing her paws down here and there, smushing his skin to her appropriate comfort level, and then she curled into a ball. Mr. Relish gave a mighty sneeze, and stared at the papers on the desk before him, and on the ground. He sneezed again, and a small smile crept onto his face.

It was Marcus' turn to offer up a slice of his mind, just enough to whet the appetite of his companions without revealing too much of himself.

"I should have known about Clara. She has been 'off the radar' as the phrase goes, for a few years now. She was so young...so young when you broke her heart, Theophilus. I had thought that she destroyed her Libri, so that I could not track her movements. Her sister Liber

Libri was here in the Panopticon, but it had stopped traveling, and so I thought only that she had retreated back to the world of the ordinary. I thought that she tired of the Lector world, never imagining that she was so shaken, like a young tree, that her roots had transferred to an evil soil. I should have done more for her, comforted her... searched her out."

Isadora clucked at him soothingly and shook her head.

"She did not want to be found, ducky. It will not do to mire yourself in blame. She had written herself into my book, after all, and if I'd cared to pay more attention to the people around me, I would have known her for what she was."

He nodded, realizing that there are those that go dark so suddenly, that they no longer can see the illumination of brighter days ahead. It was everyone's fault and no one's blame.

All of the Lectors turned back inward, a thoughtful circle, marveling silently at the changes come to pass. They sipped their champagne and nibbled on the strawberries that had appeared suddenly, near Isadora's hand. After the contemplative pause, they began trading stories, telling Lively of her father's feats, of the many great books he had written, and Julian learned of his illustrious grandfather and great-grandmothers. Lectors of the past that had moved through the worlds of books easily, shimmering brightly in many of his most well-loved stories. They talked for hours and hours, the champagne keeping them giddy, but never sick. Until, one by one, the Lectors stood and took their leave, assuring Julian that they were excited to read his next work, as his first would have to be locked away.

"What can you mean?" Lively asked Mr. Fernsby after he shrugged his disappointment that he might never read the full tale. Julian turned to her, and parted a few stray waves from her brow.

"My first book, is this one. It is our story, and the story of the Tenebrae. It is the story of Clara, previously a Lector, your lady's maid, and the spurned former lover of Mr. Bythesea. It is the tale in which I have trapped her and the spirit of confusion and disillusionment. The malignant Spirit has doubtless moved on already infecting the minds of other unhappy souls, but it is a weakened spirit. For that reason, my first book cannot be read by anyone. It is too dangerous. Mr. Birdwhistle will keep it here, safe."

Marcus' eyes glimmered, and he gave Julian an odd look. "Yes, for a time it will be kept safe. But, you know, as you have seen it before…that it will one day be read. And widely, I believe." He winked at Julian, whose mouth curved into a strange smile, remembering an unusual book, once held in his hands, emblazoned with his own name.

Lively nodded her head, understanding as well as she could. There was still too much about book magic that she didn't perfectly comprehend. Which, she supposed was probably how it should be. Magic, after all, defies explanation. If it didn't, it would cease to be magic.

Finally, they were alone with Isadora and Marcus Birdwhistle. The older people stood up, gesturing for Julian and Lively to follow. They walked silently back to the space on the wooden floorboards where they had landed, all of their thoughts spinning and twirling about within their minds. Julian embraced his aunt, and then Mr. Birdwhistle. He asked if Mr. Relish would be all right, and Marcus replied he was certain that the poor man had never been better. Lively, realizing then that this was the time, knew full well that there was an important something she must do. She reached into her back pocket and reluctantly drew out her father's Libri, the diary that had connected her to Julian, and her constant companion through her harshest sorrows.

"Mr. Birdwhistle, I believe this belongs here now." There was no more sadness in her voice. Her father had died for something he believed in, and in his death had brought her to Julian. There was nothing left to cry over. To do so, would disgrace his death.

"No, no, Miss Lindenwood, This is undoubtedly yours now. And I retain the other copy here, in the Panopticon. So that I will always have an eye on you and young Julian. Though, I cannot imagine that the two books will ever be apart."

He winked at them, kindly, and Lively hugged her father's book, *her* Liber Libri, to her chest.

"A question, Mr. Birdwhistle. Why didn't Clara simply use my diary to come right here to the Panopticon? The book was in her reach for months, why not just use it?"

Marcus laughed and scratched his head, eyes focused far away.

"An excellent question, my dear. And the answer is deceivingly simple. Your father disguised the book. He cut off the writing on the spine with his penknife, and wrote a diary entry or two in the front, in order to throw anyone off of his trail. It is well known in our world that one never writers in their Liber Libri, as the account of one's journeys is writ invisibly inside each time one moves from one story to another. She may have read the words, and torn out his diary entries, thinking they would give clues to the book itself, never realizing that which she was seeking was in her hands. Brilliant man, Alistair, a most dreadful loss to the Lector world."

When her heart subsided into a manageable level of bursting, she risked one more question.

"I know it is silly, and that they are not *real*, but what of

Victoria and James? And even my ogre Aunt Charlotte? What will happen to them?"

Mr. Birdwhistle laughed, the reverberations of it echoing off the mighty stacks of books.

"My dear girl, just because they exist in a book, does not make them any less real than you or me. Some of the best and most real people I have ever met live their whole lives within a book. You can see them anytime you like... just pick up the novel and *read.*"

He bent down, his spine bending so completely she feared she was breaking him in half. He kissed her pearly cheeks softly, and clapped Julian again on the shoulder, gesturing for him to get his Liber out. His aunt kissed him again and again, and the cat wandered out from the stacks, licking her paw casually, before darting between his legs, meowing loudly for a rub.

His aunt rolled her eyes theatrically at the cat, and took Julian's hand into her own.

"Where are you off to, pet?"

"Don't worry Aunt, we will see you soon. There's a few matters that need tying up."

His aunt shook her head again, and held her arms out in a gesture of surrender. Stepping away, she watched as Julian and Lively both opened their books, and holding hands tightly, vanished into the pages of their new life.

Marcus looked about the room, and realized that Marmalade had disappeared again. He knew he shouldn't be disappointed, after all, she had always been Julian's cat, but it was so pleasant when she was near. Looking down, his face hung in a frown, he caught the eye of Isadora, who smiled with her nephew's half smile on her face. She offered him her arm, and stooping to take it, they walked back to his office, a few dozen books sailing above his great grey head.

CHAPTER THE ALMOST LAST
In Which The End Feels Like A Beginning

It was funny, the longer he'd been away from Julian, the more he thought about him. For a guy he had never really thought of as a close friend, it sure was strange.

At first it was only once in a while. The gallery he was working in would do a show, it would be the kind of modern art nightmare that he knew Julian hated. Stuff like old industrial laundry bins nailed to the wall with gold paint splashed onto it. Or, an old boot on a pedestal. Weird stuff that Julian always rolled his eyes at. He would've said something like, "If me not understanding this means I'm not a true artist, then I guess I'm not an artist." and then he'd snicker into his sleeve. Patrick hadn't admitted it at the time, he'd always been so careful to appear apathetic about everything to do with art back home, but he'd felt the same way. Still did.

So now, when he was surrounded by his new art community friends, debating in coffee shops or in a dive bar in SoHo or Chelsea, his mind always wandered over to Julian. A part of him would miss the familiar presence beside him, two minds in tune, without having to discuss anything at all. This was just such a time.

An exhibit at the gallery he worked for had just come to a close, and his friends Mark and Siobhan were arguing about the meaning of a smashed car that had been painted metallic bronze. In the midst of their impassioned argument, a memory of something Julian had said came to Patrick's mind, and he couldn't help but cut in to the discussion to share it.

"Do you guys ever think that maybe it's just a smashed car? What if it's just a big, ugly hunk of metal that someone painted to look like something beautiful and classical?"

When they began to look doubtful, he added almost sarcastically,

"Or maybe it's modern God and Goddess worship, like where the Greeks made bronze sculptures of their deities. Some type of commentary on technology being God. Who knows."

They mulled over it a minute their thoughts getting behind Patrick's idea. He rolled his eyes, and stood up, draining his beer. "Or maybe it's just a smashed car."

He laughed, loud and deep, the ghost of his former self, the raucous team-spirited man who had been his personality for so many years coming out of his mouth in that laugh. His friends looked at him strangely, then shook off his out-of-character behavior like a dog after a bath. Their facial expressions changed immediately, all disagreement forgotten when they remembered where Patrick was off to. They called out any words of encouragement they could think of, promising to be at the gallery as soon as it opened for his show.

His show. It had all really started with the gallery owner serendipitously looking through his sketchbook. The gallery had a few free days in the schedule for the year, a few days between two well-known artists who were coming in to exhibit. The owner had seen Patrick sketching behind the desk, seen his strong, dark hands flying over the paper, possessed with an image he didn't want to lose before he had the chance to commit it to the sketchbook. The owner had watched him, silently, for a few minutes. When Patrick had finally looked up, his cheeks coloring a dusky rose at being observed, the owner had asked him if pencil was his medium. Patrick had told him no, he was a painter. The owner had nodded, and asked him if he had any canvases completed. He'd told his boss, yes, quite a few. The owner had nodded again, and then said to complete three more before the free days in

May, and had calmly walked off. As if he hadn't just changed Patrick's life completely.

It was an amazing opportunity, and Patrick knew it. Most painters would sell their own mothers for the chance to exhibit at this gallery in SoHo. He had easily selected some Michigan studies to include: a few landscapes, some work he had done of the more depressed areas of downtown Detroit. Abandoned mansions that had been the glittering jewels of the early 20th century. Factories closed and rotting to dust. Picking the best things to show of his completed work was simple. It was creating new work that had seemed impossible.

His hands drew only Julian, or that damn orange cat he'd brought home. Julian painting, Julian laughing, Julian walking, alone. Patrick wasn't in love with him or anything, but it hit him that he thought of Julian more than he'd like to admit. And Julian was the one person that Patrick had really *seen*. Someone who had opened himself up to Patrick, even if it was done silently. It wasn't like he wore his heart on his sleeve, it was more like…after spending so much time around one another, suffering their own personal sorrows, Patrick had seen Julian's soul. A soul that was thereafter reflected in every expression, every movement. That was what he missed.

He had tried to look him up when he'd come back to Michigan for Christmas, but their old apartment had been rented by someone else. The leasing office downstairs said a moving company had come and stuck all of his things in storage. They had taken everything except for a canvas, the moving company had been afraid to damage it. Patrick had asked for it, and since his name had been on the lease, the girl in the office had no problem handing it over. It looked like she was glad to be rid of it.

Patrick had taken the painting back to New York with him. He had hung it on the wall in his tiny studio walk-up.

His own work sat tenderly on the floor, a sheet draped over top of his paintings. But Julian's depiction of the girl with the cinnamon hair, the same Patrick had watched him painting last year, stared at him all night long, his own guardian angel.

All through his work days, his rides on the subway, whenever his mind was free to wander, he wondered. Where had he gone? Was he finally traveling around Europe once again? Had he simply moved to a smaller place in Ann Arbor? Of all the possibilities, Patrick hoped that wherever Julian was, that he was with this girl. He hoped she was real. Working on her picture had been the most passionate he'd ever seen his roommate get about anything. He hoped that skinny-ass punk Julian had found some peace, because that dude needed it.

But tonight was his show, and so as he stepped through the doors of the gallery, he straightened his tie and looked down to be sure he didn't scuff his shoes. The owner raised a glass filled with clear liquid, a bright green lime threatening to fall off the edge, in Patrick's direction. He nodded back and said hello to a few of the other people that he knew in the room. He didn't even look at his own paintings. He had seen them. He had seen them far too much, actually. Patrick was almost tired of them. Instead, he looked at were the people in the room, the ones who were inspecting his art. Those that were scrutinizing, deciding if he was a rising star or a passing talent.

There were a small number of people surrounding each of the canvases, hung now in large gilded frames. It reminded Patrick of the Monet seascape series he had seen in Detroit, he had thought the golden frames added depth to the masterpiece within. Not that he was a master, but the frames complimented his own work in the same way. Each of his paintings was well attended, critics and admirers pointing and discussing his subjects. The only painting in the place that was completely surrounded though, was the large canvas on the back wall. It was the last work he had completed. Done partially from copy, and partially from memory, he hadn't been sure if he should include it at all.

But it obviously had created a buzz. He walked across the small gallery, catching Siobahn calling his name behind him, apparently just now arriving. He ignored her though, he was concentrating on trying to hear the murmurings of the people around the painting. Patrick raised his eyes to take it in again, and it was disarming, even to him, to see Julian's green eyes staring back at him. It wasn't that it was an exact likeness, but more how Julian had appeared to *him*. His olive skin, gleaming coffee-colored hair, and expression of comfortable nonchalance. This was the face that had made him feel comfortable in his own skin since the day he'd first met him on campus. Someone who carried as much pain, although of a different kind, as Patrick did. He had realized too late that it wasn't friendship that he felt for Julian, but kinship. A closeness that doesn't come from having everything in common, but instead in the comfort of the other's presence. And next to Julian, the girl from the painting. Her hair sometimes strawberry red, sometimes honeyed yellow, and mostly spiced brown. Julian was looking at her in the canvas, his face in profile. She was staring out from the painted strokes, almost a challenge. A challenge that Patrick had issued to himself. She was asking him, "what do you think, Patrick? Am I real? Am I a memory? Or do I only live in the tortured mind of the disappeared Julian Cole?"

Patrick shook his head and exhaled. He had used more vibrant colors than he normally did, which was strange, because he'd only ever seen Julian in black or grey. But something about the painting, the mood of it, the joy he wanted for his friend, demanded it.

"Some painting, Pat."

Patrick nodded, Mark and Siobhan must have caught up to him. He turned to ask what they thought, but the voice and the person it belonged to froze him in place.

"I'm not sure if my eyes are really that green though. It's definitely flattering. Though, you didn't quite get Lively right."

A girl stepped forward, her long hair waving and tumbling as she turned her head to examine the painting. Julian's arm was draped around her shoulders lovingly, and he kissed her hair quickly, pointing out some technique in the painting. She looked at Pat and grinned.

"I think it's perfect. Although, I must say that you've made me look terribly intimidating, almost regal. I think I will adopt that expression as my ordinary one going forward." Her smile was mischievous and playful, and Julian half-smiled back at her.

Patrick was still staring, and it had begun to attract notice from some of the other people standing nearby. Pulling Julian and the girl swiftly into the corner of the gallery, Patrick scooped Julian into a bear hug, lifting him off the ground.

"Where you been, man?"

"Ah, Pat, that's a really long story." Julian was looking around, obviously uneasy. Patrick realized he didn't care where Julian had been. He was just extremely happy he was here now.

"Shoot, Jules. I don't have the time for a story. Write it down and send me a copy. You and me and this mystery girl of yours have a lot to celebrate. Meet me after the show, about 11? Right outside? We'll have a real Detroit-

City revival, eh?"

Julian nodded and reached up to clap Patrick on the shoulder, smiling ear to ear. He and the girl, Lively, walked over to a different painting, and Pat overheard Julian explaining something about the mansion in Detroit. Feeling his gaze on her, she looked up and met Patrick's eyes, sunrise starting on her lips, and startling grey eyes that lit like the dawn.

Some new beginning was in her expression, and suddenly everything had meaning and magic was everywhere. Patrick laughed, and turned back to his show, his story, that somehow now belonged to all three of them.

EPILOGUE

"You are so like Izzy."

That had been the first words the strange grey-haired man had said after Mia had invited him into her home. His oddly quiet knock had summoned her more forcefully than a thunderclap. She had opened the door to find her eyes directed, up, up, impossibly high up to the smooth face and waving silver hair to this funny old man. He had told her that he had some important information about Julian. So she had brought him into the living room, thinking he was someone from the school or somehow connected to the University nearby.

Once in the living room the man had looked about for a few minutes, as if Mia wasn't there. Pictures of the family climbing to the top of Vesuvius, or Julian at the Hagia Sophia, his father hoisting him on his shoulders. She cleared her throat and his attention was drawn back to her.

"Yes, ah, Mr.?"

"Oh, my apologies. Birdwhistle. Marcus Birdwhistle. You will have to excuse me, I don't get out much in my line of work."

He smiled at her bizarrely, like he didn't have opportunity to practice the expression often and had forgotten the way of it.

"You said something about Julian? And my sister? You must be mistaken. That is, there must be some error. Julian has never even met his aunt."

Marcus smiled again, and took a drink from the glass of water she had offered him.

"No, no mistake. Isadora is one of my dearest friends. I am here on her behalf, and that of your mother."

Mia's mouth opened and an expression of crushing pain crossed her features. "My mother...that's impossible she's...well, she's in Italy."

"Well, yes. She is currently in Italy. The year 1443, if I remember correctly."

Mia made a choking sound as her own water glass tumbled onto the floor.

"You're one of *them*, aren't you?"

The man before her never lost the air of casual benevolence he had come in with.

"Yes and no, Mrs. Cole. I do not travel through books myself. But I am an...advisor of sorts. Your son is a great reader, in a time when not many are born with the gift. I understand it is your intention to protect him, but he is, even now, growing into a man."

Mia hung her head. She had made them travel for so long, but these past few years they had settled in Detroit. She, Finnegan and Julian traveled more than ever, except now it was temporary, always returning back to this house. Sometimes they even left Julian alone when they traveled, and she had to admit, there was a small part of her, that hoped the books were seeking him still. There was a piece of her that wanted to tell him of his gift, and what it meant. She longed to ask forgiveness, to explain her decision.

"Yes, Mr. Birdwhistle. He *is* growing into a man. And you are too late, I'm afraid, to counsel me. I...we, his father and I, have already decided to tell Julian the story of our family. After graduation. It will be his choice then to decide the course of his future. We will fetter his choices no longer."

He nodded his great, grey head slowly, his eyes never leaving the anxious expression on her face.

"I hope you are not here to tell me that he is special, or the chosen one or any other such thing." Her expression was teasing but something in her attitude was serious. Marcus laughed, loud and heartily.

"No madam, I have never experienced such a thing in my time. There is no chosen one to lead anyone into, or out of anything. We are all the heroes of our own story. I have simply come to ask if you would allow your son to live his."

There was nothing more to say. He smiled warmly and they both stood, Mia following him to the door. Marcus turned around, his tall, gangling form perched over her like a young tree.

"You were right to do exactly as you have done. Do not feel guilt. You taught him love and kindled a sense of adventure. Those are the things that set imaginations on fire, these are the most essential traits for truly great Readers."

He smiled again and stepped off the stoop of their house, and Mia watched him walk down the side of the street not yet shaded by the sun. He was whistling quietly, and a moment later both man and whistle had vanished, the street seeming somehow emptier, barren without his looming presence.

It didn't rankle her, as it did when she was young. Seeing her mother and sister disappear into the air. Mia's old fears had changed with age, and she was able to examine them without her emotions clouding them.

Her husband and son would be home soon. She still needed to finish up an article she was writing and get dinner started. She and Finnegan were leaving for Russia and a helicopter piloting lesson in a few days. Though how they'd picked this location for a trip, she couldn't remember. And in a few months, Julian would graduate and she would tell him everything. But until then, he would be an ordinary young man.

Soon another whistle could be heard outside the kitchen window, and her lanky, black-haired son burst in the door, kissed her cheek and threw his backpack on the table before running up to his room to get changed.

Mr. Birdwhistle's words lay over her like a warm blanket, assuring her that Julian would master his own future.

"We are all the heroes of our own story...allow your son to live his."

She smiled. What a future that would be.

ABOUT THE AUTHOR

ALEXANDRIA NOLAN was born and reared in Michigan's second motor city, Flint. She attended the University of Michigan, earning a Bachelor of Arts in English. After graduation from university in 2008, Alexandria moved to Texas to teach History, English and Writing in the public school system. In the spring of 2013, she left teaching to write full time.

She is the author of "Wide, Wild, Everywhere" a collection of short stories for those who love to travel, "Shears of Fate: A novel of Memory & Madness", a historical fiction novella, and "Starlight Symphonies of Oak and Glass" a historical fiction/fantasy novel set in 1820s Michigan.

Alexandria maintains a travel + lifestyle blog, *Greetings from Nolandia*, and is a frequent contributor to various online and print publications. She loves to read, travel, and read about traveling.

She resides in Houston, Texas with her husband.

www.ingramcontent.com/pod-product-compliance
Lightning Source LLC
Chambersburg PA
CBHW022155170626
46807CB00005B/2220